Offside Attraction

CANADIAN PLAYED
BOOK SIX

CYNTHIA GUNDERSON

BUTTON PRESS

With Gratitude

Editing and Critique
Jordan Truex, Scott Gunderson

Cover Design
Mitxeren

For the women who protect themselves. And the men who prove they can let down their walls.

Prologue 1

RHONDA
MARCH 25, 2023

RHONDA TAPPED the elevator call button and glanced over her shoulder at the still-packed bar. She could've used the washroom there, but she'd binged the first season of Germ Squad while at a hospital event the month prior and preferred not to contract Hep C. Yes, as a pharmaceutical professional, she understood that wasn't possible. No, this fact didn't matter to her slightly buzzed lizard brain.

"Come on." She jabbed the button again, like prodding the elevator would make it move faster. She wanted to cross her ankles and bounce on the balls of her feet like a three-year-old.

She should've returned to her room an hour ago, but the Jets game was in overtime, and missing a tie-breaker goal was a sin basically equal to dipping her hand in a bowl full of holy water. Waiting had paid off. In the last seconds, Nikolaj Ehlers slipped the puck right through the Preds' defence and fed it to Scheifele, who slapped it home, top corner. The crowd went insane, and so did the entire hotel bar—probably the whole city of Medicine Hat. Tina and her migraine had missed out big time.

The elevator dinged, and Rhonda straightened. As the doors slid open, she gave a small nod to the woman in her overcoat and scarf stepping out, then moved inside, pressing the button for her floor. She turned and shoved her hands into the pockets of her wide-legged slacks as the doors slid closed.

As the elevator crawled upward, she inspected the faux wood panelling on the walls. The buttons ringed with a dull shade of brass. At least the mattresses were firm, because this hotel looked like it hadn't been updated since the seventies.

Rhonda stepped out when the doors finally opened and walked briskly down the hall, her mind replaying the night's events. Perfection. A Jets win, along with the Snowballs securing a spot in the semi-finals for the Rose Cup. The only thing that could've been better was if they'd beaten Pucks Deep to do it. There was always next year.

Rhonda reached the room she shared with Tina and pulled out her keycard, swiping it over the panel above the door handle. All she got was a red light. She tried again with no luck. "Ugh, come on." She swiped it twice more before giving up and pounding on the door. "Tina! Sorry, my key's not working." Now, she crossed her ankles, the urge to relieve herself becoming more emergent. "Tina, I don't care if you're naked, babe. Just open the—"

The door swung open, and Rhonda started to push in when she froze. Standing in the doorway was *not* Tina. The guy was tall, well past six feet. He was built, athletic, with a tattoo sleeve that was wholly visible since he wasn't wearing a shirt. His dark hair was wet and messy, clinging to his forehead, and he wore a pair of grey sweatpants that looked soft enough to rub your face against. Thick enough to be well made. Thin enough to leave nothing to the imagination. Her eyes snapped up, and the smug grin on his face told her he knew exactly why she was suddenly experiencing cottonmouth.

Rhonda cleared her throat. "Sorry. Tina didn't tell me she had company."

The guy raised an eyebrow. "Hmm. She doesn't. Yet. But if you can tell me who she is and where I can find her naked—"

Rhonda stumbled back into the hall and stared at the room number. 306. That was her number. She was—

She squeezed her eyes shut and exhaled. "Damn it. Wrong room." Six-oh-three. Her room was—

"Or is it the right room?" He grinned at her.

She rolled her eyes. "Ah, nice. Seizing your moment."

He pointed down to her popped hip and crossed legs. "Yeah, no. It just looks like you might piss your pants in the hallway."

Rhonda cursed under her breath, her cheeks flushing. She was vaguely aware that she intended to walk into a perfect stranger's hotel room to use his toilet, but rational thought was drowned out by her screaming bladder. "Can I—?"

He nodded and opened the door wide so she could come in, the grin never slipping from his face. Her arm brushed his chest, and her breath hitched. He smelled like sandalwood body wash, her personal kryptonite. His hockey bag with a big Grande Prairie logo, skates, and stick lay in a pile next to the half-open closet. Not a surprise. There were at least four hockey teams, including the Snowballs, there in the hotel.

She didn't have time to ponder any of it. Rhonda lunged into the washroom, closing the door behind her. It was humid, the mirror still fogged from his apparently quite recent shower. She quickly pulled down her pants and sat on the toilet, relief washing over her as she finally released.

Her eyes scanned the counter. A name-brand electric toothbrush, a bottle of clear mouthwash, a stick of deodorant with black recyclable packaging—*why was that hot?*—and a comb. You could tell a lot from someone's toiletries. This guy was simple. Probably someone who preferred to spend more and buy one good item instead of wasting time with the cheap versions. He knew what he liked. *He knew what he wanted.*

Rhonda shivered and finished up, thanking the heavens that there was toilet paper because she *always* checked after being stuck in a staff washroom in Taber for over an hour last summer but had forgotten in her rush.

She pulled up and buttoned her pants, then turned on the faucet and washed her hands, noting the water was already turned to warm. Rhonda drew a deep breath, then dried her hands on the towel that sat next to the sink.

His towel. *His* hotel room. She didn't even know this guy's name, and now she had to go back out there and face him when he was highly aware she just dropped her pants and peed in his toilet. And inspected his personal hygiene items. She'd had plenty of experience exiting a man's washroom, but the peeing usually came after he'd seen more than her cringing in the hallway.

Rhonda exhaled and opened the door. Tall Dark And Smug was leaning against the wall, scrolling on his phone. Still shirtless. That seemed purposeful.

He glanced up as she stepped out, his eyes moving lazily up to her face. There was something boyish about him. How his cheek almost dimpled when he smiled, but not quite, or how his left eyebrow had a little nick out of it. Like he knew both how to get in trouble and talk his way out of it.

A flush of heat crept up her neck. "Thanks for that." Rhonda motioned to the washroom with a stiff thumb, like she was trying to hitchhike.

"Anytime." He pushed off the wall, his grin widening. That dimple wanted to happen, and Rhonda wanted to watch until it did.

She swallowed hard. "Well, I should . . . get back to my roommate."

"Naked Tina?"

Rhonda snorted. "Yeah. She's hopefully asleep by now. And my key should work on *that* door, so . . ."

He nodded, then glanced down at the floor. It gave her a few seconds to look at all the places she'd been working so hard not to. The mole next to his belly button. The way his skin moved over his ribs when he shifted his arms.

When he looked up, his hair fell over his forehead, and his blue eyes peered out from behind long, dark lashes. He scraped his teeth over his lower lip, and all the blood in her head rushed south.

For all the talk about men being visual creatures, it didn't take much for Rhonda to be interested in all things physical. Maybe not a breeze in gym shorts, but this was more than *much*. His abs flexing as he pushed off the wall and set his phone on the suitcase that sat open on the luggage rack. *He used a luggage rack.*

"Have a good night then, I guess." He put his hands in his pockets and took a step toward her and the door.

"I—" Rhonda cut herself off. She hadn't moved, and he noticed. He froze, his pupils expanding, his eyes locking onto hers. Her heart may as well have been the bass line to YYZ by Rush.

It had been a while since she'd been tempted to do something this spontaneous. She wasn't reckless in her love life under normal circumstances, but when she was on vacation, all bets were off. *Did driving two-and-a-half hours to Medicine Hat count as a vacation?*

It didn't matter. Truthfully, she'd known something like this was coming. She'd been too busy with work, and since the whole thing with the doctor next door to Anne and Tina's hadn't worked out, she'd been flying miserably solo.

And this guy was standing in front of her. Looking *like that*.

Rhonda tried to plant a hand on her hip and missed. "Do you have a roommate?" He shook his head, and she swallowed hard. "Do you have a game tomorrow morning?" It was already past midnight. She wouldn't proposition him if he had to be up at six in the morning. Even though the look in his eyes insisted he'd say yes regardless.

"You want to watch a movie?" he asked at the same time she said, "Do you want to have sex?"

He opened his mouth and closed it. The corners of his lips lifted. "Uh, yeah." His eyes narrowed in amusement. "What's your—"

"No." Rhonda strode forward, putting her hands on his skin, her heart pounding against her ribs. He felt exactly like she thought he would. Warm. Firm, like a perfect mattress. "No names. Just—"

His finger hooked the belt loop of her jeans, and he tugged her closer, then dropped his head and pressed into the space between her shoulder and jaw, kissing her neck.

Yeah. That.

Prologue 2

JORDAN
APRIL 13, 2024

THE SPORTS BAR in Okotoks buzzed with energy. Teams from all over Alberta and beyond mingled, which surprised Jordan a little. His team, Pucks Deep, had no problem sharing beers with C-Biscuit, but they circled the wagons when the Snowballs were around.

He didn't get why Sean still hated his ass. Well, that wasn't true. Sean held grudges better than a raccoon held onto garbage. He'd seen that back when they were friends. Before the whole thing with Lisa. Now, here they were in their mid-thirties, and Sean still acted like he'd kicked his dog last weekend.

Jordan leaned back as their waitress slid a fresh pitcher of beer in front of them.

"Boys." Nate grabbed the pitcher and poured himself a pint. "Tell me we didn't just play like a bag of rusty wrenches out there tonight."

"It wasn't that bad," Nate grunted.

Cam exhaled. "We got lucky."

Steele snorted, clinking his glass with Nate's. "It wasn't pretty, but we put 'em in the woodchipper, bud. They'll be coughing up splinters till Tuesday."

"The woodchipper, eh?" Chubs piped up, shoving a fry in his mouth. "Seemed like you barely chipped the ice with that twiggy shot of yours."

"I chuffed *one*, asshat. More than you can say," Steele grumbled.

Nate poured from the pitcher. "You see how those Rocky View boys looked at us tonight?"

Jordan grabbed a wing. "They had their wheels greased in game one, for sure."

Cam raised an eyebrow. "Plenty of stink eye from the bench."

"They'll do more than that after tomorrow." Jordan stripped the meat from the wing and set it down, wiping the buffalo sauce from his fingers with his napkin.

Steele snickered. "Passed their goalie in the hall. He asked if I was ever going to get a haircut. I told him, 'Only if you buy me one, bud.'"

Chubs nearly spat his beer. "If he can afford to pay for that, he must be pulling oil money."

"Weren't you a rig pig back in the day?" Cam asked.

Chubs balked. "I don't have the hands for it, bud." He held up his fingers. "Too delicate. These are built for finesse."

"Not what Ellie says," Nate quipped, then jumped out of his seat to avoid Chubs' shoulder.

The table erupted in laughter, and a few people across the room turned their heads. Jordan reached for the pitcher, and that's when his insides rearranged themselves.

She was there. Copper skin. Black, curly hair. Sitting at the end of the Snowballs' table, leaning in, laughing at something the petite blond woman beside her was saying. But she wasn't paying attention because her eyes were locked on his.

Jordan's heart rate kicked up. He hadn't seen her since that night in Medicine Hat. He hadn't known enough about her to even think about trying to track her down. Well, at least not specifics he'd want to type into a Google search.

Now she was right in front of him, and he was instantly back in that hotel room. He knew what was under that cream sweater that offset her bronze skin perfectly. Or how her mouth looked when she was breathing hard.

A thought splashed cold water over his memories. *She was with the Snowballs.* Did that mean she lived in Calgary? Or was she an out-of-town friend? A puck bunny that followed them to tourneys?

Jordan's lips parted in a slow smile. How much would it piss off Sean if he knew what had happened between them? He was a bad person for thinking it, but Sean made it easy to be the worst version of himself.

It only took seconds for any thoughts of their Elite League rivalry to dissolve as his body remembered that night. Her laugh, her breathy moans, the way she arched her back when he pressed her against the wall of that hotel room. Jordan's blood pulsed harder in his veins, and he shifted uncomfortably on his stool.

He filled his glass and did a double take to ensure his memory wasn't playing tricks on him. It wasn't. It was her. She remembered him, too, since she was still flicking her eyes in his direction every half a second.

Her hair was a little different. Shorter. Hell, from across the room, he already knew her lips were a slightly lighter colour. He barely remembered what he had for breakfast, but he remembered that exact shade of coral. How it looked on his sweatpants the next morning.

He took a swig of his beer to hide his fixation while his teammates still jabbered around him. She continued to laugh at her friend's jokes, her eyes crinkling at the edges. She brushed her hair behind her ear, her fingers lingering on her earlobe, then picked up her drink.

Her lips wrapped around her straw, and Jordan's muscles tensed. She still looked at her friends, but invisible energy sliced toward him. *This was for him.* Heat shot between his thighs as she idly played with the straw, using her tongue to tease and twirl it.

So. She was an asshole.

It was a good thing people like that created his natural habitat. Jordan leaned back in his chair, glancing down as if he'd just spotted something on his T-shirt. He pulled up the sleeve, exposing more of his tattoos and twisting his arm, flexing his triceps.

She loved his arms. Especially his ink. He'd known that the second she looked up at him outside his hotel room door.

He glanced up to find her eyes wider than a cat at midnight, the straw caught between her teeth. *Damn straight.* Two could play this game.

She rocked in her seat, her tongue flicking out to wet her lips. Jordan exhaled. There was no way that was an accident.

He waited two slow seconds, then leaned forward to grab his beer. He held up his hand, showing five fingers, then pointed to the door. Her cheeks flushed, and her nostrils flared.

Jordan's lips curled into a smile. He lifted his beer and took a long drink, then turned his attention back to his teammates as if he hadn't just made a plan to hook up in the parking lot. One that he was ninety percent sure she would participate in based on the way she started searching for her purse.

Jordan cleared his throat and set his beer on the table.

"Wiped out, bud?" Nate nudged him.

Jordan chuckled. "Not more than you. How's the knee?"

"Like a bag of gravel."

He winced. "Want me to tape it up tomorrow?"

Nate nodded, and Jordan glanced at the clock on the wall above the bar. He'd told her five minutes. It had been forty-five seconds, and it felt like a half-hour. He picked up his beer and took another gulp. His leg bounced under the table.

"Hey, Nurse Betty. I have a serious question." Chubs glanced around, pretending to make sure no one else was listening. "Hypothetically speaking, if a guy had a rash—"

Cam stifled a laugh. "Pick something up in your extracurriculars, bud?"

Steele exhaled. "Is it in the crease?" He mimicked a goalie stretch, and Chubs shot them both a glare.

Jordan smirked, stopping his fingers from tapping impatiently on the table. Chubs was a high school teacher. He deserved all the extracurriculars he could get. "Can't be out there giving the boards a lap dance every game and not expect a little burn." Chubs grinned at that, and Jordan slid off his stool, clapping a hand on his friend's shoulder. "I've got some cream at home. I can bring it tomorrow. You know, theoretically."

"You leaving then?" Nate asked.

Jordan nodded. "See you at ten thirty. South locker rooms."

Steele picked up his beer. "We play on rink five?"

Jordan nodded, trying his damndest to look relaxed when every cell in his body was buzzing like a hive of bees. He hugged and fist-bumped his way around the table, then didn't look back as he pushed through the door and stepped into the evening chill. The sun had already set, and the parking lot was dimly lit by a few garish post lights.

He walked past the first row of vehicles, his breath visible in the cool night air, until he reached his truck parked in the back corner. He'd never been more grateful to have chosen a spot far from the main entrance. In the dark.

He leaned against the hood of his truck, the metal cold against his palms, then turned to look at the front of the sports bar. His pulse quickened.

There she stood, framed in the doorway.

She glanced up, and her posture shifted like all the air in her body had left in a single rush. She wrapped her arms around herself and started toward him. His hands were trembling. They'd already slept together once, so he shouldn't have been nervous, but something about this girl made him feel like he was back in grade ten getting to second base for the first time.

Jordan turned and leaned into his truck, shoving his gym bag and a box of extra pucks into the front seat. He barely had time to straighten before Rhonda was in front of him, her cheeks flushed from the cold. She looked up at him with those dark, curious eyes, and he decided right then that he wouldn't give himself a chance to open his mouth and ruin this.

He reached out, and his hands found her waist, pulling her forward. He twisted and flipped her between him and the side of his truck, and she let out a surprised gasp. The scent of her perfume wrapped around him, and he breathed her in for a split second before her hands ran up his arms, slipping under the sleeves of his shirt.

"I knew you were watching," he murmured, dropping his head. He hovered there, feeling her quickening breath. And then her lips were on his, and he was lapping up her lip gloss like a damn kitten. Sweet, with a hint of berries. He swept his tongue into her mouth.

Her fingernails trailed over his neck as she tilted her head, deepening the kiss and rolling her hips against his. The cold metal of the truck must've been seeping through her thin jacket, but she didn't push away. Instead, she twined a leg around his, pulling him flush against her.

Jordan's pulse pounded in his ears as he shuffled them toward the truck bed, then reached for the door handle. He fumbled for a moment but finally yanked it open. He lifted her off the ground, put a hand up to duck her head, then dropped her on the backseat. She laughed in surprise, her eyes glittering in the street light. Then she fisted her hand in his shirt and shim-mied back on the bench seat, tugging him in after her.

Prologue 3

RHONDA
SUMMER 2024

HE WAS THERE. The Grande Prairie Guy. Parking Lot Guy. He was standing at a table on the other side of the dance floor. Rhonda turned away and swayed to the music, popping her hips a little more than necessary. She was desperate to turn and confirm he'd noticed her—be sure he was watching.

They weren't at a hockey tournament or at a new rink for playoffs. They were out at the Dusty Rose on a regular weeknight. Her mind spun, all her previous assumptions cracking as they crashed against this new information.

Sean and the other Snowballs seemed to know exactly who he was. Had they looked at him like that at that bar in Okotoks before she'd met him in the parking lot?

Jenna and Anne were more than happy to mirror her sexy energy on the dance floor, though the second Country saw some guy with a half-unbuttoned shirt move into their circle he was at

Jenna's side, his hands clamping protectively over her hips. The "move along" message may as well have been tattooed on his forehead.

Anne leaned in. "Would you go home with *that* guy?"

Rhonda jolted, then realized Anne wasn't looking in the direction of Parking Lot Guy. She raised an eyebrow and motioned to Half-Unbuttoned Shirt Guy instead.

"Uh, doubtful." Rhonda kept her eyes trained forward.

"So how do you choose then? How do you know a man isn't looking for something more serious?"

Rhonda laughed. "Why? Are you thinking of trying things my way?"

Anne shrugged. "I don't know. I'm not having much luck making anything else work."

Rhonda wrapped her arm around her friend. Anne, Tina, and Jenna were more than that, really. They were her family in Calgary, but she often took for granted how well she knew them. Anne talking about random hookups was like a fish wondering if it would be a good idea for him to try living on land. "Girl, you would hate it."

Anne scoffed. "What, you don't think I could pull it off?"

"No, you could definitely pull it off. You'd just want to throw up. And probably cry?"

"I'm not that fragile!"

Rhonda dropped her arm and gripped Anne's shoulder. "Anne, would you avoid peanuts if you didn't have to?"

Anne frowned. "No, but—"

"Exactly." She shrugged, but Anne didn't accept the question as case closed.

"You're saying you're allergic to relationships?"

"Yup." A new song came on with a bass line that shook her bones. That was the perfect description. It wasn't that she hated the idea of a relationship. She could see how they worked for other people, she just knew they didn't work for her. It was like clockwork every time she was interested in someone new. Attraction could be off the charts, but within a few weeks, it all started to fall flat. They were too into her, not into her enough, too many red flags, not any red flags–which meant they were definitely hiding something. Probably a true self they'd never discovered between their multiple degrees and promotions. Or a gambling addiction.

"What if you just *think* you're allergic?" Anne asked.

"Ha! And now you understand my childhood. I'll tell you, ending up in the ER Halloween night put those conversations to rest." Rhonda pulled back and moved to the music, not giving Anne a chance to make another argument. There was a part of her that wondered if it was only in her head, but she'd seen what promises of forever had done to her mother—to her whole family. She'd learned her lesson, and she wouldn't let anyone else convince her she should "try it and find out." That was how you ended up with a tube down your throat.

Rhonda leaned into Anne, trying to be nonchalant. "Who is Sean giving death stares to?" She shouted over the music, nodding her head in Parking Lot Guy's direction.

Anne followed her gaze. "I don't know." She reached out and pulled Jenna into their trio. "Who's that guy at our eleven o'clock? Dark hair. Tattoo sleeve."

That damn tattoo sleeve. Tonight he wore a light polo shirt that hugged his arms and shoulders. She pretended her shortness of breath was due to the dancing.

Jenna rolled her eyes. "Jordan. Captain of Pucks Deep."

Pucks Deep. Rhonda blinked. That may not have been the last thing she expected to come out of Jenna's mouth, but it was close. *Pucks Deep?* That was a Calgary team. Their *rival* Calgary team.

Both of her encounters with Jordan flashed through her mind. The first in Medicine Hat—he'd had a Grande Prairie bag and was staying in the hotel. Obviously from out of town. Then in Okotoks, she'd assumed the same thing since it was the play-offs. It's not like they talked much. She hadn't even thought to ask the question.

And she'd been to Pucks Deep games. She would've noticed him, wouldn't she? Her mind raced, running over every minute of those games still locked in her memory. No. The Snowballs had such a deep-seated rivalry, she was only ever booing their team. She never looked at their faces on the bench. Didn't wait to see any of them after. They usually left the arena and met the Snowballs at the pub or wherever their after-party was, and Pucks Deep never once chose the same location. It was like their teams were opposite sides of a magnet, only meeting when they were forced to on the ice.

Sean continued to look like someone had spit in his drink, and Rhonda couldn't stuff down her curiosity. "Does he hate him because of the crap they pull on the ice?" She'd seen plenty of dirty plays, though if she was being honest, the players on Pucks Deep weren't any worse than some of the other teams they played. Mills Hoodie could high stick and trip with the best of them.

Anne waved her hand. "You know these guys. They've played together since PeeWee. There's this whole sword fight happening under the surface."

Country was close enough to overhear that comment. "You think this is some petty rift? That dipshit slept with Sean's girl-friend. They'd been together for over a year, and Jordan purpose-fully sought her out just to make a point."

Rhonda's stomach dropped. "He slept with Kelty?" She thought she was going to be sick.

Country shook his head. "No, this was after high school. They were both in the NHL draft. I don't know all the details, but it was bad. And you don't even want to know all the shit he's pulled with the league—"

Jenna put a hand on his puffed-out chest to push him back

toward the tables. "Okay, let's bring it down a notch. We don't need to create a fuse to light tonight."

Rhonda watched them go, then glanced up at the bar. She was suddenly parched. "I'm going to get water. You want anything?"

Anne shook her head but walked with her back to the others. Rhonda wove through the tables, her mind still smashing together two stories into one. The lore of Pucks Deep and her personal timeline schema. *Jordan.* That was his name. Knowing it somehow changed everything—added a layer to both of the nights they'd spent together.

Both. Ugh, she was so stupid! Why had she met up with him a second time? Probably because seeing him now was doing the same thing to her blood pressure as seeing him in that sports bar. But now if she saw him, there was no way she could pretend she didn't remember.

And she needed to be able to pretend because the Snowballs could never know what had happened between them. If Jordan's sex life was what sparked Sean's hatred of him, knowing she'd jumped into bed with him at their tournament wasn't going to make things better. And yes, she'd been a willing participant in the rivalry banter, but she'd only ever cared because the Snowballs cared. She didn't want to add more fuel to the fire. Hockey was violent enough as it was.

Rhonda leaned over the oiled wooden counter and caught the attention of the bartender. He nodded when she asked for two glasses of water, and she sat on one of the stools to wait. With the number of people already standing there, she doubted her free request would be at the top of his list.

Someone slid in next to her, and the bartender looked up mid-pour. "Two pints," he said, and the hairs rose on the back of Rhonda's arms. Her body recognized him like he was her childhood blanket. If a blanket could make you momentarily disassociate from your body.

She clasped her hands in front of her, keeping her eyes

trained ahead, pretending to be riveted by the bottles the bartenders were grabbing off the shelves.

"Pucks Deep," she murmured.

Jordan let out a puff of air next to her. "You say that like it's a curse word."

"In my neck of the woods, it definitely is." Rhonda turned her head away from him, just in case anyone was watching. He was silent long enough that she started to get antsy.

He scraped his stool closer to the bar. "You were the one who said no names."

"You had a Grand Prairie logo on your hockey bag!" she hissed.

Jordan chuckled. "You noticed my hockey bag?"

"Of course I noticed. I do a little research before . . . you know."

"Very thorough. Did you check my toiletry bag for condoms, too?"

She almost broke and turned to him. Instead, she clenched her jaw and tapped her fingers on the counter. Hard. "If I would've known—"

"You would've missed out on the best sex of your life."

She scoffed. "Okay, cocky. It wasn't the best." That was a lie, and by the smile she heard in his voice, he knew it.

"Well. If you ever want to compare and be sure." A piece of a napkin slid into her field of view, along with his left hand. The edges of his tattoos curled over his wrist, and those fingers . . .

The bartender handed Jordan his beers, and Rhonda knocked her knees on the underside of the counter as she tried to shift over so his arm wouldn't brush against hers. She wasn't fast enough.

And then he was gone. Her heart was pounding like a squirrel that had barely escaped oncoming traffic. She barely eeked out a "thank you" when the bartender set the glasses on the bar in front of her.

Water dripped onto the wood, soaking into the napkin, and

she quickly swiped it off the bar. She wasn't going to keep it, but she also wouldn't leave it there for some rando to find. She'd throw it away in a second, after she dropped off the waters.

Rhonda stuffed Jordan's number into the back pocket of her pants, then blew out a breath, grabbed the drinks, and walked back to her table with a smile on her face.

CHAPTER
One

RHONDA SHIVERED as she dropped her yoga pants on Tina and Anne's patio. The steam rising from the hot tub curled like smoke in the chilly night air. Her fingers fumbled with her shirt, the cold making them clumsy. She laughed as she finally got it over her head, then slipped into the water with a contented sigh. It was dark enough this time of year that she didn't even bother putting her swimsuit top on in the first place.

Emma grinned as she took hers off and draped it over the edge of the tub.

"That's my girl." Rhonda laughed and quickly pulled her hair up with a clip so she could sink to her neck.

Penny opened the cooler. "You're a terrible influence."

"Don't knock it till you try it." Rhonda grinned as Penny dropped her coat and pants, holding her drink above her head as she slid into the water. "It's like a warm massage, and they just float."

Tina rolled her eyes. "Yours float since they stick out more than an inch from your body."

Rhonda shrugged. "All the more reason to set them free—they don't even *need* to be restricted." It was her personal mission to bring more non-sexual nudity into the world, or at least her small piece of it. Women hated their bodies when they thought everyone else looked like the airbrushed images they were bombarded with. But in her experience, everyone pretty much looked the same. A different mole or roll here or there. None of it mattered, and baring it all was a good way to convince her brain of that truth.

"I think I'm going to dye my hair," Tina started.

Rhonda laughed. "We've been talking about this since August."

"I know, but now I'm really thinking about it."

"Darker for fall?" Penny pulled her jet-black hair up into a ponytail.

"Maybe a balayage? Dark undertones?" Tina squinched her face.

Rhonda sighed. "You white girls have it so hard. Too many options."

Tina rolled her eyes. "More like I'm pretty sure my hair is thinning, and I need to do something to distract myself."

Anne took a sip of her drink. "Collagen. They sell it in bulk at Costco now . . ."

The mention of a supplement snapped Rhonda back into work mode. She let the conversation flow around her, white noise as she mentally ran through the list of meetings she needed to set up for next week. Dr. Henson in Lethbridge, Dr. Patel in Edmonton, and that new clinic in Banff. She'd been waiting for shoulder season to approach them. No ski accidents to fill up their waiting rooms for at least another few weeks.

She closed her eyes, letting the chilly air and hot water create a delicious contrast on her skin. She peeled one eye open as Emma started recapping the Snowballs game they'd gone to the night before. "I swear, I haven't seen that kind of energy this early in the season ever."

"Well, we've missed the cup for the past two years, and the team is damn good. We want momentum," Penny said.

Tina nodded. "It was electric. Even without Jack, the offence was solid."

"Ugh. I'm happy for him, but we need a deeper line." Emma leaned her head back on the tub.

Rhonda shifted in the bucket seat. "Sean's still recruiting, isn't he?"

Emma nodded. "Yeah. Tyler's working on it, too."

"Brett found a guy through his AA meeting. I think he's practicing with them next week," Penny added. "After Pucks Deep stole—what was his name, Patrick or something?"

Emma jumped in, but again, Rhonda snapped into herself. Pucks Deep. She'd tried to avoid thinking of Jordan since the summer with some success. She hadn't seen him again at Dusty Rose, thankfully. In her current drought, she didn't know if she'd be strong enough to say no to another hook up.

She thought about that plenty. They'd been more than compatible, and late at night, when she was alone in some hotel waiting for a meeting the next morning, she'd been tempted more than once to look him up and slide into his DMs.

Which was the worst idea ever. They'd met up twice, and that was one time too many. Three would be bordering on a relationship, especially since they knew too much about each other at this point.

"Did you hear Jack and Delia are going to be at Sunday Supper tomorrow?" Tina reached for her water bottle.

Emma grinned. "Mom's making her famous lasagna in celebration."

"Has she met Delia before?" Anne asked.

Emma scoffed. "Sharla is positive they're besties."

Rhonda laughed. Sharla Thompson was positive she was

besties with everyone. And she was right. "Didn't you try to recreate that lasagna once?"

Emma shot her a look. "My mom won't give me the actual recipe. She's holding out so hers is always better."

"Uh-huh." Rhonda grinned and took a sip of her sparkling water. "I'm going to be bringing my world-famous bagged salad. So, be jealous."

Anne put her feet up on the side of the tub. "You love food too much not to cook."

"I love other people's food. I wouldn't like it nearly as much if I had to do all the work." Rhonda pushed up on her knees, laughing as Tina did a quick check over the fence to make sure the neighbours weren't out. "We don't even have the lights on. Chill!"

Penny sat up across from her. "You just need a boyfriend who can cook."

"She needs a boyfriend, period."

Rhonda blew out a breath. "Fine. Get it out of your systems. We're in, what, Q3? I haven't had this lecture since first, so I'm overdue."

Emma laughed. "It's not a lecture, we just want you to be happy."

"I am happy!" Rhonda threw out her hands, and her bobbing breasts accentuated her point.

Tina groaned. "Okay, but sexuality oozes from you like—"

"Can we not use the word oozes?" Rhonda wrinkled her nose.

"Oozes like what, though?" Emma leaned in.

Tina paused. "Like, I don't know, garlic from your pores?"

"Gross!" Rhonda flicked water at her.

"She's not wrong, though." Emma sighed. "You walk into a room, and men just *know*. You can see it in their faces."

Rhonda sank back into the water. "Exactly! Which is why I don't need to settle down. I can just have fun with it."

"You don't know *that's* more fun than finding someone to be with permanently." Penny cocked her head.

Rhonda took another sip of her drink. "You don't know that it's *not* more fun." Penny had no rebuttal to that. They'd known each other long enough to be well-versed in each other's pasts. Penny had gone from one serious relationship to the next. Emma had crashed and burned in a long haul, then tried the whole casual thing with Tyler. The ring on her finger was proof she'd failed miserably.

Penny stayed on topic. "Brett was telling me about this friend of his. He's a contractor, rugged, loves the outdoors. I thought—"

Rhonda laughed, rolling her eyes. "Oh, Penny, you're adorable."

"No, this guy is very non-committal."

Emma laughed. "I can't believe that is a selling point for you."

Rhonda leaned back against the tub. "Does he meet my top qualification right now?"

Penny pursed her lips. "I told you he's a contractor, not a doctor."

Anne shook her head. "She was seriously searching up staff at Rocky Ridge Medical Centre the other day."

"And?" Emma raised an eyebrow.

Rhonda leaned forward, sending a low wave of water across the tub. "I'm not going to get physically involved with any of them, I just need to know who's most likely to be . . . interested. At least enough to hear me out on Reviact."

"This drug works, right?" Emma teased.

"Of course it works." Pharma reps got a bad rap, but she couldn't do this job if she didn't believe in the drugs she worked to get on formularies. She was particularly passionate about this one. Reviact was a medication designed to help manage opioid addiction, a unique formulation that combined an extended-release component to reduce cravings with a blocker to prevent relapse. The independent trial results were beyond statistically significant, and with the number of opioid addiction and abuse reports through the roof, there was never a bigger need for a medication that brought real hope.

But this was Canada. It took more than stellar results to supplant the old favourites, especially when shiny new drugs didn't yet have federal approval or funding and cost ten times more.

"They haven't even phoned you back?" Tina frowned.

Rhonda shook her head. "It's like trying to convince my mom that tofu is a real food. They're not budging."

Penny smirked. "Well, I don't know any doctors there, but I do know a very masculine contractor who—"

"Thanks, but no."

Penny pursed her lips. "It's been a while for you, Rhon."

Rhonda sighed. "I know. I'm just . . . busy. You know that."

Anne nudged her knee under the water. "Yeah, but you need a life outside of work."

Rhonda shrugged. "I have a life. I have you guys." And her mom, but she didn't see any of them as often as she wanted to. Not with all the travel.

Emma blew out a breath. "You know I'm not judging you—"

"Here we go." Rhonda leaned over and made grabby hands in the direction of the cooler. Tina laughed and passed her a beer.

Emma waited for her to use the bottle opener and take a sip. "'Kay, but hear me out. You make great money, you're hilarious, sexy, and you're not superficial or arrogant—"

"Thank you." Rhonda nodded gravely.

Emma held up a hand, ignoring her sarcasm. "I don't understand how someone hasn't locked all of this down."

Anne pointed a finger at her. "Do not use the peanut allergy metaphor. We've already discussed how that doesn't hold up."

Rhonda snorted. "Because I need therapy?" Anne shot her a look. "When would I have time for therapy?"

Anne dropped her chin onto her arm. "No. If you're happy,

I'm good with that. I just—" She blew out a breath. "I don't like the idea of you being alone."

Rhonda grinned. "You've been dating Gary for six weeks, and you're already one of those people? Pitying me?"

"Not pity! You're just travelling all the time by yourself. What if one of these times you bring home a guy that . . ." Anne shrugged, and Rhonda looked around the hot tub.

"Exactly! I travel too much to be in a serious relationship. You guys are the only thing I have time for when I'm home." She paused, chewing her lower lip. "Is this what you're all thinking, though? That I'm pathetic? Sad and alone all the time?" Her heart picked up speed. She was very aware that her lifestyle choices weren't pedestal-worthy, but she didn't love the feeling that her best friends were secretly judging her, too.

She stiffened and was about to push up out of the water when Tina said, "Sit your ass down, Rhonda. You know we love you. This is what friends do. They worry about you and your lady parts. So just accept that you'll get a version of this lecture every six months or so."

Emma nodded. "You're over thirty-five. It's like a mammogram."

Penny gave her a serious look. "And if you're still happy, fulfilled, and alone in another forty years, I'll scour Rocky Ridge and find you the hottest medical student to change your bedpans."

CHAPTER
Two

JORDAN

IT WAS eight forty-five on a Monday night, and Jordan's lungs burned. He skated a lap, then stopped at centre ice, his eyes scanning his players as they moved up and down the rink. Steele took a shot on Chubs in the net, Wyatt charged at him, then Cam and Nate fought for the puck and lost it to Sam.

Jordan's breath condensed in white puffs in front of his face. The rink was old, the boards scuffed and dented from decades of pucks and bodies crashing into them. The bleachers, mostly empty except for a few die-hard fans and the occasional girl-friend, creaked with age. The ice itself was a patchwork of old and new, the scars from previous games and practices barely covered by the fresh layer laid down by the Zamboni, but he lived for this. For the smell of the rink, the snap of the puck, the camaraderie.

Jordan blew his whistle, and his teammates circled back, their blades carving arcs into the ice. "That was a shit show. Nate, you were out of formation."

Nate grunted. "Yep."

"Fix it." Jordan led them back to the boards where they switched out pairs, then started again. He partnered up with Wyatt on defence and got in line for the drill.

"Left your balls in the dressing room!" Steele shouted as Cam skated past him.

Cam flipped him off, then got back in line. They'd been practicing breakouts, and he needed to get his defence more in sync. They were up against Mills Hoodie this weekend.

After a few more rounds, Jordan called his players in, then they ran through their final set of rushes. He banged his stick against the boards, and the guys circled up. "Alright, strategy for the weekend. We know their boys are bruisers, so we need to close those gaps and play smart, not just hard. We can't afford to let them break through the blue line. No free lanes to the net.

"When they're cycling the puck along the boards, I want our defencemen to play tighter, force them to the outside. If they're digging in deep, stay low, cover the slot, and don't get drawn out by their forwards. We'll use our wingers to press high and cover the points, so defence can stay focused on protecting the net.

"Offensively, we need our puck movement sharp and our heads up. They're big on clogging the middle, so we'll work it from the perimeter and draw them out. Quick passes, work them until they're spread thin, then hit those seam passes to catch them off guard. When we're on the rush, if you see an open lane, go for it, but no hero plays—we need that support trailing behind. If they come at you along the boards, chip it in deep and go to work below the goal line. Keep the zingers. They can't hit what they can't catch."

His players nodded around him, and Steele clapped him on the shoulder. "Nice speech, Cap. Almost brought a tear to my eye."

Jordan gave him a gloved finger as the metal door at the end of the ice creaked to life. The team worked to get the pucks and nets off the ice, then clomped down the hall into the locker room.

They found their lockers, stripped off their gear, grabbed towels, and walked over the peeling rubber mats to the showers.

"Hey Nate, is the Zamboni driver gonna be disappointed you didn't get her number?" Cam called out from under the spray.

Nate laughed. "Shut your hole. I was being polite, admiring her work ethic."

Chubs snorted. "Yeah, nothing says hard work like driving in circles."

"You know what, Chubs? Maybe you should look into dating a Zamboni driver. That way, you can finally have someone who knows how to handle a short knob."

Jordan laughed as the hot water beat down on his neck, running in steady rivulets over his shoulders and back. He grabbed the soap, scrubbing at the sweat and the layer of grime from drills and sprints. His shoulders ached from the weight room yesterday, arms heavy from passing drills, but that would all be gone soon enough. Replaced by the fluorescent lights and antiseptic smell of the ER.

He worked the soap over his chest and stomach, then braced a hand on the tile and tipped his head into the spray. The guys' voices drifted from the locker room, laughing, joking. They'd be out the door soon, heading home for leftovers, Netflix, maybe a couple beers. Simple, easy.

He rinsed off and grabbed his towel. He'd be off by dinner time for the rest of his shifts that week, but he'd swapped his Friday afternoon for a night to ensure he wouldn't miss the game. It would be brutal coaching his youth team the next evening, but he'd get to nap all morning. Hopefully, since it wasn't a weekend, the urgent care would be quiet.

Steele grabbed his towel and started drying off. "You think they'll ever fix these showers? I swear, every time I turn it on, it's like playing Russian roulette with scalding hot and freezing cold."

Cam nodded. "It's like trying to wash off with a dribbly garden hose."

Nate snorted. "Hey, at least we have showers. I remember playing in rinks where we had to change in the parking lot and use wet wipes."

Chubs grinned. "Sounds like your sex life, Nate."

Jordan stalked back to his locker, his mind wandering back to that parking lot in Okotoks. He'd thought about her after Medicine Hat, regretted not getting her name or something to go off of, but after his truck . . .

"Hey, Jord. You got plans for the weekend?" Cam pulled on his shirt.

Jordan shook his head. "Nothing special. Why?"

Cam shrugged. "Just thought we could grab a beer or something. It's been a while since we all hung out off the ice."

Jordan nodded. "Sounds good. Let's set something up." He was about to say more when Steele caught his attention.

"Be right back," Jordan said to the guys, then walked with Steele into the other room, standing in front of the line of sinks. This was standard procedure. Every one of these guys had taken him aside at one point or another, especially after barely joining the team. Steele wasn't green, but he'd had to overcome a lot to be there.

"Hey." Jordan leaned against the wall, arms crossed.

Steele shoved his hands in his pockets. "So, you still doing weekends at the hospital?"

Jordan nodded. "Sometimes, yeah, but I dropped to part-time. Now I pick up shifts at the urgent care. I can work that around our games better." Steele nodded, and Jordan pressed, knowing it would be difficult for him to say what he needed to. "What's on your mind?"

Steele ran a hand over the back of his neck. "An article came out. Just an online news site or blog post or whatever. Talking about NHL has beens, or would've beens."

Jordan sucked in a slow breath. This was a constant occurrence on Pucks Deep. Sometimes one of their players did something to incite media attention, but mostly, it came like a sale catalogue in the mail. Unannounced and unwanted. "How'd you find it?"

"Old teammate in Ottawa."

"Nice."

"Yeah." Steele exhaled in a whoosh.

Jordan waited until Steele lifted his eyes. "You're not that guy anymore."

"No, I know." He shifted on his feet. "I just wish—maybe if I could've figured things out sooner . . . "

The regrets, the wishing they could go back in time and make different choices. Jordan was all too familiar with that. But it was a losing game. One that only led to more suffering in the present. "You have to accept it, bud. Who knows what would've happened if you stayed in the NHL? You have this story in your head that life down that path would've been easier, but you didn't know how to deal with your shit. That's why you got arrested. If it wouldn't have been that, it could've been something worse."

Steele nodded. "I know."

Jordan pushed off the wall and clapped a hand on his friend's shoulder. "I have a shift tonight, but if you want to come by tomorrow?"

"Yeah."

"Stay with Chubs and Nate tonight."

Steele sniffed. "Thanks."

"We've got you." Jordan followed him back into the locker room.

After packing up and saying his goodbyes, Jordan walked down the hall, climbed the stairs and pushed through the rink doors. He exhaled and watched his breath billow out like smoke into the night air as he walked to the parking lot. His shoulders eased. It was always a rush at practice, but now that the adrenaline had done its job, the fatigue settled in. No sleep tonight.

He'd be raiding the hospital's supply of energy drinks within the hour.

He pulled his keys from his pocket, but his fingers froze when he spotted someone standing next to his truck. Jordan's steps slowed. Standing on the passenger side, a thin figure shivered in a too-thin hoodie and jeans that looked two sizes too big. Her hair was bleached blond, and she had a ratty backpack slung over one shoulder.

Jordan clenched his jaw. "Claire." *What the hell was she doing here?* She turned, her eyes darting as she wrapped her arms around herself. "Did you drive?"

Claire shook her head. "A friend dropped me off."

Jordan took a step closer. "Who's the friend?"

"Just . . . a friend."

"What's his name?"

"It's a she, and you don't know her."

Jordan stared her down, but Claire looked away, her breath coming out in quick puffs. "Get in the truck."

He unlocked the doors, and they both climbed in. Jordan turned the key in the ignition and cranked up the heater. Claire held her hands up to the vents. They sat in silence for a moment, the only sound the fan blowing warm air.

"It's been . . . what? Three months?" Jordan finally said.

"Four, I think." Claire nodded, her eyes fixed on the dashboard. "I'm staying with a friend. I can't go there until Wednesday, though."

Jordan frowned. That was two days away. "Where've you been staying?"

"Here and there."

Jordan ground his teeth. Here and there meant she'd been sleeping in places he didn't want to imagine. He ran a hand through his hair, then gripped the steering wheel. "Alright. Let's find you a place for the night."

Jordan pulled out of the parking lot and headed down Macleod Trail, his mind spinning. He should've been more surprised to see Claire, but considering the last few months, it wasn't a shocker that she'd show up unannounced. Especially since she didn't answer his texts. Hard to do when your phone was being shut off every couple of weeks.

His hands tightened around the wheel. He couldn't take her home. Not because he didn't want her there, he did. More than anything. But he'd learned from past experience that he couldn't have her around when she wasn't sober. He talked with his patients about healthy boundaries all the time. Harder to implement in real life.

"You still playing with the same team?" Claire broke the silence, her voice hoarse.

"Yeah, Pucks Deep. Same crew."

"How's Cam? Still working that landscaping job?"

Jordan tensed. "Yeah, but he's been talking about going back to school. Something with engineering, I think." He hoped the message was clear. *Cam's doing well. Don't mess with him again.*

"Good for him." Claire smiled faintly.

They drove past a Tim Hortons, and for a split second, Jordan was tempted to pull in and get them both a coffee. Just to drag out the time they had. But Claire never seemed to turn up on a day off. It was like she had radar attuned to the brief moments between his other responsibilities.

He turned onto seventy-second and headed toward the industrial area where he knew there was a hotel that wouldn't ask too many questions. Jordan pulled into the parking lot, wincing at the neon sign. "This place, okay?"

Claire nodded. "Yeah, it's fine."

They walked into the lobby, the air smelling faintly of disinfectant and something chemically floral. The receptionist barely looked up as they approached the desk. Jordan pulled out his wallet and handed over the credit card he kept for exactly situations like this. It had a five hundred dollar limit.

The receptionist ran the card and handed him a key. "Room 214."

Jordan turned to Claire and handed her the key. He pulled out cash from his wallet and handed her a couple of twenties. "For food or anything else you need."

Claire took the cash, her fingers brushing his. "Thanks."

Jordan hesitated, then looked her in the eye. "You know, Alpha House is still an option. If you want to get clean."

Claire nodded, her eyes glued to the floor. "I'm doing okay."

Jordan's throat tightened. "Right. Okay." He pulled her into a hug, holding her tight. "I love you, Claire."

"I love you too." She pulled back, her eyes glistening. "Thanks."

Jordan forced a smile, then watched as she walked to the elevator. The doors closed, and he stood there for a moment, his heart aching. He wanted to believe her. She was his sister. But he spent all day with patients just like Claire.

He knew better.

CHAPTER
Three

RHONDA

ON THURSDAY, Rhonda stepped out of her car and walked up the sidewalk to Penny and Brett's house, her heels clicking on the concrete. Burnt orange and brown leaves collected along the path, nestled into every nook and cranny of the yard like they were huddling together for warmth.

She ascended the freshly stained porch steps and took a deep breath, then rang the doorbell, her stomach doing a little flip of nerves. As she waited, Rhonda inspected the porch swing and the welcome mat. It was a beautiful house. Penny and Brett had bought it together in the spring, and every time she stopped by, it looked a little more like they'd lived there forever.

The door swung open, and Penny, wearing a mustard yellow sweater and tight black jeans, grinned at her. "Hey, you made it!"

Rhonda raised an eyebrow as she stepped in and hugged Penny. "Did you think I was going to bail?"

"I gave it a twenty percent chance."

"I said thirty!" Brett called from somewhere deeper in the house.

In summer, the place had been light and airy, with large windows that let the sunlight pour in like liquid gold. Now that it was dark by five o'clock and Penny had put up window treatments, the house had transformed into something cozy. The walls were painted a soft, soothing grey, and the furniture was a mix of modern and eclectic pieces that screamed Penny. It was all clean lines and pops of colour.

Rhonda slipped off her shoes and followed Penny down the hall and into the newly remodelled kitchen where Brett was loading the dishwasher. "You've got him trained."

Penny grinned. "Yeah, he's a keeper." She slapped his butt as she walked by.

Rhonda sighed. "If only my date were here, I could offer him the same greeting."

Penny laughed. "I'm sure he'd appreciate it. Water?" She pulled a glass from the cabinet. Rhonda nodded and sat on one of the barstools at the counter. "So, Aaron should be here any minute."

"Did you tell me his name was Aaron? Or was it just 'masculine, non-committal contractor.'" Rhonda took the glass of water Penny handed over the counter.

Brett closed the dishwasher. "I took that straight from his dating profile."

"Mmm. Nice. Great hook." Rhonda set her glass on the counter. "If he only added his favourite sexual position, he'd fit right in with the others."

"Do you spend time on those apps?" Penny asked.

Rhonda shrugged. "Sometimes. When I'm out of town. So far, no murderers."

Penny gave her a look that said *Plan on every three months for that safety lecture,* but before Rhonda could assure her she always shared her location and the information of said dates with someone—usually Anne—the doorbell rang.

Penny jumped and grabbed her purse. Rhonda took another drink, then leaned over and set her glass in the sink. They walked together behind Brett and watched as he opened the door.

"Sorry I'm late, I got held up at the site." His voice was deep, but Rhonda couldn't get a good look with Brett standing in the way.

Aaron stepped through the doorway, and suddenly, the room felt smaller. He was tall, with dark hair that was still damp from his shower. Without permission, an image of Jordan standing in his hotel room popped into her head. *No, thank you.* Rhonda stood a little taller, willing herself to focus on the man in front of her. He had a strong jaw, broad shoulders, and a very nice lopsided smile.

"Hey, I'm Aaron." He put out a hand, and Rhonda shook it. His fingers were rough, his eyes a deep, rich brown. He wore a simple button-down shirt and jeans. Yeah, he would do. He would do nicely.

Rhonda slipped back into her heels and the four of them walked out to the driveway. Brett pulled his truck out of the garage, and she slid into the back seat with Aaron, the scent of the leather seats mingling with the faint aroma of coffee from a travel mug in the cupholder.

Another flash. Jordan's hand behind her head as he lowered her to her back, her feet pressing against the door as he—

"So what do you do?" Aaron asked.

Rhonda swallowed hard. She hadn't thought about Jordan in weeks, and tonight was the night her brain decided to take a trip down memory lane? "I'm a pharmaceutical rep. I work for Cantra."

"She doesn't just work for them," Penny added. "She's their top sales rep in the Calgary region."

Rhonda grinned. "Thank you for that."

"It's true!"

It *was* true, but her experience was that most men didn't love hearing about her accomplishments right off the bat. They wanted to know she was successful but only to a point. Especially when they worked in corporate sales.

Aaron shifted on the seat, and their legs brushed. "That's impressive." Rhonda was about to smile and shrug it off when Aaron asked, "Are you happy in that role or do you want to move up?"

It was a simple question, but Rhonda had never once been asked that by a member of the opposite sex. Usually when they heard about her work, they jumped into stories about their own job, levelling the playing field a bit.

Rhonda paused, not sure if she should answer honestly or say something safe. *What the hell, right?* Reason number one hundred why not getting into a serious relationship was less stressful. She could say whatever she wanted, and if Aaron didn't like it, he could move along.

"I want the regional sales manager position. I'm hoping to hit some sales goals by the end of the quarter that should solidify my application." Rhonda watched him for his reaction.

Aaron nodded. "Would that be better pay or a better work-life balance?"

Okay, so this guy was good. She caught Penny's eye and noticed her friend already grinning. "Both, actually. It would mean less travel. I could manage a team mostly remotely, and the pay wouldn't necessarily be more, but it would be similar and guaranteed, not totally commission-based."

Aaron leaned back in his seat. "Guaranteed income. What would that be like?"

Brett laughed from the driver's seat. "Don't give me that. You like the risk."

"When it pays off." Aaron grinned.

Brett pulled into a parking spot outside the restaurant, and they all climbed out of the truck. Part of her wanted to pull Aaron aside and ask if he wanted to skip the whole date thing and just head back to her place, but that was also something men didn't like. They wanted to feel like they'd earned something—like they'd put in the effort and won. They didn't want to feel like they were the ones being used, and Rhonda had gotten good at playing the game their way.

Aaron held the door for her, and they entered the restaurant, the rich aroma of spices and grilled meat enveloping them. They were seated at a table near the back, and Rhonda slid into the booth next to Penny. Aaron sat across from her, and Brett took the seat next to him. The waiter handed them menus, and Rhonda scanned the options, her stomach growling.

"I think I found my happy place." Penny sank into the booth.

"It smells really good," Rhonda agreed.

Brett looked pleased. "You haven't even tasted the food yet." He leaned back in the booth, stretching out his legs as he looked over the menu. "So, Canucks game tonight. You think they've got a shot this season?" he asked Aaron, who was still shrugging off his jacket.

Aaron snorted, shaking his head. "They've got a shot, sure, but it's probably not a great one. New coach, new system—it'll take a few more months to settle into anything that looks good." He slid a hand over his arm as he leaned over the table. *Tight T-shirt. Tattoo sleeve.*

She was back in that sports bar in Okotoks. What. The. Hell. "I'm going to the washroom. I'll be right back." Rhonda flashed a smile as she slid out of the booth and walked toward the only obvious hall at the side of the restaurant.

All of these flashes of memories were probably just because she was meeting someone new. She'd been slammed with work and had spent as many nights in hotels as she had her own bed in the past two months. Her body remembered him. That was normal, and of course, she was excited at the prospect of connection.

She loved the game, the chase. It was a rush, and she hadn't made time for any of it as of late. While she didn't want to admit

Penny had been right, she would eventually thank her and admit she clearly needed a break.

She pushed open the door to the washroom and found herself in a small, well-decorated space with two stalls and a large mirror above a stone sink. There were fresh flowers on the counter, and the air smelled faintly of lavender. Rhonda stood in front of the mirror for a moment then washed her hands and reached into her pocket for her lip gloss.

As she fished for it, her fingers brushed against something else. Something that wasn't supposed to be there. Rhonda frowned and pulled out a folded napkin. She stared at it for a moment, trying to remember where it had come from. Then it hit her. These were the same pants she'd worn to the Dusty Rose. She hadn't washed them.

She laughed out loud. First because she'd put them back in her closet after sitting on sticky barstools, and second because now the night made perfect sense. That napkin had been crying out from her pocket for hours, throwing itself back into her life like a bad penny.

Rhonda held it up to the light, half-worn numbers scrawled in Jordan's handwriting. Why hadn't she thrown it away like she'd planned to? She'd completely forgotten about it. But she always washed her jeans after a night out. Had she really not worn this pair since the summer?

That was strange. All of this was outside her normal routine, and that made her skin start to buzz. She believed in this kind of thing—energy and all that cosmic mumbo jumbo. She'd had too many experiences in her life to write it off.

Like the time in college when she'd been dead set on skipping her friend Maya's engagement party because she was in one of those *Don't talk to me, I'm moody and existential* phases. She'd tried three times to leave the house that night, but each time, something pulled her back. She lost her keys, couldn't find her phone, and then realized her car battery was dead. Finally, she threw her hands up and went out in defeat, only to bump into a woman in the living room—a total stranger—who gave her the exact piece of advice she hadn't realized she'd needed about her job. That stranger had rattled off an entire pep talk, like the universe had sent her an undercover angel who just happened to be sipping a gin and tonic.

Then there was that time she actually lost her phone for an entire week—vanished without a trace. She'd been tearing her place apart, fuming, annoyed at the cosmic unfairness of it all. It finally turned up in the fridge, of all places, when she went for the almond milk. But by then, she'd spent days unplugged–forced to go out in the world, read an actual book, talk to her mom for an hour without "checking" anything.

That whole week had made her feel like she was living someone else's life for a change—and she'd liked it. She'd taken it as the universe telling her to unplug, to stop rushing for once. Now when she saw a pattern of "out of the ordinary" occurrences, she was immediately skeptical.

Rhonda stared at the napkin, her heart speeding in her chest. Texting Jordan would be a terrible idea. He worked strange magic when she was around him, and now that she knew he was on Pucks Deep?

No. She couldn't risk betraying the only family she had in this city just because his hands were capable of things that were borderline otherworldly.

The door to the washroom slammed open, and Rhonda jumped, shoving the napkin back in her pocket and thrusting her hands under the faucet for a second time.

———

Rhonda walked back to the table and sat down next to Penny

who was saying, "Oh, he's tough on the ice. Not so much when my dad's grilling him about grandkids."

"Wait, what is this?" Rhonda reached out for a piece of papadam.

Penny rolled her eyes. "My parents at Thanksgiving."

"Ooh, did you get the whole 'what are your intentions with my daughter' talk?" Rhonda dipped the cracker in tamarind sauce.

Brett scoffed. "That happens over text at least every couple months."

Rhonda laughed. "Sounds like lectures run in the family."

Penny rolled her eyes. "So what are we getting, family style?" she asked, looking over the options.

"Definitely need the butter chicken," Aaron suggested. "And maybe a couple orders of naan?"

"Vegetable biryani, too," Rhonda added.

"And let's do the lamb vindaloo," Brett said, folding his menu. "Spicy enough to make sure we'll all regret it tonight."

The waiter approached, and Rhonda gave their order. Brett specified half garlic naan, and Penny ordered a mango lassi. Brett and Aaron talked about work, they all joked about the American election coming up—so much fodder it was almost depressing but also sadistically entertaining since it took the spotlight off their own political woes.

When the food showed up, Rhonda's stomach was grumbling. The colours were vibrant, the aromas intoxicating. She couldn't wait to dig in. They passed the basmati rice around the table, followed by the dishes they'd ordered.

She and Aaron took their first bites at the same time, and Rhonda held back a sigh.

"Good?" He grinned at her from across the table.

Rhonda nodded, her mouth full. She reached for a piece of naan and tried the butter chicken. "So good. Great choice, Brett."

He puffed out his chest and started to say something, but Rhonda didn't hear it. Her stomach dropped when she felt a familiar irritation at the back of her throat. She frowned and took a sip of her water.

"Something wrong?" Penny asked.

Rhonda shook her head. "No, just—" She cleared her throat. Indian food didn't use peanuts. She'd eaten it a hundred times and never had an issue. But she knew this feeling, and it was getting progressively worse.

"Is there any chance there are peanuts in this?" She asked as the waiter passed by their table.

The waiter looked puzzled. "Peanuts? No, ma'am."

Rhonda's throat felt like it was closing in on itself. She tried to take a deep breath, but it felt like she was inhaling through a straw. "I don't think—"

Penny's eyes widened. "Rhonda, are you okay?"

Rhonda's mind raced. She always had her EpiPen with her, but she'd switched purses before she left the house. "I need my EpiPen. I think I'm having a reaction."

Aaron stood up, dropping his napkin. "Where is it?"

Rhonda shook her head, her hands trembling as she dug through her purse. "I don't have it. I—" She couldn't focus. Her heart was pounding, and her vision started to blur at the edges.

Brett was already pulling out his phone to dial an ambulance, but Rhonda shook her head. "No, we can't wait. I don't think I can wait."

Penny grabbed her purse and reached for Rhonda's hand. "Let's go. We'll find—"

"There's an urgent care clinic just a few blocks from here." Rhonda coughed. She had it mapped for a potential sales visit in the new year.

Rhonda's face flushed as she stood. She felt sluggish, like she was moving through molasses. She could barely focus on anything. Brett called something to the waiter as they rushed out of the restaurant and into Brett's truck.

Rhonda was legitimately starting to freak out as she stumbled into the back seat, Aaron's arm steadying her as her legs felt like Jell-O. So embarrassing.

She'd never had a reaction like this when she wasn't prepared. Why had she left her EpiPen at home? What the hell was she reacting to?

She fought to stay calm, breathing in through her nose, out through her mouth, forcing herself not to think about the fact that she was starting to wheeze. In. Out.

Brett revved the engine and peeled out of the parking lot. It was fine. If she died here, at least someone would know about it instead of her choking on a piece of steak in her living room or something.

Tears pooled at the corners of her eyes, and she gritted her teeth, willing herself not to cry in front of this masculine, noncommittal contractor she'd barely met. *Hey, you wanted a fun night out? How about holding my hand while my face blows up until I look like one of the Muppets.* Wasn't one of them named Rhonda? She squeezed Aaron's hand. No, it wasn't Rhonda. It was Janice. The one with blond hair and big lips.

Damn it, she was getting weird. Soon, she'd be full-on hallucinating. Her heart pounded in her chest as Brett swerved onto Macleod Trail. Rhonda's vision blurred, the streetlights and storefronts blending into a kaleidoscope of colour.

"We're almost there," Brett said, his voice strained. Rhonda nodded, tears now streaming freely down her cheeks. Her lips were tingling. She probably already looked at least partially like Will Smith in Hitch.

Aaron rubbed her back. "It'll be okay," he soothed, his voice barely audible over the thrum of the engine. The fact that he was trying to comfort her only made her cry harder.

This was what her friends were talking about. Someday she was going to be sitting in her hotel room, and she was going to have to stab her own thigh with an EpiPen and phone her own ambulance and lie alone in a hospital bed, and nobody was going to be rubbing her back and telling her it would be okay.

"Rhonda, you need to calm down." Penny turned in her seat, her eyes wide.

Rhonda tried to answer, but her throat was constricting, her breath coming in ragged gasps. She was right. She was always right, and Rhonda was an idiot. A sad, pathetic idiot with an allergy to a freaking nut that was currently trying to kill her. She gripped Aaron's hand harder and shook her head.

They pulled into the parking lot of the urgent care clinic, and Brett didn't bother finding a spot. He parked right in front of the entrance, and Aaron and Penny helped her out of the truck. Her legs wobbled as they hurried inside.

She couldn't smell anything. Could barely suck in a full lungful of air. Rhonda's eyes adjusted to the harsh fluorescent lights as she stumbled up to the intake desk. A nurse with a tight bun and dark circles under her eyes looked up from her computer.

"She's having a reaction," Brett snapped. "Peanut allergy."

The nurse's eyes widened. She motioned for another nurse, and Rhonda fumbled to pull her Universal Health Coverage card out of her purse. Penny reached over and took it, handing it to the nurse as Rhonda's hands started to shake.

"You're Rhonda Hart?" the nurse asked, her fingers hovering over the keyboard. Penny nodded for her, and the nurse typed it in, then handed the card back. "We'll get you in right away."

Brett looked like he was about to bash through the doors, and Penny put a hand on his arm. "They're coming. It's okay." She turned to find them all a place to sit, but a nurse appeared and motioned for Rhonda and Aaron to follow her.

"Can we—" Brett started, but the nurse shook her head.

"One person only."

Rhonda glanced at Penny, wishing she could come with instead of this guy she barely knew, but the nurse was already walking. They strode through the doors and down a sterile hallway.

It felt like she was sucking air through a cocktail straw. The nurse led them to a room, motioned for her to sit on the paper-covered lounger, and immediately started prepping something at the side counter.

Aaron stood next to her, shifting back to leave space for the nurse. The door creaked open, and when Rhonda looked up, her heart stopped in her chest. A man walked in. Tall with dark hair that curled slightly at the ends, a five o'clock shadow that added to his rugged charm, and a full tattoo sleeve on his left arm.

Jordan held a clipboard in his hand. He set it on the counter and said something to the nurse before turning around and looking at her.

Her lips were swollen, her face flushed, and still, he stopped dead. Jordan blinked, then looked up at Aaron.

She should've thrown out the damn napkin.

Jordan

JORDAN BLINKED. He felt like a bird that had just run full-tilt into a sparkling glass window. Rhonda. That was her name. He'd asked a few people at the bar that night, but they weren't sure, and he wasn't going to waltz over and ask Sean.

She sat stiffly on the edge of the exam table, looking pale and drawn, her breathing shallow. Some guy stood next to her, one hand resting on her shoulder, and he was rattling off the details like he had intimate knowledge of her life.

"She's having an allergic reaction," the guy was saying. "We think it was peanuts in the sauce."

No shit. Jordan's eyes flicked over him, assessing. Tall. Built. The guy's hand on Rhonda's shoulder, trying to look like he could do anything to help this situation. What an asshole.

Jordan stepped closer, keeping his gaze firmly on Rhonda, who was still looking at him like a deer in headlights. A deer with severe facial edema. "How long ago did this start?" He kept his voice steady. Cool. Professional.

"A few minutes," the guy answered, but Jordan barely registered the response. His focus was solely on getting her stable. "She only took a few bites of dinner." Her date shifted, fingers brushing over her arm like he was trying to comfort her.

Jordan gave a curt nod, barely acknowledging him, eyes on Rhonda as he reached out and took an epinephrine auto-injector from Ally, the nurse at the counter next to him. He sat on the stool and rolled up to her, sitting close enough he could feel her shaking. He put a hand on her thigh, hoping her date was watching.

"Rhonda, we've got this," he said, voice low and calm. "This'll get you breathing better in just a few seconds." She nodded once, and her fingers gripped the edge of the table. Tight.

He administered the epinephrine with a single quick motion, inserting the needle through her jeans on her outer thigh, then scanned her face for a reaction. It was ridiculous the way his chest tightened at the sight of her like this. *Just a patient.* That's all she was supposed to be tonight.

The guy next to her cleared his throat, and Jordan left his hands on her a few seconds longer than necessary just to screw with him.

Ally turned from the counter. "This is an albuterol inhaler. Have you used one before?" Rhonda nodded, her pupils already dilating from the shot. "Great, so take one deep breath and hold, okay?"

Ally held the inhaler to her lips, and Rhonda took it like a pro. Jordan turned, grabbing the IV kit from the counter, all of it muscle memory at this point. Assessing her veins took only a second. He scanned the inner crook of her elbow, spotting a prominent vein that barely needed a tap to rise to the surface.

His fingers grazed her skin as he positioned the needle. "Little pinch," he murmured. "You're doing great." A quick swipe with the antiseptic, and he was in, sliding the needle into her vein with the kind of smooth, practiced precision that made the whole thing look effortless. He secured the IV, glancing briefly to make sure the line was running smoothly.

Rhonda's date leaned in, and Jordan's voice came out sharper than he intended. "Give her a little space, eh?" Ally gave him a look, and he stepped back, too. Rhonda's wheeze was gone, but she was shaking. That was fine. A normal response to the epinephrine.

Jordan opened the cupboard behind him and pulled out a blanket. He laid it over her lap, tucking in the edges a little more than necessary. "What did you eat?"

Rhonda swallowed hard, pressing her fingers to her still-swollen lips. That was going to take a few hours to go back to normal. "Indian food. I can't remember exactly what we ordered—"

"Biryani, vindaloo, naan, and butter chicken." The guy next to her piped up. "The waiter said there weren't any peanuts."

Jordan set down the clipboard. "Fenugreek."

Rhonda's eyes widened. "What?"

"Some chefs put fenugreek in butter chicken. Seeds or powder."

Rhonda blinked. "Okay, and?"

Jordan dispensed hand sanitizer and rubbed it between his palms out of habit. "Fenugreek is in the same family as peanuts. If you're allergic to peanuts, there's a good chance you'll react to fenugreek." Rhonda's mouth opened, then closed. "It's not common knowledge. I only know because of my sister. She has a peanut allergy and found out the hard way."

Jordan picked up her chart. Peanut allergy. It was noted. "Is this your boyfriend?" He didn't look up.

"Uh . . ." Rhonda hesitated.

"Blind date. I'm Aaron." The dude put out a hand, and Jordan glanced up from the clipboard. He shook it then reached for more sanitizer.

Rhonda exhaled and leaned back against the reclined chair.

"It was a double date. My other friends are still in the waiting room."

Jordan turned to Ally. "Can you get this chart approved with Dr. Petrov? I'm guessing he's going to want Benadryl and Solu-Medrol before we discharge."

Ally nodded, taking the chart and exiting the room. They had other patients needing attention, and they only had one doctor on staff for the next couple of hours. Rhonda probably wouldn't meet Petrov in person.

Jordan nodded toward the door. "Aaron, you can go get your other friends. Tell them she's stable. They can come see her."

Aaron hesitated a moment, then glanced at Rhonda. She nodded, and he shuffled past the two of them and exited into the hall.

Rhonda dropped her head back. "What a shitty date."

Jordan pointed back at the door. "Because of that guy? Yeah. I get it." Rhonda laughed, then winced and pressed her non-IV hand to her forehead. "You might be a little out of it for a bit."

She turned her head to look at him. "Thank you."

Jordan wheeled the stool over to the computer, putting a few notes into her chart. "Just doing my job."

"Yeah. I didn't know you were a . . . doctor?"

"Nurse." He glanced over, and to her credit, she kept a smirk off her face. "Just say it." There it was. A puffy-ass grin.

"Say what?"

"I know you're thinking it."

She laughed through her next words. "I wasn't thinking anything."

"Bull shit." He turned from the computer, smirking.

Rhonda pursed her lips. "Okay, I might've been thinking that it's kind of funny—"

"Funny how, exactly?"

She groaned. "You're going to make me say this?"

"Definitely."

She lifted her head. "It's funny because you're this, like, hot, built hockey player."

"And hot, built hockey players can't be nurses?" He deadpanned.

Rhonda grinned. "You're the worst."

"You're smiling. Plus I got you to admit you think I'm hot. I win." He stood up from the stool.

She scoffed, ignoring him. "I think it's the name. 'Nurse' sounds so feminine. They should have a different title, like 'emergency responder' or something."

"That's an actual job."

"Well, you know what I'm saying."

Jordan grabbed the blood pressure cuff and sidled up to her. He reached for her wrist and wrapped the cuff around her arm, then pressed his stethoscope against the bend in her elbow. "You have to breathe."

"Right." Rhonda swallowed hard.

"It's a little high." Jordan flicked his eyes to her. "Probably the epinephrine."

"Mmm. Yep."

Jordan slung the stethoscope around his neck and stepped back so she couldn't hear his own heart hammering in his chest. The door to the room swung in, and there was Aaron with Bouchard and his physical therapist girlfriend. Penny, was it?

"Hey, Copper." Jordan grabbed his clipboard and waited for them to fully enter the room.

Penny's eyes opened in surprise. "Oh, hey. Jordan, right?" He nodded, and Brett's jaw tensed. "You work here?"

"I mostly work at Rocky Ridge, but I pick up shifts here off and on," he said. Penny's mouth fell open, and her head swung to Rhonda. Rhonda's eyes were narrowed, boring into him. "Ah, alright then. I'll be back in a few." Jordan rapped his knuckles on the countertop, then got the hell out of there before something else happened that he had no explanation for. He sucked in a deep breath and released it, shaking out his hands as he walked back to the nurse's station.

"You were right, as usual." Ally waited for him, holding two IV bags in her arms. "Want me to administer it?"

Jordan nodded. He didn't want to walk back in there two seconds after he left, even though the pull to ditch his shift and sit bedside next to Rhonda for the rest of the night felt worse than watching Burrows in game seven, 2011, stickhandling in double overtime.

He forced himself to take his time making his rounds, giving the Benadryl Ally administered a chance to kick in. When he got back to the room a half hour later, Rhonda's eyelids were drooping. She smiled when he walked in, and his chest clenched. The bed was reclined, the lights dimmed, and she looked so small on the bed, her dark curls spreading out like a halo on the crappy pillow.

"I'm glad you're here." Her words were slurred together as she reached out her hand, and Jordan's breath caught in his throat. For a split second, he thought she was reaching out for him before her hand landed on Aaron's arm.

Jordan's eye twitched. He cleared his throat and inspected the numbers on her pulse ox. "Your oxygen levels are good. The meds in your IV will prevent a secondary reaction."

"That happens?" Penny asked.

He nodded. "Sometimes." The three of them were crammed in like sardines. Bouchard and Aaron were half sitting on the counter.

"How much longer will she need to be here?" Bouchard asked.

"I'm going to stay here for a while. I can't move my legs." Rhonda grinned, and Jordan's stomach did a backflip.

"That's the Benadryl. It's doing its job." He willed his voice to steady and crossed his arms in front of him. "Shouldn't be more than another half hour now that everything looks good. She'll be sleepy. She can't drive."

"I can drive her car home," Penny offered, and Bouchard nodded. Penny leaned back and put a hand on his arm. "Why don't you two go out to the waiting room? I'll stay here with her, and we'll meet you out there . . . "

Jordan snuck out before they did. He tapped his pen against his palm then walked to the next room. He checked in with Ms. Simmons, a woman in her sixties who was battling a bladder infection, and updated her chart. He discussed her treatment plan with Dr. Petrov and noted her medication adjustments.

Next, he visited a man in his forties with a fractured wrist. He checked his vitals, made sure his pain was under control, and updated his records. At the nurse's station, he reviewed the notes from the previous shift and added his observations. He grabbed a coffee and a couple of non-peanut granola bars from the break room, then headed back to the printer. Rhonda's discharge paperwork was there, so he snagged that, too, and walked to her room.

He paused at the door at the sound of conversation.

"I think that's the Benadryl talking." Penny laughed.

"You don't think he's hot?" Rhonda sighed. "Probably because you're betrothed or whatever."

Penny chortled. "Okay, I'm definitely filming now."

"Staaahp."

Jordan pushed the door open and stepped in, wishing he could ask who Rhonda was talking about. He was just going to believe it was him. That was best for his ego.

Jordan set the granola bars on the counter. "Alright, looks like you're good to go. Brought these in case you need a snack." He might've been listening when her blind date said she only got two bites of dinner.

Penny smiled and took two bars as Rhonda sat up. Her face was mostly back to normal. It looked like she had just a hint of lip filler. A surprising sense of relief washed over him.

He blinked and handed the papers off to Penny. He was about to launch into instructions for her care overnight but hesitated and turned to Rhonda. "Do you have anyone, um, someone at home with you? That could watch you overnight?"

Rhonda threw up her free hand. "Ugh, now it's you, too? Is everyone just going to keep rubbing it in my face that I'm going to die alone in my house?"

Penny snorted, her phone camera still rolling. "Rhonda, I think—"

"Do you want to come watch me overnight, Jordan? Would that make you more comfortable?" Rhonda slapped her hand on the bed next to her.

Jordan wet his lips, trying not to laugh. "So. Might be a good idea to let her crash on your couch."

"Yeah." Penny tried to keep a straight face.

"Keep an eye out for any other symptoms. She's had her dose of Benadryl and steroids, but if she starts to have trouble breathing or you notice any swelling, get her back here imme- diately."

Penny nodded, her expression sobering. She dropped her phone. "Got it. And if she wakes up in the night?"

"Just make sure she's comfortable. She can take another dose of Benadryl if she needs it, but it might make her a bit groggy in the morning. Everything's on the paperwork."

"Mmkay. Thanks for all your help, Jordan."

"No problem." He stood in front of the bed and locked eyes with Rhonda. He didn't want to say anything that would incrim- inate her. She'd made it clear at the bar that she didn't want anyone on the Snowballs to know they knew each other. But he also couldn't leave without giving her some kind of message. "Hope you feel better soon. If you need anything, I guess you know where to find me."

Rhonda slow-blinked like a cat. "I guess I do."

"Ooookay, let's get you out of here." Penny stood and helped Rhonda from the bed. Jordan turned toward the door, then stopped when Penny asked, "How's the shoulder?"

Jordan turned back. "Like new." He rotated it to prove his point.

Rhonda's jaw dropped. "You know about his shoulder?" She shot daggers at him. "Did you two—"

"Physical therapy." Jordan cut her off before she could expose their history. "Last year. She treated my shoulder. I think she does have a thing for hockey players, though."

Rhonda was still glaring at Penny. Jordan left before he could hear the end of that conversation, a smug smile still on his face. She was jealous. She thought he was hot, and she didn't want another woman touching his shoulders. Jordan made a quick trip to the washroom to splash water on his face. He still had two hours left on his shift, and he was currently pitching an average size tent in his scrubs.

CHAPTER
Five

RHONDA WOKE up feeling like her head was stuffed with cotton, every muscle in her body heavy and sluggish. She blinked at the ceiling, piecing together where she was. Right. Penny and Brett's new guest room. She lifted up the sheets. In her bra and panties. Perfect. Hopefully Brett didn't see anything he didn't want to.

Sunlight filtered in through gauzy white curtains. A tall, unmarked dresser stood against one wall, and a reading chair was tucked in the corner with an Instagram-worthy stack of books on the delicate side table next to it. A watercolour of peonies hung on the far wall, and the walls were a soft grey just like the rest of the house. It was simple but cozy, and she'd take that over the fluorescent lights of urgent care any day.

Rhonda pushed herself up on one elbow, squinting at the clock on the side table. 8:12 a.m. Her heart thudded, her Cortisol spiking—had she slept through an alarm? Had she even set an alarm?

Her phone sat on the nightstand, charging, and she grabbed it, flipping through her calendar. Nothing scheduled today. She had no hospital visits, no appointments. Her heart released its grasp on her throat and settled back in her chest.

Which made plenty of space for her mind to circle back to last night. She groaned, pressing her palms against her face as flashes of moments and conversations in the urgent care came back, hazy but vivid. Aaron had been standing next to her, his hand on her arm, but then . . . Jordan.

Her cheeks grew warm as she remembered him walking through the door. The way he'd frozen, the whites of his eyes growing. How he'd recognized her right away was beyond her. By how tight her skin felt, she must've looked like she'd run into a beehive with her mouth open.

She thought of his hands brushing over her skin as he checked her vitals, his voice saying *"just a little pinch"* as he administered the IV. The whole thing felt like a fever dream, but Rhonda glanced down at her arm and found the cotton ball and tape still there in the crook of her elbow.

Fenugreek. Rhonda shivered at the memory of her throat on fire, the sensation of a hand squeezing around her neck. How many foreign dishes had she eaten in blissful ignorance? And what else could it be hiding in? She made a mental note to always carry the EpiPen. She was going to have to purchase a larger bum bag.

She swung her legs over the side of the bed and padded to the small washroom attached to the guest room. Gleaming white tiles, an oval mirror, towels in greys and creams. It was so Penny —everything in its place, clean and functional.

Her own washroom, on the other hand, looked like she'd just checked in for a week-long vacation. It wasn't too far from reality, considering how much she travelled. Everything was out. Easily accessible. She'd tried the whole organization thing, but she didn't have the patience to put her tincture bottles away just to get them out again in eight hours. Maybe if someone else were affected by the lack of counter space, she'd suddenly acquire the willpower.

Rhonda splashed cold water on her face and took a moment, the exhaustion settling deeper into her bones. There was a profound hollowness behind her eyes. An ache in the muscles of her jaw.

After freshening up, she pulled on her clothes from the night before—they still smelled like warm spice—and shuffled out to the kitchen, where the scent of eggs and greens greeted her. Penny was at the stove, a spatula in one hand and a cup of coffee in the other.

"There's our little warrior," Penny grinned, eyeing Rhonda over her cup. "How are you feeling?"

"Like I got hit by a truck." Rhonda slid onto one of the stools at the counter. "Did I—at one point was I talking about Jord— my nurse's shoulders?"

Penny laughed and took the pan off the heat. "Yeah. You were pretty hopped up on the Dryl." She poured a fresh cup of coffee, then plated up a serving of food on a modern white plate and slid it across the counter. "I checked on you a couple of times during the night just to make sure you were still breathing. You're welcome."

"So you're the person I can blame when I have recurring nightmares about a break-in."

Penny tipped her proverbial hat. "What are the chances that Jordan Wheatfill would be your nurse?"

"Yeah. Wild." Rhonda took a drink of her coffee, hoping her cheeks weren't betraying her. She should've left the subject alone, but her curiosity got the better of her. "Anne filled me in on him when he showed up at the Dusty Rose that one time in the summer. I didn't know he was one of your patients."

Penny settled into her right hip and scoffed. "That was well before I had anything to do with the Snowballs. I was renting that extra room at Brett's, and he was kind enough to hook me up with Elite League players while I was scrambling for a job."

Rhonda nodded, working to keep her next question casual. "So Brett didn't care?"

Penny scoffed. "Oh, he definitely cared. The first session I had with Jordan—I was using the detached garage for my studio—Brett came out pretending he had to look for a lamp or something. He had his chest all puffed out, all hot and bothered." Her eyes flicked up. "It was super hot."

Rhonda laughed, her fork hovering over the eggs. "So he was mad because he wanted you. Thought Jordan was going to swoop in." She took a bite, savouring the warmth and flavour.

"I don't know. I didn't realize how much history there was there. Did you know one of the Pucks Deep players put Fly—do you know him? Old captain of the Snowballs, before Sean—anyway, one of them put him in the hospital. After the game, came at him in the parking lot and left him with two cracked ribs."

Holy shit. "This was a long time ago?" Rhonda didn't know why she was asking. It didn't matter. She'd seen the animosity between the players in person and between the fans in the stands.

Penny shrugged. "Fly only left the team a couple of years ago when he aged out, so not that long. There are a hundred other stories, and it's not just the other players. Jordan's one of the worst." She cupped her coffee mug with both hands. "I don't know. He was fine when I worked with him."

"Right." Rhonda's heart pounded in her ears. *He was fine when she'd worked with him, too.* More than fine. She'd been with men who made it obvious from the first kiss that they were only in it for themselves. Jordan had been the complete opposite. It was why she'd cruised past the caution tape that night in Okotoks.

Every moment with him in Medicine Hat was seamless. As a perfect stranger, he'd made her feel safe, and given her long list of neuroses, that wasn't a simple task. Instead of treating her like a brand new toy he got to play with, she'd felt like a gift he was unwrapping. It sounded cheesy, but there it was. Even in the cramped backseat of his truck, he'd found a way to admire her.

Rhonda swallowed hard, the dark intensity of his eyes startlingly clear through her antihistamine-hazed brain from the night before. *I guess you know where to find me.*

". . . I thought I would find him on the couch this morning."

Rhonda's eyes snapped up. "Who, Jordan?"

Penny frowned. "No, Aaron." She took another sip of her coffee. "He was so worried about you."

Rhonda blinked. Right. She'd been on a date last night. *And hadn't thought about him once since she'd woken up.* "That's sweet."

"I texted him this morning. He didn't have your number, but I told him you were fine and I'd pass his along to you."

"Mmm. Thanks." Rhonda took her last bite of eggs and carried her plate to the sink, her pulse racing when one other detail snapped against her mind like an elastic. *Jordan's number.* Probably still plastered to her hip on that thin strip of napkin at the bottom of her pocket. "Thank you so much for breakfast. Text it to me?"

Penny nodded and checked the clock on the stove. She blew out a breath. "I have to get going. But no rush. You can stay as long as you need."

"I'll clear out—I need to prep for some appointments tomorrow."

Penny rinsed out her mug. "You heard that Jordan works at Rocky Ridge, right?"

Rhonda feigned sudden remembrance. "Oh, yeah. He mentioned that last night."

"Probably not an option. Now that he knows you're with the Snowballs, but . . ." She exhaled. "I'm not offering this lightly because Brett would not be thrilled with this plan, but they do have an Elite League message board. I could have him reach out if you're desperate."

Rhonda's heart twinged. With guilt or gratitude, she wasn't

quite sure. "No, it's fine. I don't want to rock the boat. I'll figure something else out."

Penny grinned. "Kay. Just go out the garage when you leave. I'll text you the code." She rounded the counter and wrapped her in a hug. "And never scare me like that again."

Rhonda sank into her, the tension in her shoulders instantly easing. "Got it."

Penny smacked her hip as she pulled back, then waved on her way to pick up her purse from the bench in the entryway. Rhonda waited just long enough for her to disappear into the mudroom, then raced into the guest bedroom like she was a sixteen-year-old who tricked her parents into letting her skip school.

She reached into her pocket and pulled out the napkin, then wrestled her phone from its charger on the nightstand. She tapped on a new text message, her fingers hovering over the numeric keypad.

This was for work. Jordan had a connection there at the hospital, and she didn't have to go through the Elite League boards or anyone on the Snowballs to get in touch with him. Nobody on the team would blame her for accidentally meeting him at work, just like they didn't hold it against Penny when she'd treated him before she'd been wrapped into the family fold.

Rhonda typed the number, then jumped when her phone vibrated in her hand. A text from Penny with the garage code. And Aaron's number. She swiped out of that conversation and went back to her new message and began to type.

This message is for Jordan Wheatfill. Checking if this is still your number? This is Rhonda. If you don't remember me, I was a recent patient —food allergy.

She didn't want to say too much in case she was texting a random stranger, but needed to give him enough info that he wouldn't just delete it. Though remembering her didn't guarantee he wouldn't ignore it. What had she said to him when she'd gotten out of his truck? Something about how she was glad he didn't live locally because he was *too tempting?*

How embarrassing. It was bad enough she'd had to see him at the bar after that, realizing that he'd known who she was that night and not said a word, but now he had the genuinely horrifying image of her sitting on a hospital bed, sweating through her shirt, with a face reminiscent of Quasimodo's half-sister.

Rhonda pressed send. She didn't have a better option. She'd been working for years to find a connection there, and somehow Bailey Winters, the rep for TheraNova had gotten their version of Cardivex in last spring instead of hers. It had performed worse in clinical trials, and they were only offering half of what Cantra would've given for inpatient benefits and rebates. When she sent that information to Rocky Ridge, she received a one-line reply.

Dr. Mallory isn't available at this time.

It was the same response she'd gotten every six months when she dutifully responded to her calendar alert. Dr. Mallory was never available. Unless you were TheraNova.

At least they didn't have an answer to Reviact, but she'd still had no luck getting in for a presentation. Dr. Mallory had also been notably absent at the luncheon she'd held for other chiefs of pharmacy and therapeutics. Jordan was the first lead she'd had in ages, and regardless of their history, she had to take it.

Maybe the night before would make things better, not worse. All that giving-her-his-number-at-the-bar energy was probably so far gone he'd be shocked to see her text him. She could show up and make a few connections with the nurses he knew, and he'd be happy to pass her off.

Too many coincidences. She couldn't ignore the cosmos.

Her phone buzzed.

Looks like you found me

CHAPTER
Six

JORDAN

JORDAN WRAPPED up the last of his shift at the nurse's station, feeling that late-afternoon drag settle in. It always took him a solid week to recover from a night shift, but he couldn't say no when he knew how short-staffed they were, and it didn't affect his team.

Clipboard in hand, he jotted down a quick set of vitals for a final patient, then tossed the pen back in its holder. He logged off the computer, mentally checking off his list: patient files updated, meds double-checked for the next shift, his station cleared. All of it was so routine, he didn't have to leave his head to get it right.

And inside his head was all Rhonda. If she'd been serious in their text conversation that morning, she should be arriving any minute. He glanced up, scanning the lobby and ER intake area for the hundredth time.

He'd thought all afternoon about what it meant that his

stomach felt like he'd swallowed a packet of Pop Rocks. Gertie, the shift coordinator, had already commented on how frequently he was checking his phone when he rarely took it out of his pocket on normal days.

How could Rhonda think that he wouldn't remember her? Had she been that out of it the night before that she hadn't noticed the hints he'd been trying to send?

Jordan turned, flicked on the shredder, and started shoving in papers from the top of the trash pile. They'd moved to a digital record system years ago, but this stack was all the old records that were still being transitioned when old patients came back for a visit.

She wasn't out of his system. That was all he knew for certain. Every time he saw her, it was like he'd been standing in a dim room, and someone suddenly flicked on the lights.

But what did that mean? Was he intrigued? Was his mind trying to make sense of the fact that she didn't want to hook up again after the two explosive nights they'd had? Or was he feeling a bit insecure since she'd made it clear at the bar that the team he played for trumped any connection they had. Could it have been as good as he thought if she was able to shut it down that fast?

No. It'd been good.

He replayed the moment she'd left his truck that night in the parking lot. *"It's a good thing you don't live locally. This would be too tempting."*

He reached for another stack of paper and shoved it into the metal teeth. Rhonda had contacted him to get to Dr. Mallory. She'd had that napkin with his number on it for months and hadn't used it until now.

But she'd kept it.

That fact kept ringing through his head. She hadn't known at the bar that he had any connection to Rocky Ridge, but she hadn't thrown it out. He tucked that bit of information away.

A pang of guilt hit his stomach as he fed the next batch of old patient records through the shredder. He hadn't explicitly told Rhonda that he had an "in" with Dr. Mallory, but he also hadn't been honest about the fact that he was the last person in that hospital who could ask a favour from him. Jordan was a damn good nurse and that fact hadn't protected him from what happened the previous February.

Jordan turned when movement caught his eye and froze. Rhonda was there across the room, standing at the intake desk in front of the entry. She looked polished and professional, like she'd just stepped off the set of some corporate commercial. Her blazer hugged her shoulders, and her curly hair was . . . tamed. He had to admit, he liked it better splayed around her face on his leather seat.

Jordan caught himself staring and dropped his eyes. What was he doing? He'd wanted to see her again, but now that she was here—

"Here we go," Gertie murmured.

Jordan looked up and frowned. *When had she arrived?* He turned just in time for Rhonda's eyes to meet his. The corner of her mouth twitched as she smoothed her blazer, her heels clicking on the linoleum as she strode toward the nurse's station. The closer she got, the harder it was to ignore the pull low in his stomach.

Rhonda stopped in front of the counter, her hands lightly folded in front of her, the faintest flush on her cheeks.

"Where can I direct you?" Gertie asked, her voice gruff. It was disturbing and impressive how she could transform from a kind-hearted granny into a hardened prison guard in a matter of seconds.

Jordan had worked at Rocky Ridge long enough to know what Gertie's greetings meant. "Hello, sweetheart," meant she knew the person approaching was having a shit day. "How can I help you?" meant that person had already bothered her or one of the other nurses on shift, and "Where can I direct you?" was as good as a middle finger.

Rhonda hadn't done anything wrong, but Gertie had taken one look at her outfit and made the assumption—correctly—that Rhonda was one of the many professionals trying to get an appointment with the hospital administration. It wasn't only Dr. Mallory that made things difficult. Rocky Ridge was as steeped in tradition as The Original Six.

"I'm right where I need to be," Rhonda answered. "I think." Her eyes flicked to him, and she looked suddenly unsure.

Jordan stepped forward. "Yep. Thanks for meeting me." He swiped his ID card to clock out. "You want to grab a coffee?"

Rhonda hesitated, looking briefly over her shoulder as if debating her options. "Sure."

Jordan would've given his left nut to know what was going through her head right then, and that was saying something. His left nut was his unspoken favourite.

"Where's your report?" Gertie eyed him.

"Already handed off to Marie." Jordan put a hand on her shoulder. "See you Sunday."

Gertie shrugged him off. "We're short-staffed with you at half-time."

He winked. "You can just tell me you miss me." He motioned for Rhonda to follow him down the hallway toward the hospital's attached coffee shop.

"How was work?"

"Good." His heart hammered against his ribs. What was it about her that made him feel like he'd just finished a round of suicides? He'd never felt like this around a woman before, especially not one he'd already slept with. His prowess in the bedroom had always been a source of pride. Confidence. It gave a strange sort of power when a woman looked at him and knew from experience what he was capable of.

With Rhonda, it was the exact opposite. She'd tasted the

forbidden fruit and had decided she didn't want it anymore. That lit a fuse that was slowly incinerating, edging closer and closer to a blast he wouldn't be able to contain.

Women weren't able to quit him that easily. And as much as he wanted to pull her into the storage closet they'd be passing in less than four seconds and remind her what she was missing, he kept to the script he'd pre-planned after receiving her text. *You don't want her either.*

Jordan matched his stride with Rhonda's as they moved down the fluorescent-lit hallway, passing the rows of curtained-off exam bays. Antiseptic seemed to be ground into the grout between the tiles, the scent was so overpowering, and the low mechanical beeps and shuffling footsteps barely registered.

They passed two other nurses, and both of them gave Jordan a raised eyebrow. He was going to hear all about this on Sunday. He was the minority in this hospital, and working in a sea of women meant that his love life was always under scrutiny. He didn't date his co-workers. But he hadn't seen a problem with dating a few of their sisters.

Jordan guided Rhonda down a side hall to the coffee shop. It was a small, unassuming place, wedged into the corner just past the gift shop, but for him, it was a kind of refuge. Every morning, he stopped by here, talking with the same staff who knew his order by heart.

He'd hoped it would be dead at that time in the afternoon, but the place buzzed with activity—doctors grabbing a caffeine fix, patient families picking up snacks since it wasn't quite late enough to justify a full dinner. Rhonda took it all in as he motioned for her to join him at the counter.

Oscar, the barista, caught sight of them and flashed a grin. "Hey, Jordan. Usual?"

"Yeah, thanks," he said, then turned to Rhonda. "What are you having?"

She scanned the chalkboard menu. "I'll take a caramel

macchiato, please." Jordan swiped his card, and Rhonda frowned. "You don't need to—"

"It's fine. Coffees are free for staff." Technically, he only got two free coffees a day, but he'd given up his morning cup so he could use both that afternoon.

They waited a moment, then took their drinks and found a corner booth.

"So last night was a little embarrassing." Rhonda tapped her fingers on her cup and took a sip.

"You know I regularly look at people's assholes, right?" he said. Rhonda nearly snorted out her drink, and Jordan grinned. "Sorry. It felt like saying something extreme would get my point across."

Rhonda searched for a napkin, but there weren't any on the table. Jordan stood and walked over to the dispenser and grabbed her one. When he returned, she'd mostly mopped it up with her fingertips, but her bottom lip was still wet. Jordan had the sudden urge to reach out and wipe it.

He set the napkins on the table and sat back down, forcing his hands to his lap.

"It was kind of a shock to see you there." Rhonda dabbed the napkin to her lips.

"Would it have been less shocking if you didn't have someone with you?" he asked.

Rhonda looked at him quizzically. "I doubt it. Would it have enhanced your experience?"

Jordan smirked. "I'm pretty good at keeping work and plea-sure separate." The statement didn't ring as true as it would've in the past. He did not enjoy seeing Aaron, or whatever the hell his name was, standing with his hand on Rhonda's shoulder.

Rhonda's pupils dilated just enough that he knew that comment hit. So, she didn't hate him enough to not be thinking about what had happened between them. Even when she was in the midst of a full-on anaphylactic attack. But it wasn't good enough. He was still dying to know exactly what she thought about their prior encounters. Maybe if he had a little closure, the buzzing in his head every time she was in his vicinity would stop.

Jordan had never been one for finesse in conversation. He'd pissed off plenty of people in his personal life and at work because of his brusque nature. In his twenties, he may have cared, but in his mid-thirties, he just didn't give a shit anymore. He'd learned when to keep his mouth closed, but if he was going to open it, he was going to say what he thought. Or in this case, ask what he wanted to ask.

"Do you regret it?" He didn't need to know if the sex was good. That had been obvious.

Rhonda blinked, then set her drink back on the table. "Regret what?" she parried, knowing damn well what he was asking. He didn't give her the satisfaction of an explanation. He leaned back in the bench seat and waited.

Rhonda opened her mouth then closed it again. "I gave up regrets a long time ago."

That wasn't a full no, but it wasn't a yes, either. He would take it. "What made you stay in my hotel room that first night?"

Rhonda blew out a breath. "I actually came here to talk about—"

Jordan held up a hand. "Yeah. I know. Doctor Mallory. But if I'm going to help you with this and we're going to be seeing each other again, I need to clear the air."

Rhonda raised an eyebrow. "Clear the air? Do you have a problem with me?"

Jordan nodded. "Yeah."

Rhonda's mild look of amusement turned to a frown. "I—" She looked down at her coffee cup. "Did I—"

"My problem is that every time I see you, I want to strip your clothes off and lift you back onto the seat of my truck." Jordan lowered his voice. Rhonda didn't look up, just tightened her grip on her coffee cup. He took a deep breath and continued. "That's not usually a problem for me. Once I've been with someone, I don't have strong feelings about whether I'm with that someone again. Considering how we met, I'm guessing it's the same for you?"

Rhonda swallowed. Her breathing had quickened, and if he had to guess, he would put her blood pressure right where it had been the night before when he pressed a stethoscope to the inside of her arm.

Her shoulders visibly relaxed, like she suddenly became aware of her own body and told it to back down. She looked up and met his eyes. "Yes. Same for me."

"But you came with me in Okotoks."

Rhonda flicked her tongue over her lower lip just like she had in the bar that night. "I did."

"Why?"

She gave him a look. "It was a weak moment. And I still didn't know that you lived here."

"So . . . was that your plan then? I was satisfactory enough to hit up when I was in town?"

"I didn't have a plan."

He huffed a breath. "Yeah, people like us aren't really good at that."

Rhonda scoffed. "Okay, I may not have linear, forward momentum with relationships, but that doesn't mean that I'm not serious about my job. Is that what this is? Trying to weed out whether I'm going to be flighty and noncommittal with your boss before you give me access to him?"

Jordan cleared his throat. He should tell her. He should admit that he wouldn't be able to get her a meeting with Mallory. That she had a better chance of landing an audience with him if she pretended she'd never met him.

But then he thought about her standing up and walking away like she had at the Dusty Rose, about her never using that number he'd scrawled on the napkin, and something inside of him locked down like a table brake.

Jordan ran a hand through his hair. "Yeah. Exactly."

Rhonda's face grew serious. "I can show you all the data on the drug I want to get on the formulary here. If that would help." She picked up her phone then set it down again. "Might be easier on my laptop, but I didn't bring it."

Jordan nodded, his pulse rushing in his ears. "Where do you live?"

CHAPTER
Seven

RHONDA WALKED down the sidewalk between the ultra-modern apartments on either side of her. They were painted in earthy colours, all straight lines and metal railings. It had only been half an hour since she left the hospital, but it felt like a year with all the thoughts playing battle bots in her head. *She wasn't going to tell him where she lived.*

Listening to Coldplay on the way over had only accomplished so much. She couldn't expect Chris Martin to put her completely at ease in a situation like this. Especially when she knew damn-well she shouldn't be here. But what were the other options? Do this at her place? Automatic no. Meet at a Tims and talk about addiction recovery with every Grandma in the Northwest?

She shivered. A cold front was blowing in, and she was grateful for her thick wool tights and the fact that she'd picked a thicker blouse to go under her blazer. She pushed through the doors to building A, then smoothed her skirt and straightened her back, replacing her laptop bag strap over her shoulder before walking forward and pushing the button for the elevator.

She glanced around the lobby. Took in the calming, abstract art. This would be simple. She'd already presented in front of hundreds of doctors and medical professionals at three other medical centres in the past month. She'd prepared for this conversation meticulously. She had every detail about Reviact memorized, every potential question Jordan could throw at her thought through, and every answer polished to a sheen. After seeing the data, he wouldn't be able to turn her away in good conscience.

The elevator dinged, and Rhonda took it to the third floor, then exited and followed the signs to Jordan's door. She drew a deep breath and knocked. This was business. It was the mantra she'd repeated the whole drive over. She needed Jordan to take her seriously because, after last night, she'd already blurred the lines more than she'd intended. There couldn't be any hint of impropriety—she wasn't manipulating Jordan to get to Dr. Mallory, just presenting the facts.

Jordan was a contact. Just another hospital employee who could help get her product to the people who needed it. Her heart beat a little faster than it should, but she attributed that to the fact that she was about to enter the house of a man who'd seen her naked. More like *heard* her naked.

She groaned, then closed her eyes and forced another deep breath in.

Within seconds, Jordan answered the door, and Rhonda's pulse stuttered. He had changed out of his scrubs and was dressed in jeans and a white T-shirt. She didn't know which was worse, but what did her in was that his hair was wet. Exactly like it was the first time. *Had he done that on purpose?* Her eyes traced the lines of his collarbone, barely visible above the collar of his shirt.

"Come in." Jordan stepped back, and her stomach flipped. That was a normal thing to say, but hearing it out of his mouth . .

. Ugh. It was like his voice was laced with ginseng or whatever other eastern medicinal herbs Tina had been talking about that boosted libido. She clearly didn't need any of them.

Rhonda slipped off her shoes and set them next to the door, then followed Jordan down the hall and into a small living room. The whole place smelled like his body wash. It wasn't cologne. It was too subtle. She found herself wondering if he was a bar soap or loofah guy. She could use his washroom and—

"Can I get you anything? Water?" Jordan asked.

"Umm, sure. Water would be good." She opened her bag, pulled out her laptop.

The space was cozy, with a deep chocolate brown leather couch and a rustic coffee table. The walls were clean and minimalist with a few pieces of art and some hockey memorabilia. Rhonda set her laptop bag on the coffee table and took a seat on the couch, her pulse still thrumming from the sight of him standing there in his own space. It was how she'd felt when she'd gone on a behind-the-scenes tour at the Calgary Zoo as a middle schooler and first walked through the "Staff Only" door.

Jordan sat down on the couch next to her, and she slid a little on the cushion. He set the water down on a coaster in front of her, and Rhonda opened her laptop. She scooted to the edge of the couch, not looking up as she clicked through her files. "I know this isn't your first rodeo, so I'll skip the sales pitch and get straight to the important points." Might as well get into it.

Rhonda pulled up the first blue slide. "Reviact is a long-acting medication for addiction management. It's designed to reduce cravings by stabilizing neurotransmitter levels, specifically those linked to reward and dependency pathways in the brain."

She scrolled through the next few slides then paused to show tables and graphs as she launched into the clinical data. "In our third-party trials, we've seen a seventy-three percent success rate in reducing relapse rates over a six-month period. Patients have also reported a sixty percent improvement in adherence compared to standard treatments." Rhonda glanced at Jordan, who was watching her computer screen, his face unreadable.

She continued, outlining the patient benefits and potential for improving addiction treatment outcomes. Her words were measured, her tone calm, but inside she was tangled up like a fitted sheet in the dryer. He was giving her nothing. No smile. No "hmms" or other sounds whatsoever. Was he impressed? Skeptical? Bored?

Rhonda blew out a breath. "So, in summary, Reviact offers a more effective and sustainable solution for patients struggling with addiction. It's not a magic bullet, but it's a significant step forward." She clicked to the next slide, her finger hovering over the mouse. "Any questions so far?"

Jordan leaned closer, his knee brushing against hers, and Rhonda's breath hitched. She forced herself to look at the screen, but she couldn't ignore the way his hand slid along the back of the couch near her shoulder. The scent of his soap, fresh and clean, filled her senses.

"You mentioned patient adherence. How exactly does Reviact improve that compared to other treatments?" he asked, his voice reverberating through her.

Rhonda sat back and turned to face him, her brain stuttering over the words she could normally rattle off without a second thought. "Right, so, Reviact has a longer half-life, which means patients don't have to take it as frequently. That alone reduces the burden of daily medication adherence. Additionally, the stabilization of neurotransmitter levels helps with overall mood improvement and cognitive function, making it easier for patients to stick to their treatment plans."

Jordan nodded, his eyes flicking to hers. "And the side effects?"

Rhonda's mouth suddenly felt like she'd taken double the recommended dose of cyclobenzaprine. She picked up her glass of water and took a sip. "In our trials, we've seen minimal side effects. Most patients experience some initial nausea or dizziness, but those symptoms typically subside within the first few weeks of treatment. The benefit-to-risk ratio is highly favourable."

The only sign that Jordan had heard her explanation was a slight tip of his head.

Rhonda clicked her laptop shut. "Cantra is offering rebates. To cover up to 50% of the cost for patients. It will be more expensive than they want. But that's the best we can do."

Jordan didn't answer at first, and the silence stretched between them like melted cheese. After an interminably long thirty seconds, Jordan pushed his hair off his forehead. "My sister has been in and out of rehab for years."

Rhonda blinked. Of all the things she'd imagined him saying, that wasn't one of them. "Oh. I'm—that's awful. I'm sorry."

Again, silence. Rhonda's pulse quickened as Jordan stared at the top of her closed laptop. She wanted to put an empty glass up to the side of his head and press her ear against it to get even a snippet of what was going on up there.

"She's tried it all." A muscle in his jaw flexed, and he dropped his arm back to the couch.

Rhonda's skin prickled. Heat flared across her neck and into her cheeks. That was all it took. Four words and a deep sadness moving through his eyes, and Rhonda was suddenly blinking back tears.

What was wrong with her? Plenty of people shared personal things about their family or their own life after presentations like this one. Every drug she educated people on was meant to alleviate human suffering, which meant there were plenty of people struggling in the interim, waiting for new innovations.

But this was a sister.

"Can I use your washroom?" she croaked, jumping up from the coach and rounding the table before Jordan could look up and catch a glance at her red-rimmed eyes.

"Down the hall," he said behind her, but she was already moving. She found it, first room on the left, and slipped inside, closing the door behind her with a soft click. She leaned against the door, her chest heaving as she tried to catch her breath.

She walked to the sink and splashed water on her cheeks, hoping to shock herself back into emotional stability. Rhonda stared at her reflection in the mirror, watching the water drip from her chin.

Breathe.

Rhonda pulled her phone from her pocket and scrolled back in her texts. Beginning of September. The timestamp proved what she'd already been thinking. It had been six weeks since she sent a text to Cassie and hadn't even received a read receipt.

Jordan knew things about his sister. Currently. They seemed to have a relationship. That was good. Just because she didn't have a relationship with her sister didn't mean nobody else could. She needed to pull herself together.

Rhonda took two more deep breaths, stuffing that wave of emotion back into the box labelled "Family and Childhood" where she'd kept it for years. Cassie had written her off along with their parents. It was her sister's choice, and it wasn't personal. It all had to do with *him.*

"Hey, you okay in there?" Jordan's voice sounded from the hall.

Right. *How long had she been standing there?* She should've flushed the toilet or something, but doing it now would make him think she'd needed a long time on the toilet. So, it was either pretend she dropped the kids off at the pool or admit she had a momentary emotional breakdown because of . . . nothing.

She couldn't decide which was worse.

Rhonda's skin was already dry, thank you Alberta, so she straightened her shirt and shook out her curls. She was fine. Now, she only had to convince Jordan of that since he was already skeptical of her meeting Dr. Mallory. Could she blame her period? It was damn near time menstruation came in handy.

Rhonda stepped out into the hallway and paused. Jordan was leaning against the wall, his arms folded across his chest. He looked up as she appeared, and for a moment, neither of them spoke. Rhonda's heart pounded in her ears as she stood there, a different flashback screaming into her mind's eye.

"I'm sorry about that," she whispered.

Jordan opened his mouth, but nothing came out. It was like they were both watching the same movie in real-time. Different main characters, but the same scene. The wrong hotel room. *"I should probably get back . . ."*

But standing in this hallway, Rhonda didn't want to be the one to hesitate. She couldn't give in to the slow ache building in her middle and step forward to run her hands over Jordan's bare chest because—

He moved so fast, Rhonda barely had time to inhale before his lips were on hers in a desperate, searching kiss. His hands grasped onto her like he was drowning and she was his life preserver. Her insides dropped out as she threaded her hands in his hair. Not damp anymore, but she didn't care.

Her back hit the wall, and she gasped as his hips ground against hers. "I've wanted to do this since I saw you at the bar," Jordan rasped. His hands were everywhere, kneading the curve of her waist, sliding under her shirt to splay against her bare skin.

"Yeah." Rhonda sucked in a shaky breath, her body arching into him as his fingers fumbled over the clasp of her bra. "You look hot in scrubs."

Jordan chuckled low in his throat.

Somehow, she'd successfully convinced herself that her memory was fantasy. That those nights with Jordan had been exaggerated in her head because of the raw excitement of it.

She was wrong.

His touch was just as intoxicating as she'd remembered. Rough and powerful. *Hungry.*

Her heart pounded in her chest, her pulse racing as his lips found her neck. She clung to his shoulders, her nails digging into his shirt as he clamped his hands under her thighs and lifted her to his hips, still running his tongue and teeth over her skin.

Somewhere alarm bells were going off in her head, but they were drowned out by the war drum of her heart and Jordan's panting breaths.

Then they were moving. She clamped her legs around his hips as his hands pressed into her back and he peeled her off the wall. Jordan whisked her down the hall, hurried and clumsy, through the bedroom door.

They fell together to the bed, Jordan sliding on top of her. She pulled at his shirt, and he reached over his shoulder, tearing it over his head and tossing it on the floor. Rhonda sighed as her hands met skin, her head turning just enough to see his muscles flexing under his tattoos.

This was a bad idea. She tried to access the truth of it, but her head was vastly undersupplied with resources at that moment. Jordan pulled her shirt off, along with her already undone bra, and she shivered as the cool air hit her bare skin.

It was all rushes of breath, the rustle of clothing, and pops and releases as Jordan's lips found new skin to press against. Rhonda clasped the shoulders she'd been thinking about since the urgent care. Well, off and on since the parking lot, if she was being honest. Jordan's heart beat against her hip as he moved down her body in frenzied desperation, his hands venturing under the hem of her skirt, and Rhonda suddenly wondered why she ever wore pants.

He slid his body back up, wrapping himself around her and threading his legs with hers. How were they this physically compatible? They didn't have to say a word, and everything felt right. Like perfect pacing in a great novel or a waiter at a restaurant knowing exactly when to fill your water glass. Effortlessly. Subconsciously.

Rhonda was so utterly present, the raw physicality was startling. Every thought in her head was silenced by the symphony exploding from her nerve endings, and the rest of the world faded into nothing. For the next twenty minutes, she existed fully in the space between Jordan's humming skin, his racing heart, and his soft cotton sheets.

And then she was surfacing, her skin cooling, her heartbeat slowing. Her body buzzing with aftershocks, her blood thrumming in her veins. Her hands rested limply on Jordan's lower back, her legs tingling and heavy. Jordan's lips were still on her neck, his breath hot against her skin as his breathing evened.

The ceiling came into focus. The blinds over the window. The modern moulding. The matte paint on the walls. It was like a momentary death and rebirth.

Rhonda lay there beneath him, basking in the weight of him —the warmth of him. And then the reality of their situation finally diffused past the physical high.

They were going to have to move now. To look at each other and say something.

Jordan kissed her cheek, then pushed up and broke the silence first. "I'm going to go clean up."

Rhonda nodded. Good. That was good. That would give her a moment to—

TO WHAT?

Panic crept up her throat. She'd come over here to talk to him about Reviact and ended up *naked in his bed?* She rolled over and groaned as soon as Jordan had maneuvered off her body, entered the washroom, and shut the door behind him.

She wanted to slap herself. This was pure idiocy. She'd shown up for a professional meeting, and now the waters were muddied. Would Jordan introduce her to Dr. Mallory because he thought she was going to sleep with him again? Would he tell people on staff that she'd wanted to snag an audience with their clinical team so badly that she'd hopped into bed with him?

Beyond that, would the Snowballs get word of this? So far, she didn't think any of them had heard anything, which meant Jordan either hadn't told his team or his players were tight-lipped. Something she obviously hadn't mastered yet.

Or—or—they hadn't played each other yet.

Ugh. Maybe that was the only reason the Snowballs didn't know? If they'd found out before, she could've claimed ignorance. Sean and the others still would've been pissed at Jordan, but she would've been innocent. Embarrassed but innocent. Now? Her actions were indefensible.

She clutched his pillow to her face, squeezing her eyes shut. Jordan was like a bag of Salt and Vinegar chips. Or a package of Cadbury Mini Eggs. You put one of those on the counter, and sure, she could have some self-control for a few days, maybe even a week, but eventually, she was going to rip open the bag and eat the entire thing during an episode of Bridgerton.

Her stomach twisted, and she untangled herself from the sheets, hunting for her clothes. She found her skirt, underwear, and tights on the opposite side of the bed and wriggled back into them, then threw on her bra and shirt. She searched through the twisted sheets and duvet for anything else she might've missed.

They were nice sheets. They smelled like him—the whole room smelled like him.

Rhonda jumped as the door to the washroom opened, standing at attention so fast her spine cracked.

Jordan stood in front of the door, completely nude. He took a step toward her, and Rhonda moved back an inch toward the door.

"Jordan, I . . . I don't know what happened. I mean, I know what happened, but I didn't think—I didn't come here with the intention to—"

"No, I know." His brow furrowed.

She pursed her lips, then did a final scan of the bed. "Okay. I'll—" She pointed to the door and escaped to the hall.

Like a coward.

Rhonda gathered her things, measuring time in her head by how fast she thought Jordan could clothe himself. She figured she had about twenty seconds left by the time she swung her laptop bag over her shoulder and ran to the front door.

She didn't hesitate. She swung it open and rushed out, striding down the hallway, her cheeks flushed and her hair a mess.

She reached the elevator and pressed the button, her breath coming in short gasps. After what felt like ten minutes but was probably one and a half, she pressed the button again, glancing down the hall and willing Jordan's door to stay shut.

When the doors finally slid open with a ding, she took a step forward and nearly ran into a man exiting the elevator. Rhonda jumped back and looked up.

She froze, both of them staring at each other.

Darcy McClellan.

Her chest felt like it was being squeezed in a vice. Darcy was on the Snowballs. He'd taken a year off last season, but he was back on the roster and standing in front of her with his blond faux hawk.

His brow twitched. "Hey. What are you doing here?"

"Nothing." She clutched her bag tighter. "Just a meeting."

Darcy's throat bobbed, and he stepped out of her way. "Mmm. Nice."

Rhonda hurried into the elevator and gave a small wave, then dropped her eyes to the floor, praying the doors would close. Or that the elevator would plummet to the main floor and offer her a quick and painless death.

Because she was still holding her tights.

CHAPTER
Eight

JORDAN

JORDAN'S HEAD was spinning as he geared up in the locker room. He had the whole day off, which was terrible. He hadn't been able to get to sleep Thursday night after Rhonda left, and after tossing and turning all night, he had a day of laundry and grocery shopping. Neither of which produced an eighth of the serotonin needed to compete with what had happened the evening before.

His head was filled with Rhonda. The scent of her on his sheets. The image of her in his apartment, in his hallway—his bed—seared into his brain like a brand.

He sifted through each moment, trying to diagnose Rhonda hurrying out like a patient at the hospital. Something he'd said about his sister had struck a chord. She'd been emotional, and it was the first time he'd seen that side of her. The first time he'd seen her raw and unguarded. That look in her eyes haunted him, and the curiosity over what had been behind it gnawed at his insides.

What had happened? One moment they'd been standing in the hall, and the next? He didn't know who moved first. Since they'd pressed against her side of the wall, he guessed it was probably him.

But that look. Sadness. Desire. It was the same one she'd given him in his hotel room that first night. Like she was trapped, begging him to reach out and pull her free. It hijacked all his rational thought.

It wasn't that different from the looks he'd been given his whole life, though, was it? He grunted as he tied his skates. Hell, the end result was the same. Women looked at him like that, then got what they wanted, and then they left. They always left.

Jordan stood. The arena felt sharp and intrusive as he taped his stick. He should've been used to the fluorescent lights and the cold air permeating the locker room, but tonight, everything seemed brighter, louder, more intense. Chubs and Cam were halfway through gearing up while Steele and Nate were jawing.

"It's starting to look like pubic hair." Nate's voice echoed in the enclosed space.

Steele stroked his beard. "You're just jealous."

"Damn right I am," Nate shot back. "I've got patchy stubble, and you've got a Chia Pet. It's not fair."

Jordan finished his tape job, smoothing out the rough edges with the flat of his thumb. He looked up just in time to see Chubs yank up his hockey pants. "I told you, man, it's all about the oil. You want a glorious beard, you've got to use Squalene to hydrate."

Cam snorted. "Squalene? Is that what you're calling it now?"

The guys groaned, and Jordan whistled. It was their thirty-second warning to sort their shit and get into a huddle. He grabbed his stick and waited in the open space between the showers and the sinks.

It didn't take long for everyone to circle up. Jordan wasn't in the mood for a peppy speech, but then again, that wasn't really their style.

"The Cherry Pickers." That was all he needed to say to get a chorus of head nods and grunts. "Tough team this year." That wasn't an understatement. In 2023 they'd upset Zambone It in the semis, and word was they picked up another winger with handles.

"Let's breathe." Jordan dropped a hand on Steele's shoulder and watched the gesture move around the circle like a wave. When they were all connected, he dropped his head and inhaled through his nose.

Other teams might need to get jacked before a game. Lock in, get laser-focused, aggressive. Pucks Deep was not that team. Each of his players was already wound too tight to reach their full potential on the ice, and thanks to a dickhead comment from Nate three years ago, he'd forced them all to meditate before the game. Now it was a tradition bordering on superstition. Especially after they'd won the cup two out of the last three years.

They exhaled together, filling the locker room with white noise, then inhaled deeply a second time.

Bronze skin. Dark curls.

Jordan blinked, his shoulders tensing. The opposite of what should be happening on his exhale. He forced his lungs to refill and pushed the images out. Along with the sound of Rhonda's breath in his ear. Her fingertips pressing into his back—

"Damn it," he muttered under his breath, and Steele gave him a look.

Exhale.

Three repetitions. No more, no less.

"Pitter patter, let's get at 'er," Nate quipped after the last exhale, and Jordan snorted. If there wasn't a Letterkenny quote at some point in the locker room, it wouldn't be a proper pregame.

They lumbered as a team down the hall and made their way to the home team bench. Fans started cheering when they pushed out onto the ice. The rink was a modest one, with seating for maybe a couple thousand at best. The usual crowd was there —friends, family, and a handful of youth players from the area.

He took a few warm-up laps then joined his teammates for some passing drills. As he'd hoped, dropping into the game cleared his head of anything other than his skates and stick on the ice. Adrenaline coursed through him, and by the time he crouched at the face-off, he felt like the pressure in his chest might split his ribcage.

The moment the puck dropped, he snapped forward, his body coiled like a spring ready to snap. Jordan charged like a bat out of hell, his blades punishing the ice as he pushed himself harder. Faster.

Steele barreled up the right side, and with a flick of his stick, Jordan sent the puck hurtling over. Steele caught it just before number eighteen—a brute with shoulders like a barn door— decided to try his luck with Jordan. He braced for the hit against the boards, then jostled the dude, and took off.

A pass came his way, and he scooped the puck, cradling it briefly before slashing it forward toward the net. The goalie locked onto the puck, dropping low into his pads. In a split-second decision, Jordan veered right, aiming for the corner of the net just as he felt the solid smack against his stick. The puck spun high, arching up, and a slap of rubber on leather echoed as the goalie deflected it high.

Damn, close.

Jordan huffed, already tracking the puck as it spun down. A defender snagged it and took off past the blue line.

The game was fast and physical, just how he liked it. Since their two new guys weren't starting until January, they all got plenty of ice time—too much sometimes—but it allowed them to get into good flow.

Jordan slammed into a defender, sending him sprawling, then took the puck and passed it to Wyatt. They worked their way up the ice until the crowd erupted in boos, and the referee signalled a penalty. Jordan glided to see Chubs skating toward the penalty box, his hands thrown up in frustration.

Chubs let out a string of curses, echoing in the arena. "That was a clean hit!"

The referee pointed to a spot on the ice. "Tripping, number twenty-two."

Chubs' eyes widened in disbelief. "He fell on his ass! Tripped over his own dumb ankles!"

The referee shook his head and motioned for Chubs to get in the box. Jordan skated over, dropping a hand on Chubs' shoulder. "Cook it."

Chubs grumbled but nodded, stepping into the penalty box. Jordan turned and skated back to the face-off circle. They were in the neutral zone, which meant Cam was going to attack the middle. Jordan kept his eyes trained on the ice so he didn't tip the Cherry Pickers off.

He could already see their strategy. They were pulling pucks back and trying to spread his team out. They only had to survive the power play and then disrupt them. Make them uncomfortable, or they weren't going to end with a W.

"Angles, boys," Jordan called out.

They barely scraped by without giving up a goal, mostly due to Matty, their goalie, somehow spotting a puck going backdoor and diving for the save. When Chubs exited the penalty box, they were able to recover and stop playing on their heels.

Steele scored late in the first off a pass from Tobes, then Matty missed a puck in the second, which meant they were tied going into third period. After battling it out for eighteen minutes, Cam won a scramble, exploding along the boards toward the net. He kicked the puck up to Steele. He barely had time to flick it to Jordan to shoot it blind at the net. The crowd erupted as it barely rolled in past the post.

"Helluva pass, bud," he bumped mitts with Steele, who grinned back, cocky as ever.

Back in the tunnel, the team was buzzing. Chubs was still

yapping about his penalty while Steele replayed his assist like it was worthy of a Gordie Howe nod. Jordan tugged off his helmet as they reached the locker room, shaking out his damp hair.

The locker room buzzed with victory-induced swagger. Jordan dropped onto the bench, tugging at his laces.

"Boys, you see those beauties in the first two periods? Had their breakouts looking like a herd of blind cattle. Couldn't transition for shit," Chubs crowed, slapping Steele on the back.

Steele tossed his gloves into his bag. "Yeah, 'til the third, when they started lobbing pucks behind us. We were playing fetch."

Jordan nodded. "They started dumping in and grinding us down low, and we got caught puck-watching."

Matty grabbed his towel and headed to the shower. "You boys done analyzing yet, or do you want to go back out and play the third again?"

Steele flipped him off as Jordan peeled off his gear, his muscles starting to cool. He stripped off his jersey then his pads, then sat down and pulled his phone from the locker.

There were a couple messages from work, but the credit card notification caught his attention first. He tapped on it, and the hotel total popped up on his screen. There must have been a few extras from the total, but he didn't care.

He pictured Claire sitting alone in that hotel room, ordering room service. Jordan's chest tightened. This bill meant she'd checked out, but where had she gone next? Had she found another hotel? Crashed with a friend? He hated that he didn't know.

He thought about the Reviact information Rhonda had shown him. The results she'd shared were impressive, and he'd gone down the rabbit hole after she left. Everything he'd read lined up with what she'd told him. The drug reduced cravings, helped with withdrawal symptoms, and had a high success rate in keeping people clean.

Jordan laid his equipment on the bench, grabbed his towel,

then stalked to the showers. He wanted to believe it was that simple. That he could just hand his sister a pill and everything would be solved. But after watching her for ten years, he knew better than that. Addiction was a beast. It dug in deep and didn't let go without a fight.

He hung his towel on the hook and cranked the shower handle, the tile cold against his feet. As the hot water hit his skin, Jordan let out a long breath and dropped his head under the spray.

What would it take to get Reviact approved at Rocky Ridge? He knew convincing the hospital board would be a gauntlet. And he certainly couldn't be the one to push for it.

Dr. Mallory still looked at him as a liability after what happened with Claire. He'd been the one to give her access to the cabinets at the hospital, albeit unknowingly. He should have questioned why she was suddenly interested in visiting him at work, but was it so terrible that he wanted to believe she could've been there for him?

She'd been struggling, and he'd thought he was helping, but all he'd done was give her the keys to the kingdom. When bottles of oxycodone were unaccounted for and Jordan's card was linked, he'd taken the blame. Even after Claire was caught and admitted everything, his relationship with Dr. Mallory had been torched.

He'd been naive, and it was his responsibility to keep hospital resources safe and the people around him accountable. He was still working on clawing his way out of that hole.

Jordan scrubbed himself down, then turned off the water and towelled off. He couldn't afford to ask for any favours from Dr. Mallory now. Possibly in another five years, but even that wasn't looking promising.

Before he could finish drying, Cam called his name. Jordan walked out of the shower area, towel around his waist. Cam was sitting on the bench, holding up his phone. "You see this?"

Jordan frowned and walked over. Cam handed him the phone, and he read the text from their rink's manager.

"Due to unexpected emergency renovations, our rink will be closed for the next month. All practices and games, including youth programs, will be relocated to the Ice Centre . . ."

Jordan's stomach dropped as he scanned the rest of the message directing him to the attachment for changes to some practice times. He re-read the name and location of their new home.

The Ice Centre. In the Northwest.

The Snowballs' home rink.

Cam's expression mirrored Jordan's. "Looks like we're about to get a lot more familiar with our competition."

CHAPTER
Nine

RHONDA'S SUITCASE GAPED OPEN, awaiting her offering of Anthropologie skirts and Eliza Faulkner tops. Transitioning to fall colours was part of her job description. It was a tough life, but somebody had to do it.

She tossed her hair over one shoulder as she surveyed the piles of clothing strewn across the duvet, then grabbed a seersucker white blouse from the pile. It was tempting fate to wear white to dinner, but if she paired it with a blazer, she could close the button as needed if she spilled or splashed salad dressing.

Rhonda folded the blouse in thirds and packed it. She arranged the slacks, skirts, and tops like seven-layer dip on one side of her suitcase. Then she slid her favourite heels in a shoe protector bag and put them on the other side. After adding workout clothes, flip-flops for the sauna, and most of her toiletries, she was feeling quite accomplished. All she had left were chargers, her yoga mat, and snacks for the road.

Her phone buzzed on the nightstand just as she turned and

started walking toward the door. She strode back and picked it up. Rhonda's stomach clenched at the name flashing on the screen. Derek Paulson, Regional Sales Manager.

Her boss wasn't a terrible guy. He was annoying, with his bro marketer energy and inability to give bad news without a Mr. Clean smile, but he was mostly reasonable. Unfortunately, that meant he was probably analyzing the crap out of her lack of sales growth in Q3.

Rhonda swiped to answer the call, forcing her voice into a cheery lilt. "Hey, Derek! What's up?"

"Hey, girl, hey!" Derek's voice came through warm and smooth. Great. He'd been watching reels again. "Kidding. I thought that would be funny."

"It was."

"Ready for Edmonton?"

She dropped to the bed. "Of course. Everything's lined up. Should be a productive few days."

"Atta girl!" Derek gave an easy laugh. "I always say you're one of the sharpest out there. You've got a way of making everyone feel like they're the most important person in the room. Not everyone has that energy, you know?"

"Thanks, Derek. That means a lot," she braced herself. After being forced to attend an HR seminar on leadership and team motivation, Derek had been converted to the sandwich method of giving feedback, which meant she was about to get a doozy.

"I mean it," he continued. "Though, I wanted to check in on your strategy. Both in Edmonton and Calgary . . . "

And there it was. "I'm working on Rocky Ridge and McKnight, if that's what you're referring to."

"Oh, good. Great." He laughed as if she were bringing it up out of the blue. "It seemed like you were more interested in the smaller clinics from what you'd submitted, so I wanted to see how I could support you in that."

Rhonda chewed her lower lip. Support. That's definitely what she felt from him. "I'm hopeful I'll be able to get into a couple of big centres in the coming weeks." She started to sweat. How was she going to text Jordan again after what happened? Not optional. She needed to get into Rocky Ridge, or she would have no chance of taking over as regional manager when Derek was promoted.

"Sure, I have all the confidence."

Obviously, since he was making the call in the first place. "I'll let you know how it goes. I appreciate you checking in." Maybe she should have been more open with him. Told him that she was struggling to make any headway with the older, more entrenched medical professionals. But to do that, she would've needed to feel safe that admitting weakness wouldn't come back to bite her. Since she wasn't going to suddenly go blond or sprout male genitalia, she was much safer holding her tongue. There were plenty of men who suggested she use her mouth to her—and their—advantage, but that was a game she refused to play.

Or did she? That same pang of guilt hit her stomach. That wasn't why she'd slept with Jordan. Whatever intense energy they had between them had started far before she knew he had connections at Rocky Ridge. Still. It didn't look good on paper.

"I look forward to the update. You know, I was so impressed with . . . "

And there was the last slice of flattery to close the sandwich. Rhonda nodded and uh-huh'd until Derek finally said he needed to hop on another call. Then she resisted the urge to hurl the phone across the room. Instead, she channeled her frustration into slamming a pair of flats into the suitcase with unnecessary force.

Rhonda snapped the suitcase shut but didn't zip it. She could toss in her last-minute things when she got back. She grabbed the veggie tray she'd picked up from Co-op and headed to the garage.

Her Accord sat waiting—the perfect blend of practicality and a hint of flash. She slid into the driver's seat and pressed the start button. The engine purred to life, and she pressed the garage door opener. She pulled on her puffy coat from the passenger seat. Even in summer, she kept it there just in case, but now the weather required it. She'd need to get her snow tires on when she returned home.

Rhonda pulled out of the driveway and turned onto the street. She hated being late for Sunday Supper, but she had to leave early enough the next day, she didn't want to stress pack later that night when she got home. That was how she ended up forgetting phone chargers and flushable wipes.

The streets of Calgary blurred past her windows, and as she approached the Thompson's neighbourhood, Rhonda scanned the street for a parking spot. There was already a line of cars along the curb, but she spotted a gap a few houses down. It wasn't perfect, but she could make it work with a five-point parallel park.

She made it happen, then turned off the engine and grabbed the veggie tray from the passenger seat. The air outside was cold and sharp, the kind of chill that seeped into her bones and made her shiver involuntarily. It was going to snow. Just in time for Halloween, as usual. The number of times she'd dressed up as a sexy angel or devil in her twenties and then had to ruin the effect with a toque and winter coat was maddening.

Rhonda's pulse quickened as she reached the Thompson's front door. She was being irrational. Just because Darcy had seen her in the hall, it didn't necessarily mean he knew Jordan was there. She could make up any number of stories about a friend who lived there, especially since she hadn't left at an indefensible time of night. She had to figure out what story she was going to tell. She hadn't successfully lied since she took a cat from a friend in high school and claimed she found it on the road.

The door swung open, and Rob Thompson greeted her with a wide smile. "Rhonda! Come on in, it's freezing out there!"

Warm air and the scent of roasting meat wafted over her as

she stepped inside. Rhonda slipped off her boots and coat, then made her way to the kitchen to drop off the tray.

"Thank you so much for bringing something." Sharla Thompson's eyes crinkled at the corners.

It was as if Rhonda had set down twenty pound weights she'd been carrying and slipped into cozy sweatpants. Socializing was so much easier than sitting in her own head. She smiled brightly. "Of course. It's the least I could do."

She chatted with Sharla for a minute, then squeezed past Boyd, Steve, and André from the team, making her way to the living area. The space was a hive of activity, with people chatting and laughing, everyone holding plates of finger foods or drinks. She spotted Jenna standing with Country, Brett, and Curtis, and made a beeline for them.

"Hey, guys!" Rhonda stopped next to Curtis's wife, Sasha, and threw an arm over her shoulders. She was just so glad to be there all of a sudden. It was like she turned away from the screen playing Derek's phone call and her night with Jordan on repeat and was now watching her favourite channel.

"You decided to honour us with your presence." Country grinned, and Jenna rolled her eyes.

"She's only half an hour late." Jenna pulled her into a hug. "How are you?"

Rhonda squeezed her hard and pulled back. "Great, I just had to finish packing."

"Is this your trip to Edmonton?"

Rhonda nodded. "I leave tomorrow morning."

Sasha sighed. "Do you ever need an assistant? Or a publicist?"

Curtis threw an arm over her shoulders. "I told you I'd take tomorrow off. You can go to the spa or something."

"Not by myself," Sasha groaned. "I need a girls' weekend, but all my mom friends are busy, and you all are working."

Jenna raised an eyebrow. "I could probably sneak away for an hour or two."

Rhonda reached over the banister for a sparkling water from the table. Suraj saw her reaching and passed it to her. She thanked him, then opened the cap and took a sip.

"Supper's ready!" Sharla called, and they all knew the drill. Jenna took Rhonda's arm, and they moved to line up with Anne.

"I didn't know if you were going to come tonight." Anne gave her a hug. "Don't you have to leave early?"

Rhonda nodded. "Not too early that I can't eat pot roast and talk to you two."

"Ah, I notice the pot roast came first." Jenna raised an eyebrow.

"I mean . . . how can you argue with that?" Anne pointed to the steaming roasting pans Rob was setting out on the island.

Rhonda froze as a head full of blond, shaggy hair turned. Darcy was there. Only two people in front of them. She spun so he couldn't see her face. "These Sunday suppers are so great. I've really missed you two."

Jenna gave her a look. "What's wrong?"

Rhonda scoffed. "Wrong? Nothing's wrong. I just wanted you to know that."

"You're standing backward in the line." Anne cocked her head to look over her shoulder.

"Only so I could talk to you instead of craning my neck." Rhonda grinned then turned to the side to shuffle forward. "Tell me what you and Country are working on."

Jenna was hesitant at first, but then happily launched into their recent online creator conference where they digitally met people with some of the biggest online news and broadcasting platforms. Rhonda listened and nodded, all while trying *not* to accidentally meet Darcy's eyes as they approached the plates and cutlery.

"I have so many ideas, especially since we're getting so many calls from agents and players," Jenna said.

"Mm-hmm." Rhonda reached for a paper plate, then handed two behind her for her friends.

Jenna exhaled. "Which will be hard since I've been doing so many renovations lately." Rhonda nodded and grabbed a napkin. "And I've got so much furniture to buy."

Rhonda was about to nod a second time then stopped. She blinked and met Jenna's eyes, and her mouth dropped.

"Are you—?"

Before Ann could finish, Jenna put a finger to her lips. "Shh. We're not telling everyone yet. But I couldn't keep it from you guys a second longer."

Rhonda pursed her lips, willing herself not to throw her plate on the ground and scream in excitement. Jenna and Country had been trying to adopt since the second they got married that summer. They'd looked into every option, but Jenna hadn't heard anything since they'd fostered a six-week-old baby for a few weeks at the beginning of September. "You're serious?" she hissed.

Jenna nodded, her eyes glassy as she motioned for Rhonda to turn and dish up. *Holy shit.* Jenna and Country were having a baby. She wanted to ditch the supper and drag Jenna outside for all the details. Before she could drop the plate, she looked up. Darcy was staring straight at her. He knew. *Damn it, he knew.* She hadn't said two words to Darcy since he came back, and that was a full on *look.*

"How much do you want?" Rob held two slices of roast beef up between a carving knife and fork. Rhonda nodded, and he dropped them on her plate.

"Thank you."

"When can we talk about this?" Anne asked, her voice low. Rhonda's heart jumped into her throat until she realized Anne was looking back at Jenna.

"We can text or phone. Later tonight." Jenna's cheeks were flushed. She was positively glowing. They moved through the line as Rhonda continued to fill her plate. Veggies and dip. Mashed potatoes. Gravy. Yorkshire pudding.

Suraj grabbed a Yorkshire. "The Oilers had more holes in their defence last night than these puddings."

Tyler scooped enough potatoes to feed a small army. "Did you see Matthews try to thread that pass? Might as well've been sending it to Narnia."

Brett guffawed, drowning his own mountain of mashed potatoes in gravy. "And Campbell out there flopping like a fish."

Suraj snorted. "Juggling pucks like a street busker."

They devolved into laughter, and it was stupidly contagious. Rhonda was almost smiling normally when she reached the end of the line and retrieved her cutlery. She walked to one of three tables set up in the kitchen and dining room, hoping that any weird facial expressions would be ascribed to her inability to process Jenna's news. Which was true. Until she knew details, the fact that they were expecting a baby in some shape or form felt no more real than the Snowballs hoping to win the cup at the end of the season.

"Rhonda!" Penny, Brett's girlfriend, stood from her seat and hugged her around her full plate of food. "How are you?"

"So good!" Her voice was too high. It must've hit that pitch everyone talked about, the one that cats and babies exploited with their cries, because everyone at the table turned to look at her.

"Carry on. Nothing to see here." Rhonda shooed them back to their food, hoping it came off naturally. She sat next to Penny and glanced around the table. "I'm heading to Edmonton in the morning."

"Soooo, you were being sarcastic?" Penny grinned.

"I'm actually staying at a new Marriott. It's supposed to be great. The restaurant I'm meeting my doctors at is in the hotel."

Penny nodded. "Well, good, because it's going to be freaking freezing up there."

Rhonda laughed, then picked up her knife and fork and started cutting her roast into pieces. She scooped one up with her fork, dipped it in mashed potatoes and gravy, then dropped it in her mouth. She closed her eyes and sighed. "Mmm."

"Kind of makes me want to take up cooking."

Rhonda gave her a look. "You cook."

"No, Brett cooks. Unless it's a family recipe, I microwave."

Rhonda laughed. Penny was downplaying her skills, but she decided to let her live in her truth for the time being. She took another bite and caught a glimpse of Darcy from the other table. His back was to her. He was far enough away he wouldn't hear anything.

"So great that Darcy is back this season."

Penny nodded. "Honestly, I was a little worried." She glanced up and lowered her voice. "I heard he was a bit of an asshole."

"How so?" Rhonda ripped off a piece of her Yorkshire.

Penny shrugged. "Just didn't make an effort to be a part of the team. Caused problems on the ice."

"Hmm. Hopefully it's better this time around." Rhonda chewed and swallowed. "I wonder why he didn't join up with C-Biscuit. It's kind of a long haul over to practice, isn't it?"

Penny frowned. "He lives in Rosemont, doesn't he?" She leaned over to Brett. "Does Darcy live in Rosemont still?"

Heat flushed to Rhonda's cheeks. Fantastic. Another witness to her asking about Darcy's living situation. Rhonda took a sip of her water, trying to look nonchalant. "Oh, I could've been wrong. I had a meeting in Mayland Heights, and I could've sworn I saw him at the apartments there."

Brett shook his head. "No, he's still in Rosemont. We just did some renovations on his house there. He inherited it from his grandma."

"Or great-aunt?" Penny asked.

Now that they mentioned it, she did remember hearing something about that. How he'd moved back because he had a free place to live. None of this helped her, but at least she knew he didn't live in that building. Maybe if he was visiting a friend, he wouldn't know who else lived there.

"I need a great-aunt. Or rich grandma." Rhonda laughed.

"Just phone Earl Jones." Brett took a swig from his sparkling water.

Penny rolled her eyes. "A grandparent scam. Excellent idea."

"Is that the guy from Montreal who stole inheritances in the nineties?" Rhonda asked.

Brett nodded. "Like, millions of dollars worth."

Rhonda speared a green bean with her fork. "I can think of easier ways to make a million dollars."

Penny snorted. "Do not say Only Fans."

"It's my feet, Pens. If God didn't want me to use them, he shouldn't have given me such delicate, slender toes."

They laughed and chatted until their plates were empty, then Rhonda pushed back from the table. "I'm going to head out. I still have some packing to do." She leaned in to give Penny a hug, then picked up her dinnerware.

Rhonda wove her way through the group still gathered by the table to take her dishes to the kitchen. She thanked the Thompsons, and was about to make an easy getaway, when she heard her name behind her.

She turned to find Jenna rushing up to the door. "We're going to talk later."

Rhonda hugged her. "I know, we already established that."

Jenna pulled back. "Uh, no. Not about me. About whatever is happening here." She waved her hands over Rhonda's general person. "When can you meet at Tina's?"

Rhonda's heartbeat sounded in her ears. "I get back at the end of the week."

"So Friday it is?"

Rhonda pulled on her coat and zipped it up. "I'm not sure about one potential meeting Friday morning. I'll check when I get home and let you know." Jenna opened her mouth to say something else, but Rhonda's phone was buzzing. She turned the screen to Jenna, proving she wasn't making it up. "Mom" flashed on the screen.

Jenna waved her out, and Rhonda swiped up to answer. "Hey."

"Hey there, baby." Her mother's voice came through chirpy. Too bright. "I wanted to check in before your big trip. How's my star sales rep holding up?"

Rhonda's gut twisted. "Oh, you know me, Mom. Just your typical tornado of packing chaos. The usual."

Her mother's laugh was thin. A sound of habit rather than true joy. "Well, I'm sure you'll nail it. You always do."

To anyone else, those words may have sounded like a vote of confidence, but from her mother? They were a faithful plea. Rhonda opened her car door and slipped in, turning on the engine and hitting the button for her seat warmer.

"Listen, Rhonnie," her mom began, and Rhonda closed her eyes, already knowing what was coming. "I hate to do this, but I could really use your help. The electric bill this month was up twenty percent. They charged me for prime time usage, can you believe that? I don't remember when they told us they were switching to time blocks. And the car, it's making this noise. Awful grinding."

Rhonda's grip on the phone tightened. Her jaw clenched and a flicker of anger rose up. "Mom." Her voice was gentle but firm. "We've talked about this. I can't keep—"

"I know, I know," her mother cut in, the forced cheer stripped. "I don't mean to burden you."

"You're not a burden. You know that. But you need to take him to court. Until you do—"

"I can't. You know that."

Rhonda exhaled as she turned off the Thompsons' street. She did know that. It had been almost five years since her mother had saved up enough to leave her father for good, and not once had she been willing to talk with a lawyer.

Memories of her father swarmed to the surface. The day he

cleaned out her mother's account. Zero warning. Just cancelled her cards and siphoned out all of their shared equity. Or even earlier, the time he'd refused to co-sign on a loan for her mother to go back to school. He'd sneered, saying it was a waste of money because she'd only fail anyway. That conversation had happened during Rhonda's last year of high school.

Her stomach churned when she thought about walking out that door. Leaving her sister alone with them. But what could she have done differently?

Now, her career ambitions weren't only about herself. They were about securing a future for her mother. But sometimes it felt like patching holes in a sinking ship.

"I'll see what I can do." Rhonda cleared her throat. "Hang in there, okay? I'll phone you after the trip."

Her mother's voice brightened. "Thank you, baby. I'm so proud of you."

The call ended, and Rhonda let the phone fall into her lap. She stared at the lights ahead of her, driving on autopilot. And then, she passed an apartment building. Grey. Out of nowhere, her thoughts drifted to Jordan.

Had that happened? Neither of them had texted or called since that night, and she was beginning to question herself. Maybe she'd forgotten her promise to her twenty-two year old self and had taken a blue pill from a stranger. Maybe she'd been so desperate to find someone who worked at Rocky Ridge, she'd fabricated an entire human being—an entire restaurant—to complete her midlife crisis fantasy world.

But then she felt the ghost of his hands on her, the rough timbre of his voice in her ear. It made her ache, and she pressed her palm to her cheek as she waited at a red light. The streets were surprisingly dead that early in the evening. Normally that only happened right before a storm, and she'd checked that morning. The drive up to Edmonton was supposed to be clear.

Rhonda turned onto her street. She parked outside her townhouse, the engine ticking as it cooled. She grabbed her purse and walked up to her front door.

Inside, her house was exactly as she'd left it, and a cocktail of comfort and disappointment washed over her.

So quiet.

Rhonda hung up her keys and purse, then walked to the kitchen. She couldn't have pets since she was gone so much, but she'd found solace in her plants. They were low maintenance, and after killing half of the Happy Valley Nursery, she'd figured out an efficient system for keeping them alive. A little water in the saucers at the base every few days, a misting bottle for her ferns.

She grabbed her copper can and watered them, then moved through her bedtime routine. While she waited for her light peeling mask to tingle, she scrolled and checked her meeting schedule. Nothing on Friday morning. It looked like they were going to do Thursday brunch instead. So that would be a yes on hot tubbing.

Rhonda typed Anne's name into her text message search bar, but couldn't find the chat with just her, Tina, and Jenna. Had it been that long since they'd set up a therapy night? She scrolled for a minute, then gave up and typed in their names one by one. She dropped onto the bed and tapped out a message with her thumbs.

Hey! Friday at Tina and Anne's is a go. I should be back before supper.

ANNE

Yep, Friday is perfect. I have to be out and showered by ten-thirty, though.

. . .

TINA

Because you're almost forty?

ANNE

Ha. Ha. No, because my niece has that soccer game.

Got it. Get Anne drunk so she forgets about her bedtime

ANNE

I'm great with boundaries now. New skill in 2024.

TINA

Does that mean you're dumping Gary?

ANNE

Okay, if you guys don't like him, just say it. Don't be all passive aggressive.

> We're not being passive aggressive. That was full aggressive

TINA

> I'm just jealous. He's taking all of your time, and Rhonda is too cool for school.

Rhonda laughed, but before she could finish typing out a response, Anne's message came through.

ANNE

> Speaking of which, Rhonda, you ready to come clean?

Her heart stuttered. Come clean about what? A spike of adrenaline at the thought of her friends knowing anything about Jordan made her hands jittery. But that couldn't be what she was talking about.

TINA

> Oooh what did I miss at Sunday Supper?

> Nothing. I have no idea what she's talking about

. . .

Anne

She was smiling weird

What? I wasn't smiling weird

Tina

That means she slept with someone

Anne

Exactly

Rhonda dropped the phone on the bed and stalked into the washroom. Smiling weird? She would've been mad had she not been worried the entire Sunday Supper about that exact possibility. But she'd been laughing and joking around. She hadn't even been around Anne for long since she sat next to Penny.

She peed and washed her hands, then walked back out to the bedroom and snatched up her phone.

Tina

> She's not answering. I'm guessing it was someone she met when she went to get her oil changed.

Anne

> My guess is that guy she always flirts with at the Tim's on 9th.

> She's ghosting us. It means we're right.

> Okay, wow. I went to the washroom.

Tina

> And you didn't craft a rebuttal on the toilet?

She thought long and hard about what to text next. She could deny it. She couldn't completely gaslight them. They'd known her long enough that they'd never believe her if she said nothing was off. But she could come up with some other plausible explanation. A guy at work sexted her? Or she's thinking of getting into energy work? That was always a quick way to shut down questions.

> Is there a point?

Anne

> YES!! Okay, who was it?

You don't know him.

Tina

> Pictures?

No!!

Anne

> No pictures!? This is how our relationship works. We give you emotional support. You give us pictures.

I forgot! Sorry!

Tina

> You never forget. Weird smiles and no pictures? You're going to be with him again, aren't you?

No! Stop. 😆

Anne

She has a point. It's the same thing that happened at that hockey tournament. Remember? In Medicine Hat? You showed up in the room at some ungodly hour. No pictures. And then you DID see him again.

By accident!

TINA

Parking Lot Guy??

ANNE

Parking Lot Guy

TINA

I still live vicariously through you and Parking Lot Guy. Like, more often than I'd be willing to admit

So do I

She lay back on the bed and stared at the ceiling. Now he wasn't just Parking Lot Guy. He was Urgent Care Guy. Rocky Ridge Guy. Apartment Guy. Ugh, how had she gotten into this?

All weekend she'd found herself wondering if she could accidentally run into him. If she drove a different route or stopped for coffee a little closer to the hospital. It wasn't healthy.

She would text Jordan mid-week to see if he'd thought more about Reviact and if he thought it was possible to get an appointment with Dr. Mallory. That was it. Professional. Succinct. If he couldn't, she'd delete his number and move on with a new strategy.

Rhonda rolled over and swiped up on her screen to tell the girls how whatever weirdness they'd seen on her face was going to be gone by the time she got back from Edmonton, then frowned.

A text sat at the bottom of her text chain.

J

Any more details and I might get pregnant

Her heart pounded her ribs like a gavel as she stared at the message, uncomprehending. Her body grasped the full scope of the situation before her brain caught up, but when it did, she could no longer feel her hands or feet.

J. She'd saved Jordan's number as "J" because she didn't want her friends to see it pop up on her screen accidentally. But this didn't make sense. He couldn't be part of the group chat. She'd created it minutes ago by adding Anne, Tina, and—

Ohhhhhh.

Realization slammed into her like a freight train. There were no prior messages. Why hadn't she stopped to question why there weren't other texts showing up in her history? In her haste, she must have accidentally selected "J" instead of "Jenna," and now—

She scrolled up, scanning the string of texts like one of those guys on the speed-reading infomercials.

Shit.

Shiiiit.

He'd seen all of it. The smiling weird, the hook up accusations, *Parking Lot Guy!?!?* Rhonda let out a groan and buried her face in the pillows.

CHAPTER
Ten

JORDAN

JORDAN SKATED OUT onto the rink, his breath fogging through his helmet. This arena had charm, he'd give it that. Old playoff banners hung from the rafters, but the cabinet in the entryway sat empty. He grinned to himself. The Rose Cup was safe and sound at their home rink, and he didn't have any intentions of allowing it to rehome.

"I swear, the Zamboni here is older than my grandma," Greg muttered. None of the coaches were happy about being on this side of town. Even though their home rink was nothing to crow about, it felt good to talk a little bit of shit.

"I like a little character in my ice." Jordan grinned. He was in a good mood. Hell, he was in a great mood. He drew a deep breath of chilled ice rink air and surveyed their new home for the next month or so.

The Eastfield Arena wasn't flashy, but it had ice that made you float. Hopefully that wouldn't change after the renos.

Toby, a hall-of-famer now in his sixties, rubbed his hands together. "You think they all got the memo?"

Jordan smirked. "These kids actually check their text messages."

Toby grunted, annoyed before their session even started. And that was why these guys were Jordan's people. Greg with his battered coffee mug that looked like it had seen the trenches, Toby, who always wore a toque even though he had a full head of hair, and Steve, who still donned pieces of hockey gear he'd worn in the eighties.

Their teams of kids were already warming up, skating in lazy loops and shooting pucks against the boards. Jordan glided over to his group, fifteen and sixteen-year-olds, all of them moving like derpy golden retrievers.

"Alright boys, line it up."

There were a few groans but mostly grins. These kids were good, and they knew it. more than that, they were willing to skate until they puked to get better.

He ran them through a series of warm-ups, then arced behind the net as they skated into formation and took turns cutting, receiving, and shooting. "Nice power, Carter. Maybe aim for the net next time."

Carter flipped him a mitt, and Jordan laughed. They were comfortable with him. That would be a problem if respect didn't come with it, but with this group it mostly did.

He was antsy on his skates, so he hopped into the rotation and joined the group. Their energy spiked, and it brought him right back to when he was on the cusp of something huge. He'd gone from doing coaching just like this to playing with the Calgary Hitmen in the WHL. Thirty goals and fifty-six assists his rookie season. The scouts had been all over him. His second year, he upped the ante with forty goals, and the New York Islanders had taken him sixth overall in the NHL Entry Draft.

He remembered how it felt, standing in the draft room, hearing his name called. The rush of adrenaline, the slap of his dad's hand on his back. The promise of a career that was supposed to be filled with glory and accolades.

Sean was there that night—they'd been inseparable back then. Sean was drafted twenty-fourth overall by the Blizzard. They were both living the dream, and then . . .

Jordan shook his head, trying to dispel the thoughts. It was still hard to believe how quickly everything had changed. One wrist injury and suddenly he was on the bench, his name not even on the list for Team Canada selections.

He played two regular-season games in the NHL. Two. And a single playoff game. All of them scoreless. After that, he'd bounced around the AHL and IHL, but his wrist never fully recovered. The doctors said he could play, but there was a high risk of permanent damage. At twenty-two, he made the call to walk away.

Twenty-two. He was a baby back then.

Ethan missed a shot and slammed his stick against the boards in frustration.

Jordan skated over. "Hey, it's just one shot. You'll get the next one."

Ethan nodded, still breathing hard as he joined the others to circle up for a passing drill. They had so much potential, so much time ahead of them. For some, maybe not as much time as they thought.

Jordan skated behind the net, watching them move. He loved his life now. He loved coaching these kids, seeing them improve week over week. He loved his job as a nurse, the adrenaline rush of the trauma wing.

But there would always be a part of him that wondered what might have been. What could've happened if his wrist hadn't given out on him. If he'd played more than two NHL games. If he'd been able to make good on all those promises.

He pushed the thoughts away. This was his life, and it was a damn good one. He just had to keep reminding himself of that.

It was easier than normal that morning, knowing exactly

what thoughts had been running through Rhonda's head. Or at least what she'd told her friends. He'd been given a lot of titles over the years, but Parking Lot Guy might be one of his favourites. More than that, the fact that she and her friends had a name for him meant she'd talked about him. A lot.

He chewed on that for a moment, the red flags starting to go up in his head. This was Allison and Sonya all over again. He tested well with strong women who wanted a bit of stress relief, but he wasn't the guy they settled down with. Allison was a wounded bird, but she'd only wanted an escape from problems she wouldn't deal with head-on. And Sonya. She said she didn't want commitment, but what she meant was she didn't want commitment with him.

Jordan was good at solving problems. He was good at giving people what they wanted. But he was shit at keeping his own emotions out of it. Every time he swore he wouldn't fall deep he failed. After a couple years of therapy, he realized it hadn't ever been about them.

Jordan blew his whistle and called out the next drill, then skated in to give specific feedback on their footwork. They skated hard until five minutes to the hour, then huddled up.

Ethan and Carter snickered about something, and Jordan called them out. "Care to share with the group?"

Ethan's cheeks went redder than they already were. "No, Coach, I—"

"Ethan thinks you got laid," Carter blurted, and the rest of the kids responded appropriately.

Jordan didn't miss a beat. "My typical Monday." The boys laughed. "You all need to hit puberty first, then I can give you my tips for pulling snipers." That got him a few smirks and eyerolls. "Good practice today. Hydrate. Get your calories in. You'll need it for Wednesday."

He sent them off to the showers, then worked with the other coaches to clear the ice.

"You have practice here tonight, eh?" Greg asked.

Jordan nodded as he scooped cones off the ice. "Unfortunately."

"This arena is going to be a clown car all month."

"With less laughs."

Greg guffawed. They finished up and got off the ice so the Zamboni could clean it up, then walked upstairs to wait in the lobby for parents. Their kids were old enough not to need any hand holding, but it was a courtesy their parents appreciated.

The boys were tromping up the stairs when he saw a shove. Jace, one of the older kids with blond hair sticking out under his ball cap, had Ethan pinned to the railing.

"Hey!" Jordan shouted, but Jace leaned in, getting up into Ethan's face. Ethan fought against his grip, but Jace had at least fifteen kilos on the kid.

Jordan yanked Jace back by his collar and put himself between the two of them. Jace spun, his eyes wild. Ethan, still breathing heavily, held his position against the rails, his fists clenched.

"You okay?" Jordan asked. Ethan sniffed and nodded, then stormed up the remaining stairs. Instead of heading toward the main entrance, he strode down the opposite hall. Probably taking a minute in the washroom.

"What's going on?" Greg asked.

Jordan shook his head. "Jace and Ethan."

Greg frowned. "Again?"

Jordan blew out a breath and walked back to stand next to the windows. Vehicles were arriving. This was the third time Jace and Ethan had gotten into it, and he figured it was probably time to loop in their parents.

He didn't get it. Last year, they'd been thick as thieves. Now they seemed to annoy the hell out of each other. If they'd had a falling out, whatever, but they needed to show respect at practice.

Jordan flinched a little at that thought. He hadn't always been willing to take that advice, so there was no judgement from him.

Ethan skirted past them and jogged out to a minivan. Jordan thought about following him until he saw Jace slumped on a couch in the corner.

He walked over. "You have a ride?"

"Mm-hmm." Jace pulled out a laptop from his bag.

"Looks like you're settling in."

Jace shrugged. "My dad has practice here. I have to wait till he's done."

Jordan's jaw tensed. His dad. He thought back to who he'd seen picking up or dropping off Jace in the past. It had always been his mom, which was why he'd never made that connection. "Your dad plays for the Snowballs?"

Jace glanced up. "Yeah. You know him?"

Jordan nodded. "I'm going to tell him about what happened today. Between you and Ethan."

"Coach—"

"I'm letting you know, not asking for your opinion." Voices filled the entryway, and Jordan turned to see Snowballs players filtering in through the front doors. Curtis Reeder locked onto them and left the group. So. That was his dad. Jordan didn't remember if they'd had a run in specifically, but with the Snowballs, there weren't many altercation virgins left.

Curtis walked over and ruffled his son's hair. "How was practice?"

"Dad." Jace scowled and put his white boy fluff back into place. "It was good. This is one of my coaches."

Curtis turned, appraising him. "Wheatfill."

Jordan nodded. Curtis was an inch taller than him, but not as thick. It was difficult not to be a bit of an asshole given the circumstances. He cleared his throat and ditched his player hat for his coaching one. "Can I bend your ear for a sec?"

Curtis's brow furrowed. He stepped away from Jace and followed Jordan over to the opposite wall.

"Jace has gotten into a couple of scuffles with another kid in our group. Ethan. They don't want to talk about it, but I can't have behaviour like that on the ice."

Curtis blew out a breath. "Ironic."

Jordan tensed. *Coach, not player.* "Our priority is the safety of these kids. He can't be instigating—"

"Instigating?" Curtis's jaw tightened. "I thought they didn't want to talk about it. How do you know he instigated?"

Jordan ground his teeth. "Jace seems to be the one who—"

"I appreciate the heads-up, but I know my kid. He's not one to start things." Curtis kept his voice low.

Jordan grunted. If he had a loonie for every parent that thought their kid wasn't at fault, he'd have enough for the lunch combo at Tim's. "Right. Well, if it happens again, both boys will be suspended for the week."

"Do we have a problem?" Sean walked up and stopped next to Curtis, his arms crossed over his chest.

Jordan wanted to tell him to walk his ass down to the locker room and leave the conversation to the men, but he didn't. "Youth hockey. It has nothing to do with you."

Curtis planted a hand on Sean's shoulder, and they both turned back to the stairwell. Jordan walked back to his gear, irritation itching under his skin. His eyes flicked back to Jace, who was now engrossed in whatever was on his screen.

Jordan pulled his phone from his pocket and checked the time. He still had a solid hour and a half until his Pucks Deep practice. It was a pain to twiddle his thumbs and kill time, but by the time he got home in rush hour traffic, he'd have to turn around and head back.

He swiped over to the messages between Rhonda and her friends. At least he had that to keep him company.

Jordan tapped Jace on the shoulder, then waited for him to take out his headphones. "I'm going to order food. You want anything?"

CHAPTER
Eleven

RHONDA

RHONDA DROPPED her suitcase on the floor and let out a low whistle. This place was swankier than she'd expected. Over the years, she'd stayed in a lot of bougie hotels, but this one was definitely in the top five. Maybe even top three. In Edmonton of all places.

She slipped off her shoes and sank her toes into the plush carpet. It was like walking on a cloud. The lobby had been an elegant mix of dark wood and marble, and the room followed suit with its understated luxury. No tacky floral bedspreads or peeling wallpaper here. Even the air smelled better, like fresh flowers instead of the usual faint whiff of industrial cleaner.

The bed linens looked like they defied the laws of matter and were both crisp and soft. She had to resist the urge to strip down, flop onto the mattress, and take a quick cat nap. She had work to do. A whole routine to go through before her presentation that night.

She pulled her toiletries from her suitcase and set them on

the sink, then extracted her garment bag and hung it in the closet. The presentation was at six, so she had plenty of time to prepare.

She'd already picked out her outfit, a tailored dress with clean lines. It was professional but had just enough of a dip in the neckline to keep every doctor in the room on their toes. Not that she needed help with that. Being a mixed-race woman in a room full of mostly old white men was usually enough of a hook.

Rhonda leaned against the counter and stared at herself in the mirror. She ran a hand through her curls, then pulled them back into a low bun. It was a fine line to walk. She couldn't be too pretty, or they thought she was a bimbo. But be unpolished? They'd settle into the stereotypes they already held about women who looked like her. It was a delicate balance, and one she was getting damn good at navigating.

Rhonda opened her makeup bag and started her application. She'd learned to go for a natural look that highlighted her features without being too flashy. A bit of blush to accentuate her cheekbones, a swipe of mascara to make her eyes pop. Red lips were too much, but soft, nearly translucent pink worked well. It reminded them of their mothers.

The dinner tonight was with a small group of influential doctors in the area. They served on all the boards, and she'd done her research. Dr. Harris was a cardiologist at the University of Alberta Hospital. He'd published several papers on the benefits of a Mediterranean diet. Ordering a Greek salad as an appetizer wasn't beneath her.

Then there was Dr. Singh, a prominent oncologist who'd been instrumental in starting a new cancer treatment program in Edmonton. She'd read about his work in the Journal of Clinical Oncology and was genuinely impressed.

Rhonda finished with a setting spray and stepped back to admire her work. Perfect. She packed up her makeup, then grabbed her dress and unzipped the garment bag.

She put on her shapewear, then slid into her dress and smoothed it over her hips. It fit like a glove, hugging her curves in all the right places. She paired it with a statement necklace and her favourite heels, then gave herself one last once-over in the mirror.

She closed her suitcase on the luggage stand and tidied her toiletries in the washroom. Leaving her room immaculate was a habit she'd picked up over the years. You never knew when you might want to bring someone back.

Rhonda scanned the room and grimaced. Lately, the idea of bringing someone back felt more like a chore than a possibility. Alarming, to say the least. Maybe she was just tired. Or maybe, like one doctor in Red Deer had said flippantly a few months ago, she was entering perimenopause early.

That had stuck with her. She'd read enough testimonials on Reddit to give her permanent insomnia. Were these the best years of her life? Was her sex drive going to plummet? Worse, would she have to think about chin hairs and *labial chafing?*

For the love.

Rhonda clutched her purse and strode out of the room, then walked down the hall to the elevator and pressed the button. The doors opened, and she stepped inside, her heels clicking on the polished tile floor.

She still had drive. The problem was that it seemed to be directed at one person and one person only at the moment. That moment with Jordan in the hallway . . . she couldn't remember the last time she'd felt that kind of animalistic desire.

Rhonda's chest grew tight at the thought. She hadn't heard from him since he'd joked about getting himself pregnant. He was probably laughing with the entire rest of his team right then. Showing them what an idiot she was for talking about him to her friends, or crowing about how he'd lured her back to his apartment with hopes of getting an audience with Dr. Mallory.

He was just another guy on the roster.

Even if her roster had only one name on it for the past two

months, that could change at any time. It could change tonight if she wanted it to.

The elevator doors opened, and Rhonda stepped out into the lobby. She walked past the front desk, her eyes scanning the room for any familiar faces. She didn't see any of the doctors or reps she'd been meeting with, so she made her way to the restaurant.

The place was packed, but they had a private room reserved in the back. Rhonda walked past the hostess stand and headed straight for it. She was the first one there, as planned. She liked to be early so she could get a feel for the room.

She slid into one of the leather chairs past the double doors and set her purse on the seat next to her. Their server appeared a moment later, and mmm. He was adorable. Younger than her, but that had never been a problem.

"Good evening, ma'am. Can I get you started with something to drink?" His voice was smooth, like honey drizzled over warm toast.

Rhonda smiled, twisting her earring. "I'll take a glass of your finest tap water, please. Lemon, no ice."

The server smirked. "Coming right up." He disappeared for a moment, then returned with a glass, more like a goblet, of water and set it in front of her.

"Thank you." Rhonda took a sip, then set the glass back down. His eyes flicked to her neckline. Mission accomplished.

He cleared his throat. "Are you waiting for someone, or should I bring you a menu?"

Rhonda kept her face straight. "I like to reserve the largest room. For one. It's my personal protest against the idea that perceived feminine value increases with her ability to procure relationships."

His lips twitched. "Where's the petition?" He glanced down at the seat next to her. "I want to sign." Rhonda couldn't keep the edges of her lips from turning up. He held up a finger, then walked to the stand closest to them and brought back a menu.

He handed it to her. "I would recommend the filet. Medium rare. Since you're out for blood."

Rhonda's smile widened. "I don't think they're paying you enough."

"I usually make up for it. In tips."

Hot damn. He was charming as hell. Rhonda's heart started to race, and for a moment she thought she might be cured. But then her hands grew clammy. This wasn't attraction. This was blind panic. Because even when all the right pieces were combined in front of her, she felt nothing.

He took a step back and paused. "I'm at your service until eight."

"Hmm. What happens at eight?" Flirting was so second nature, she couldn't *not* do it, even when she felt dead inside.

"I clock out. Then I usually sit at that seat at the bar." His lips quirked.

"You're a man of routine."

He grinned and his hair fell over his forehead. "Sometimes. But I'm always willing to be spontaneous." He tapped her table, then turned and walked away.

She could do it. She could work her way through dinner, then end up on the stool next to him after eight. It would be the most natural thing in the world. They'd flirt, she'd order a drink, he'd probably pay, or the bartender would pull him a solid, and then she'd tell him what room she was staying in.

The thought made her mouth go dry, and she took another sip of water. That was exactly what she needed, wasn't it? To let loose. Forget about whatever had happened with Jordan.

Rhonda didn't have much time to consider. The doctors filed in, and she stood, shaking hands and making introductions. She'd met two of them previously, and the others were colleagues they'd brought along.

The dinner went exactly to plan, besides a brief diversion when they found out she was allergic to peanuts *and* fenugreek as they were ordering. She gave the high-level story of how she'd discovered that, but it did allow her to expound on something high brow, nuanced, and intelligent within the first five minutes. From there, they discussed politics and hospital administration, then ended with Reviact and the impact it was having on patients around the country.

Even though she didn't order the filet mignon, the server was extremely attentive. Always filling her water first, his eyes meeting hers from under his dark lashes. It was a welcome addition to her toolbelt. When other men picked up on a man's pointed interest, they were immediately more tuned in to what that woman had to say.

Again. She judged herself for using all of it to her advantage, but would a man apologize for that? For using communication strategies or charisma? No, he sure as hell wouldn't. This was business, and using her knowledge of human psychology didn't make her unethical. It made her good at her job.

When the meal was over, Rhonda spoke with each of the doctors and thanked them for their time. She excused herself to the washroom as they said their goodbyes, then came back out at eight ten.

Sure enough, there he was. Sitting at the bar, chatting with the bartender. He smiled as she approached. "Fancy seeing you here."

Rhonda smiled. "I ran out of water."

He motioned to the barstool next to him. "Perfect. Because I already bought you a drink."

RHONDA

RHONDA SETTLED ONTO THE BARSTOOL, running her fingers over the polished wood of the counter. "So what am I drinking?"

The waiter nodded to the bartender. "After that spiel in the booth? There was no way in hell I was ordering for you. I just told him to get you whatever you wanted."

The bartender gave a mock bow, and Rhonda laughed. "Whiskey sour."

The server raised an eyebrow. "Didn't peg you for a whiskey girl."

She smiled, leaning in. "Mixing things up, I guess."

He shrugged. "I don't know. That's a bit of a classic."

Rhonda laughed. "It is. My mom used to make them."

"Oh? She was a bartender?"

Rhonda shook her head. "No, definitely not."

Her mother had made that drink one time. She remembered it vividly, the image burned into every cell. Her mom stood in their beautiful kitchen with new countertops and the name brand dishwasher. The drink hadn't been a celebration. It had been all she had in the house—a random bottle of whiskey her father had brought home and forgotten about, and a shriveled lemon from the back of the fridge.

Rhonda watched from the doorway as her mom poured, stirred, and gulped it back. Then, with shaking hands, she set the glass down, wiped her mouth, and quietly told Rhonda and her sister, who still lived at home, that they were getting divorced.

She'd never forgotten the look in her mom's eyes that night. Like a wild animal. A rabbit staring down a fox.

Leaving had been the hardest thing her mother had ever done, but staying would've been death by a thousand cuts. Her dad didn't hit them. He didn't have to. His control was absolute, like a puppeteer pulling invisible strings.

That summer home was when she'd rewritten her childhood. As a kid, her father had been a hero. Always taking care of anything, saying yes when her mother said no. But after being away, she saw his behaviour for what it was.

He managed every detail of their lives—what they ate, who they saw, what they wore. Rhonda didn't know it was possible to do something sinister with a smile. He kept her mom isolated, convinced her she couldn't make friends, refused to let her take classes. "I provide for you," he'd say in a tone that now made Rhonda's skin crawl. "Isn't that enough?"

But Rhonda had seen the way her mom's eyes would linger on books or commercials for community colleges. The way her hand hesitated when she wanted to call her sister but never did. Back then, Rhonda believed she was ungrateful. In reality, he'd made her so dependent on him that when she finally left, she had next to nothing. No savings, no safety net. Just the clothes she could carry and a couple bags of groceries.

Rhonda avoided the years after. Always finding excuses to stay on campus. They were filled with crappy apartments, over-drawn bank accounts, and clothes that never quite lost that thrift store patina. Rhonda's mom worked two jobs, sometimes three, and still didn't ever have enough since she didn't know how to manage her expenses.

But there was freedom in the chaos, and if Rhonda paid her mother's bills for the rest of her life, it wouldn't be thanks enough for the way she held things together growing up. How she shielded them so much that Rhonda grew up loving her father.

The bartender slid the glass toward her, and she took a drink. Awful, but she revelled in the way it burned down her throat.

"You're a woman of ritual." The waiter turned on his stool, and Rhonda felt it. That was her moment. She could riff on the line he gave earlier, make it witty and sexy. Watch as he adjusted himself, drawing her attention to the way his body responded to the suggestion.

It was simple. She'd done it before, meant it before. And, not surprisingly, never regretted it before. Maybe she'd had some regrets about people she hadn't taken to her room, but never about the ones she had.

But tonight, her tongue was glued to the roof of her mouth.

"I have a confession to make." The server leaned on the bar. "I already know your name." She gave him a look, and he laughed. "From the reservation list. I didn't google you."

She smirked. "Too bad. I have some damn good dating profiles."

He laughed out loud. "So you're single."

"Sometimes."

He reached out and spun her glass on the bar. "Depends on the night? I'm Reid by the way."

She took another drink, and he made a point to brush her thumb with his. "Correct."

"And tonight . . . "

"Taken, unfortunately." Reid's face fell a little, and Rhonda put a hand on his arm. "This week I'm married to my work." He let out a puff of air. "If he wasn't such a cruel master, you'd be the first to know."

Reid ran a hand through his hair. "But you're going to finish that drink?"

"Of course. A super sexy waiter bought it for me."

Reid grinned, and Rhonda exhaled, the tension seeping from her shoulders. Good. This was good. She did have work to catch up on, and probably people she needed to reach out to since she'd been radio silent for the past two-and-a-half hours.

She glanced up at the screen above the bar. The Avs were playing. A pang hit her in the gut so hard she almost gasped. She wanted to be home at the ice centre, sitting with her friends watching hockey. Damn it, she was getting old.

Rhonda chatted with Reid while she finished her drink, then shook his hand, blushed when he lingered too long, then exited the restaurant and headed for the elevator. The ride up to her floor was silent, but Rhonda's mind was anything but.

Who even was she?

Her existential crisis started the second she left the elevator and ramped up until she slid her keycard into the lock and pushed the door open. She kicked off her shoes and walked straight to the washroom.

She turned on the shower and stripped while she waited for the water to heat up. When steam began to fill the room, she stepped under the spray. The water was hot, almost scalding, but she liked the burn on her skin just like she craved that burn in her throat. Water rolled off her shoulders, down her back, and over her legs and feet, warming her freezing toes.

She closed her eyes and lifted her face to the stream, pulling out her bobby pins and setting them in the soap dish. After a few more seconds, she turned her head to breathe and wiped her eyes, then reached for the still-wrapped body soap. The packaging was stubborn, but when she got it open, she lathered up and ran her hands over her body.

She wanted touch—craved it. But this was the first time she

was desperate for one set of hands. Despite the heat, she started to shiver.

Rhonda cranked the temperature higher and stood there, letting the water heat her back and shoulders. Finally, she turned off the shower and stepped out, grabbing one of the fluffy towels from the rack. She dried off, wrapped her hair, then grabbed her toothbrush, not bothering to dress.

She ran through her nightly routine, and her skin glistened with moisture as she walked to the nightstand and pulled out her Kobo eReader. She grabbed the extra blanket from the closet, jacked the thermostat up to twenty-four degrees, then threw the blanket over the comforter and climbed into bed in her birthday suit.

She turned on her eReader and settled back into the pillows. Rhonda hadn't read a romance in years. Her books of choice were usually psychological thrillers or nonfiction. But tonight she was suddenly desperate for a love story.

She scrolled through the recommended books and impulse bought the first one with a review that read, "Bookmark chapter nineteen. IYKYK."

Just as the book was loading, she realized she hadn't checked her phone and it was still in her purse across the room. Cursing under her breath, she forced herself from the bed and crossed to the entryway. She grabbed her phone and froze as the notifications showed on her screen. *Seventy-five texts?*

Rhonda swiped up, navigating to her messages as she walked back to the bed. Messages from Anne, Tina, and—

What the actual!?

She scrolled back in the text chain, her stomach dropping to her knees. She needed an alibi for Friday night—because she was going to murder her friends.

JORDAN

JORDAN THREW his hockey bag into the back of his truck, then cut across the parking lot to the sidewalk.

"Coming out with us tonight?" Cam nudged him.

Jordan nodded. "It's been a while." He'd taken so many night shifts lately, his social life was suffering.

He briefly wondered if any of the Snowballs players would be inside the pub, but their practice ended two hours earlier. If they were still chugging brewskis after that long on a Monday night, they had more problems than running into Pucks Deep.

He grinned to himself as they walked in out of the cold. He may be a terrible person. He shouldn't have responded to the texts, but it wasn't him that started it. By the messages that were coming through, he knew that Rhonda wasn't telling her friends what had happened between them.

He didn't enjoy seeing them hypothesize about who she'd slept with. More concerning was that sinking feeling in his gut whenever he thought about her being with someone else. He didn't get that feeling. Ever.

That was when he told himself to delete the chat, block their numbers, and never interact with Rhonda or her friends again. He wasn't the kind of guy that girls wanted to be exclusive with, and clearly, Rhonda was no exception.

He also wasn't the kind of guy to get his feelings hurt anymore, and he wasn't going to let this situation change that.

Jordan walked across the parking lot and kept his hand on his phone. Every time he felt it buzz, his heart jolted. He was probably a tool, and Rhonda would most definitely hate him, but that text chain was just too good. He and his siblings had played pranks on each other all through high school. Then his hockey friends had taken their place in college. It had been a while since he participated in a good one, and he hadn't realized how much he missed it.

Anne—he'd gotten her name from context—and anonymous friend number two were sure that Rhonda was at a dinner with doctors and medical staff that night, which meant any second now, she was going to see at least fifty text messages on her phone. His heart raced, and his hands were clammy. As they walked inside the pub and found the other guys at a table near the back, he ordered a drink and sat down.

"That wasn't so bad." Cam reached across the table to take a handful of nachos.

"What, the rink? Or watching the Snowballs leave the locker room?" Chubbs asked. "I kind of wished we had signs. We could give them rankings. Like Miss America as they walk down the hall."

Cam snickered, and Nate snorted. "I don't think they were too thrilled with us being there."

"They can't complain," Jordan grunted. "They didn't have to change their practice time. We're the ones who have to be sweating until ten o'clock at night."

He'd been watching the hockey boards to see if there would

be any chirping about the rink closure but, so far, Sean had stayed quiet.

Jordan's phone buzzed on the table, and he glanced down. It wasn't Rhonda.

ANNE

> Just tell us how you met Rhonda. She won't care. She tells us everything

Jordan smirked. This text chain was proof of that fallacy. He'd at least told them his pronouns, but everything else had been banter. With Rhonda still MIA, they were getting desperate for facts.

FRIEND #2

> Give us a ballpark. Are you from her college days? Earlier?

Later

FRIEND #2

> Oh, damn. Okay. So . . . her twenties later or more recent?

I never ask a woman's age.

He could do this all night.

ANNE

> Are you still in Calgary?

Depends on what you mean by Calgary.

FRIEND #2

> Ugh. You're exactly the kind of guy Rhonda
> would go for

Smart? Funny?

ANNE

> A cheeky bastard.

Thank you?

ANNE

> But why does she still have your number? She
> never keeps numbers. That means you have to
> be someone she knows from work.

FRIEND #2

Or the team

Anne

Or family

Ew

Friend #2

IS IT THE TEAM?

That was hitting a little too close to home.

"You okay there?" Cam asked, taking a drink of his beer.

Jordan set his phone face down on the table. "Yeah. Just a work thing."

Cam nodded. "Your work must be a helluva lot more fun than mine judging by the grin on your face."

Jordan cleared his throat. "Yeah. Nurses are funny."

Steele scoffed. "Nurses aren't funny." He launched into a story about getting a rectal exam for a reason he wouldn't specify. "I prepared ass jokes. She didn't laugh at a single one."

"User error." Jordan grinned, and Steele flipped him off. He reached for a buffalo wing just as their server dropped off a plate piled high with loaded nachos.

As soon as she left, Nate shook his head. "I told you. Too much cheese."

Steele shook his head. "You're batshit crazy. Cheese is the best part."

"Not when it's that fake crap."

"It's not fake. It's melted." Steele pulled out a chip bathed in orange.

Nate pointed at the plate. "I don't see any strings. Do you see strings? That's how you know it's not real cheese."

Jordan rolled his eyes and reached for the pitcher of beer in the centre of the table. "You guys catch the Avs last night?"

Nate nodded. "Yeah, that was rough. Blew it in the third period."

Steele shook his head. "Gantt's gotta step up."

Chubs waved him off. "He can't do it all. The defence was a pile of steaming ass."

"And where was Trembley?" Jordan took a drink from his glass.

"What, if you're getting paid ten and a half mil, you're expected to show up?"

Nate grunted and swallowed a mouthful of beer. "Did you hear about the new kid?"

Jordan shook his head. He didn't want to admit how little attention he'd been paying to hockey news lately.

Chubs grinned. "This eighteen-year-old phenom out of Moose Jaw. He's been tearing it up in the juniors."

Nate shrugged. "He's got some attitude problems, though."

"Who doesn't at eighteen?" Chubs chuckled.

"Hell, who doesn't at thirty-four?" Steele fist-bumped Cam.

Cam nodded. "True. But from what I've heard, he's been in a bit of trouble. Fights, skipping practices, that sort of thing."

Chubs grinned. "Hey, if the kid's got skills, they'll overlook a lot."

Nate took a swig of his beer. "Yeah, but at what point does the baggage outweigh the talent?"

And just like that, Jordan was back in his head. He was thirty-six, and it felt like all he had was baggage.

Cam nodded. "True, but you gotta admit, it's fun to watch these young guns come up and shake things up."

Steele grinned. "Especially when they piss off the old guard. Did you see that clip of him mouthing off to his coach?"

Jordan worked to keep up. How had he missed all of this?

Chubs laughed. "The kid's got balls, I'll give him that."

Jordan raised his glass. "Here's to the next generation of assholes." A worthy contribution to the conversation. He drank, then picked up his phone and rose from his chair, citing a needed washroom break. Once he was out of view of the booth, he stopped in the corner between the washrooms and the bar.

FRIEND #2

> I think you're holding out on us

ANNE

> I kind of don't want him to tell us. I want more
> clues, so I can feel like I figured it out

FRIEND #2

> What's your favourite colour?

ANNE

> Ooh, what's your sign?

· · ·

Just as he was about to respond, he saw it. A thumbs-up emoji from Rhonda.

Jordan frowned, staring at his phone. That was it? Rhonda didn't respond to the group text, didn't berate them for being scumbags, nothing.

Just a thumbs-up.

The feeling of self-loathing hit him like a sack of bricks. He'd done this more times than he could count. Following a woman like a kicked puppy. Waiting for some kind of sign. A whisper of interest.

In college, he thought he was the shit. After his injury, he sank to the opposite end of the spectrum. In both cases his actions were identical. He'd spent his nights out at bars and his days recovering from hangovers.

Jordy was a good time. No commitment. No strings.

The pathetic thing was? At his core, he was a problem solver. A giver. But the women in his life never protected that. They would take until he was empty, then scrape him out with a spoon.

So now he had hockey. He had work. He took care of people who would actually let him help. And yet he was still trying to break through walls that weren't ready to come down.

Rhonda had tensed the first time he'd brought her coffee. She'd been practically itching out of her skin when he'd given her an IV, though to be fair, that could've been the Fenugreek.

He wasn't going to wait around with his tongue lolling out this time.

Just as he lifted his thumb to click off the screen, a text came through from Claire.

CLAIRE

I don't want to go to rehab.

Jordan's stomach sank. Seemed like the universe was punctuating his inner monologue.

Where are you?

Claire

Safe

But you don't want rehab?

Claire

It doesn't work

Jordan hissed air through his teeth and pulled up his browser. He typed in his search and started scrolling through the results, then clicked on Cantra's official link, scanning the page for information about where his sister could get Reviact in the city.

Not many options, but he found a private clinic. Licensed to prescribe new treatments for mental health and addiction. It was out of the way, but that didn't matter. He copied the address and phone number, then pasted it into his text thread with Claire.

> This place stocks Reviact. I've seen the results. They're compelling.

CLAIRE

> I'll phone them tomorrow

Jordan's thumbs hovered over the keys. He wouldn't be a golden retriever for other women, but this was his sister.

> I'll cover anything your benefits don't.

CLAIRE

> You don't have to do that

> I want to.

He stared at the screen for another thirty seconds, and when she didn't text back, Jordan dropped his phone into his pocket and stalked to the washroom.

RHONDA

RHONDA ADJUSTED HER STANCE, heels digging slightly into the bland carpet. Her presentation on Reviact was polished, her tone upbeat, but her mind was elsewhere. Most notably on the full novel of text messages between her friends and Jordan.

"And that brings us to the latest clinical trials." She clicked to the next slide. "We're seeing a thirty-five percent reduction in relapse rates over six months. That's significant for patients who . . ."

Somehow she kept talking as her phone vibrated against the podium. Rhonda's heart jumped. She hadn't intentionally set it where she could see it. *Or had she?* Her pulse picked up speed when she saw the text was from "J."

She prattled on, worried that she'd fully dissociated as her eyes flicked down to the screen. She swiped up.

J

My sister started on Reviact this week

Her chest tightened and she sucked in a breath. Before anyone noticed, she finished her sentence and scanned the room. "Questions so far?"

As the doctors stared at the screen, taking in the chart on her slide, she typed a quick reply.

I'm glad to hear it. Keep me updated

The room settled into silence again as she fielded a question about dosage adjustments. Her phone buzzed once more. Another glance.

J

Working on Mallory

She breathed a sigh of relief. After what happened between them, and especially after her friends had hounded him for hours the night before, she hadn't worked up the courage to ask him about that favour.

Honestly, she'd been a little pissed that he wouldn't just leave the chat alone. If he stopped responding, Anne and Tina would've lost interest.

But all of it paled in comparison to the text she got from

Jenna on their actual group text that morning. Their baby wasn't coming. Again.

Her heart was breaking for her friend, she was in the middle of a presentation, and staring at a text from Jordan. What a dumpster fire.

Rhonda's finger hovered over the heart reaction, but she settled on a thumbs-up, then tucked her phone away into the pocket of her dress slacks.

The rest of the week blurred into a series of meetings, small talk, and networking over coffee and catered lunches. On Thursday, Rhonda grabbed dinner at the hotel bar. Brunch that morning had been fantastic, and hunger didn't hit her until seven o'clock.

She set her fork on her plate and waited for the bartender to notice she was finished. Reid found her first.

"Back for more, eh?"

"Always." She smiled.

"You staying for the weekend?"

Rhonda shook her head. "Nope, heading home tomorrow." She leaned back in her chair and gave the server a wry grin. "Thought I'd soak up one last night of Edmonton's finest hotel bar cuisine, though."

Reid chuckled, leaning on the edge of the bar with a grin that asked, *"Are you still in a serious relationship with work?"* He wasn't *not* charming. "Well you know, this is the spot for anyone with an evolved palate and a passion for sticky menus."

"Stop it. You'll ruin the mystique," she deadpanned, pointing her fork at him. "How else am I supposed to pretend I'm an heiress with Daddy's card?"

He leaned in. "Is that the game we're playing tonight?" His smile widened. "If you want to do some damage, I happen to know the chocolate lava cake is worth its weight in gold." He straightened and took a step back. "I could deliver it personally."

She tilted her head, pretending to mull it over. Yes. The

answer was yes. She could lick chocolate lava off Reid's obviously toned chest and forget all about text chains and Jordan's shoulders. *Damn it, she should not have thought about Jordan's shoulders.* She wanted to be thinking about this guy—Reid, standing right in front of her. Rhonda turned to him, narrowing her eyes, willing herself to think about unbuttoning his shirt or running her hands through his tousled hair.

She bit back a groan of frustration. Nothing. All she could think about were Jordan's scrubs and his flexing forearms as he prepared an IV. This was Anne and Tina's fault. His initial "J" had flashed in front of her face consistently enough to full on incept her.

She gave Reid an apologetic grin. "I think I'll have to get it to go. The ol' ball and chain."

He dropped his eyes and nodded. "I'll wrap it up for you."

Rhonda left the bar with the lava cake in hand. She rode the elevator up to her room, which was blissfully quiet, and set the dessert box on the desk. She kicked off her heels, sighing as her bare feet met the soft carpet. Her jacket and bag landed unceremoniously on the chair before she grabbed the cake and flopped onto the bed.

She settled against the pillows and pulled out her phone, scrolling back through the last messages with Anne, Tina, and the actual Jenna this time.

Tina

> I say we invite Mystery Man to therapy

I just found out I have a meeting Friday

Jenna

LOLOLOL

Anne

Rhonda, I hope you're not mad!? It was just funny

So glad I could provide the entertainment this week

She was glad, actually. Especially with what Jenna had been dealing with.

Tina

You better be prepared to tell us everything. You're only getting away with this because we haven't been in person

She sent a GIF of someone slamming handfuls of popcorn. It *was* funny. If this had been Anne or Tina's misstep, she would've jumped in with both feet. But it wasn't them, it was her. And Jordan wasn't playing nice.

Rhonda flicked on the TV and watched a half hour of Notting Hill while she finished her cake, then walked through her bedtime routine and curled up in bed. She kicked her legs under the sheets to create some heat for her perpetually freezing feet, then eventually fell into the kind of deep sleep that felt like it came with its own weight.

She slept blissfully free of her Jordan focused brain until the next morning. She woke and ordered room service, then did yoga until a knock came at the door. She opened it and accepted the tray, then set it on the dresser and removed the covers, breathing in the scent of bacon, eggs, and avocado toast. She ate while answering emails on her laptop, then eventually showered, taking full advantage of her late checkout.

At twelve-thirty, Rhonda pulled out of the hotel parking lot, immediately turning on her seat warmer. The wind had whipped up into a frenzy in a matter of minutes. Though, that was Alberta for you.

She wound back to the highway and headed south. All in all, it had been a productive week. Northgate and Prairie Stone had both approved on the spot, which wasn't a surprise. They were traditionally early adopters of new pharmaceuticals. The question was whether Gateway and Summit Creek would take the plunge.

They were interested in the research, and they'd asked questions, which was always a good sign. But they hadn't given her any sort of commitment after the brunch. She sent a follow-up email last night, highlighting the generous rebates they were offering patients deep into 2025. She hoped that would push them over the edge.

Rhonda stopped for a donair and ate sitting on one of the diner stools so she wouldn't spill tzatziki all over her thighs. In just that short fifteen minutes, the wind had picked up again, tiny snowflakes whirling around her as she got back in the driver's seat. Fantastic. Hopefully, the weather was only there in the north and she would be able to outrun it as she drove back toward Calgary.

She topped up her gas, even though she already had three-quarters of a tank, and grabbed a bag of salt and vinegar chips and chocolate-covered almonds for the drive. She pressed play on her queue of audio podcast episodes and pulled back out onto the highway. She thought about checking the weather, but at that point, she didn't even want to know. If a bad storm had been forecasted, someone over the past week would have talked about it, which meant this was probably just a cold front blowing through.

She mentally chastised herself for not putting on snow tires yet. But the year before, she'd put them on two weeks before Halloween for a snowstorm, and then the roads had stayed dry until the beginning of December. That was a waste of good rubber.

By the time she reached Red Deer, the almonds were half gone, whereas the bag of chips still sat unopened in the passenger seat because the bag was made of raccoon-resistant plastic, and she needed her hands at ten and two on the wheel. Snow snaked across the road, and she could barely see a meter in front of her front bumper.

She drove between forty-five and sixty kilometres per hour, cranking the heat so she wouldn't get chilled from stress sweat. She could do this. Slow and steady. There weren't very many people on the road, so that was a blessing. But driving in the middle of a snowstorm was Rhonda's personal hell.

After nearly sideswiping a car a week after getting her learner's permit, Rhonda had refused to drive until she was sixteen, and even then, it was forced. She made her high school basketball team, and her mom's work schedule meant she couldn't drive Rhonda home from practice. After a month of bumming rides off friends, she decided facing a nightmare was better than burning all her bridges.

Last winter, she'd taken rideshares more times than she could count and flown both to Edmonton and Medicine Hat to avoid getting on the roads. She'd been so distracted by Jordan and Rocky Ridge over the past week, she hadn't even thought to check the forecast. Rhonda's hands tightened on the wheel. Anne and Tina were going to get an earful at therapy on Friday. Jenna was off the hook since she hadn't even been on the text chain, though she was positive Anne and Tina had been sending her screenshots.

Why the hell had they started texting him? It could have been one of her professional contacts, or a family member for that matter. Though, based on Jordan's text, it was pretty obvious that even if he was in one of the above groups, he wasn't beyond their brand of humour. As far as she could tell, Anne and Tina still had no idea who he was. But Jordan had given just enough for them to start frothing at the mouth.

She was better at BSing over text, but any story she thought of to explain this random person in their text chain sounded ridiculous. The evidence was mounting against her. Weird smiles at Sunday Supper, the admission that she *had* met somebody the week before, and then Jordan's flirtatious texts. She had to come up with something good, something just embarrassing enough that they would believe she was telling the truth.

It was a damn shame she was such a terrible liar. The idea of making up a story and saying it straight to their faces made her stomach twist. But the idea of telling them the truth about Jordan, there was no way that would stay quiet. They would be the ones giving the weird smiles after games or whenever Pucks Deep was brought up in conversation. Eventually, Country or Gary or one of the other guys would pick up on it. And she would be forced to word-vomit her shameful history to the entire team.

And over what? No matter how she spun this, it would not look good for her, and it wouldn't look good for Jordan either—especially not for Jordan. Not that she needed to do anything to protect him, but still.

That was really it, wasn't it? She'd heard the Snowballs talk about Jordan and his lack of moral standards for as long as she'd known them. And wasn't she exactly the same as him? She'd never asked anybody to prove that they were single before hooking up with them. For all she knew, she'd been just as guilty as he was. She loved her Snowball family. *If they looked at her like they looked at him?*

Of course, she could just become a more moral person.

And there was that thought spiral again, ready to kick her in the teeth. Women were supposed to love commitment. They weren't supposed to be driven by pleasure or passion, to *not* want a serious relationship.

In her thirties, she'd gotten to the point where she gave zero shits what other people thought about her life choices. But she did give many shits about the people she loved. The truth was, some people just weren't ready to love that part of her. Which was why she kept her handful of friends close. And why she couldn't lie to them during girl therapy.

But none of that mattered because she was going to skid off the road and die in an effing ditch.

Rhonda gripped the wheel, muttering prayers to any god that would listen and wishing she'd stopped to open the damn bag of chips.

CHAPTER
Fifteen

Jordan

JORDAN WAITED at the nursing station. It was 4:05, and Gertie still hadn't returned. Normally, he'd be happy not to cross paths with her before he left the hospital, but today he was counting on it. He had a game at seven in Chestermere and didn't have much time to spare, especially with the weather starting to roll in. His weather app had barely mentioned potential snowfall, but the forecaster he followed online had been predicting it would be a doozy.

He heard Gertie before he saw her. Her voice could have been used for Marge Simpson's sister in a spin-off series. Gertie turned the corner and stopped when she saw him standing there.

"What the hell are you still doing here?" she asked, straightening her scrubs. Her hair was pulled up into a banana clip that spanned the entire curve of her skull.

Jordan smirked. "I'm a dedicated employee."

She rolled her eyes and walked past him, leaning over to

make a note on a Post-It. She had hundreds of Post-Its scattered around the desk and somehow kept track of every last one of them. If any of the nurses accidentally knocked one to the floor or, heaven forbid, threw one in the trash, they all paid for it.

"Are you excited for that staff dinner on the twenty-eighth?" Jordan asked.

She turned her head, her eyes narrowing. "What staff dinner?"

"Sorry, does it have a fancier name? You're sitting at the table Dr. Mallory purchased, right?"

Gertie lifted an eyebrow. "The cancer fundraiser?"

"You're *pro-cancer?*" He looked aghast. Gertie rolled her eyes, and Jordan laughed. "Yes, the cancer research fundraiser. Lots of small talk. Probably keynote speakers." He drew out those last words. He knew how much she hated listening to other people talk.

Gertie shuddered. "They needed an extra butt in the seat, and I was promised cheesecake." She stuck the Post-It underneath the lip of the counter, then picked up her clipboard.

"What if I had an extra butt for you?"

She raised an eyebrow. "You'd have to own a suit. Or at least a shirt and tie." She stalked from the nurses' station, heading down the hall.

Gertie with the zingers. Jordan followed her. "Not for me, for a friend."

"Your friend is interested in cancer *research?*" she asked.

"Yep, and she has lots of money. Might be interested in making a donation." None of that was technically untrue. Rhonda had to make a good salary, and considering how much she believed in Reviact, she probably would be one of those people to take money out of her own pocket for a worthy cause.

Gertie stopped, and he almost ran into her hunched back. She turned to face him. "I was promised cheesecake."

"That's why . . ." Jordan pulled out his phone and typed a quick search into his browser. "I was thinking you could go here instead." He turned the screen to face her. "I'll get you a gift card. Forty bucks should buy a lot of cheesecake."

A smile played at the corner of Gertie's mouth. "You're buying me off?"

Jordan scoffed. "I'm doing you a favour. Just because I love you."

Gertie shooed him away and continued down the hall. "I want that gift card in my inbox."

Jordan smiled to himself and walked back to the nurses' station to grab his coat.

He waved goodbye to the night shift and strode to the exit. The automatic doors hissed shut behind him, the antiseptic scent of the hospital replaced by the crisp bite of winter air. The wind was being an absolute asshole.

Jordan pulled up his collar as he descended the steps, his boots disturbing the barely collecting snow. He hoped traffic wasn't backed up because of the weather. He only had an hour to get ready and book it out to Chestermere.

He crossed the parking lot, weaving through the cars until he reached his truck. It groaned to life, and he cranked the defrost, hoping to clear the iced-over windshield enough to see his way back to the apartment.

The drive home wasn't too bad. He was able to maneuver around most of the Vancouver transplants who didn't know how to drive in Alberta. He parked his truck, then jogged to the doors of his place, already pulling out his keys.

Once up the elevator and in his apartment, Jordan stripped out of his scrubs and tossed them into the laundry. He headed straight for his bedroom, grabbed his hockey bag, and started pulling out his gear. He was already in his base layer when he remembered he hadn't texted Rhonda. He tugged on his shirt and reached for his phone on the nightstand.

He'd thought about her more than he cared to admit over the past two days. Every time he looked at his bed, he imagined her back in it. The string of texts with her friends hadn't helped. Now anytime his phone buzzed, his blood rushed straight south.

That was a problem, considering Rhonda hadn't ever texted back. She was pissed. Probably. But he wasn't going to text her with news of his brilliant strategy to get her in front of Mallory just for her to give it a thumbs up.

Which meant he was going to have to phone her. He swiped to her contact and hesitated, then moved his thumb to the call button. He pressed down and lifted the phone to his ear.

This was stupid. She probably wouldn't answer. His hockey bag sat open on the floor, his pads spilling out onto the carpet.

The line rang once.

This was a mistake. He could still—

"Hello?"

His mouth went dry. "Hey." Jordan cleared his throat, his mind scrambling for the reason he'd called. Rhonda was silent on the other end, but his mind and mouth refused to connect.

"Jordan, I'm driving, so—"

"I got you an audience with Dr. Mallory," he said in a rush.

"Oh. Good." Rhonda's voice was clipped.

Jordan frowned. That was not the reaction he'd been expecting. He'd anticipated at least a little gratitude. Maybe some gushing. Or best case, a "Thank you, Jordan, you're amazing,"

He scoffed. "Okay."

"What?"

Jordan's jaw tightened. He didn't want to be petty, but he'd gone out of his way to make that connection for her. It cost him cheesecake money. "Nothing." He drew a breath, trying to keep his tone level. "Dr. Mallory has a table at the Founders Event on Monday. I got a ticket for you."

The line was silent for a beat. "At the dinner?"

"Yeah." So she'd heard of it. "I pulled a few strings."

Rhonda was again silent on the other end, and Jordan's frustration bubbled up. She had what she wanted and now didn't have any use for him. He'd seen it coming this time, at least. "You're welcome," he snapped.

"What?"

"I thought what you meant to say was 'Thank you, Jordan, for going out of your way to do me this favour.' So I'm saying 'You're welcome.'"

"Jordan—"

"No, it's fine. I get it. I'll—"

"Jordan, can you shut the hell up?"

He bristled, then paused as his brain registered information he wasn't consciously tuning in to. Her voice was shrill. Her breathing was heavy.

"I'm sorry. I can't see the road. My brain can't take anything else in," she blurted.

Jordan spun to the window. Big fat flakes swirled outside the glass. She was driving. She'd said as much a few seconds ago, but it hadn't registered. "Where are you?" he asked.

Rhonda's breath came fast and shallow through the phone. "I don't know. I passed the signs for Airdrie. I think? I don't know —" Her voice broke. The visibility didn't seem awful outside his apartment complex, but storms had a tendency to break a bit further north.

"Rhonda, listen to me. I want you to take a deep breath. Can you do that?" Jordan's voice was steady, his training taking over. "In through your nose, out through your mouth."

"The tires are slipping!"

"*Breathe.* I want you to ease off the gas. Gently. Let your car slow down on its own. Don't slam on the brakes, just let it coast." Jordan's grip tightened on the phone. "You're doing great. Just keep your hands on the wheel, and look as far ahead as you can. Try to focus on any taillights or road signs. Anything that can give you a point of reference."

Rhonda sniffed. "I can't see a damn thing! I'm going to pull over."

"Rhonda, you have to wait for an exit or a pull out. You can't—"

The line clicked dead. Jordan stood in stunned silence, staring at his phone. He glanced down at his hockey bag, then pulled a hoodie from the hooks next to his closet, and stalked out of the room.

He grabbed his keys, shoved his feet into his boots and grabbed his winter coat and a toque, then ran out the front door and into the howling wind.

CHAPTER
Sixteen

RHONDA SAT in her car with the engine running, the hazard lights blinking against the swirling snow. Her brain had drowned out the rhythmic clicking five minutes ago. The storm had come out of nowhere, a white curtain drawn across the highway, and now she was parked on the side of the road, praying she wouldn't get rear-ended by a semi. She wasn't religious, but this felt like the appropriate time to dive in.

Her hands trembled as she adjusted the heat. She inhaled, which only made her think of Jordan. She shouldn't have hung up, but her brain couldn't handle another modicum of input. She felt like an overloaded outlet ready to trip the breaker.

Rhonda exhaled and scanned the car. She had a flashlight in the glove compartment. A first-aid kit under the passenger seat. A half-empty water bottle in the cup holder. And the damn bag of salt and vinegar chips.

She reached for the chips then grabbed a pen from the console and stabbed the plastic. Once would've done it, but just in case, she drove the pen in a second time and tore it open. She shoved a couple of chips into her mouth and crunched, the tangy vinegar burning her tongue.

After a few minutes, she'd settled enough to talk to Tina. There would be no hot tub therapy for her tonight. She brushed her fingers off on her jeans and dialed.

Tina answered on the second ring. "She lives!" Someone laughed away from the speaker. "Seriously, we've been texting you for the last hour. Where are you?"

Rhonda closed her eyes and blew out a breath. "I was on my way, but I got stuck in this storm."

"I thought you were supposed to get here by, like, three?"

"Yeah, well. I left a little late."

"I mean, you couldn't have known. Everyone here was saying we likely wouldn't get any snow." Her voice got quiet for a second. "Anne says it's already up to three inches on the patio."

Rhonda stared at the fogging windshield. "I'm sorry, I'm the worst."

"You're not the worst."

"I've made you reschedule twice."

Tina scoffed. "Well, when you put it that way . . ."

Rhonda laughed. "Tomorrow?"

"Done. But you have to shovel the path to the hot tub—"

"And tell us everything about the guy in the chat!"

Rhonda laughed and said goodbye. At least she'd dodged a bullet there. She still hadn't settled on a back story for Mystery Man slash Jordan.

And as for tonight . . . She knew full well she'd let her friends believe that she'd stopped in an actual town. If she'd told them she was sitting on the side of the road, they would have sicced the entire Snowball offensive line on her, and that was not what she wanted. She was fine. She didn't need anyone to risk driving in this mess.

Rhonda set her phone in the cupholder and climbed over the

console to the back seat. She had an old blanket back there some-where, she was sure of it. She worked to pull down the middle seat, then remembered she had to climb back into the front to pull the seat release. She Catherine Zeta-Jones'd it back over the console and hit the lever, then dropped onto the back.

She grunted as she reached through the gap into the trunk. The blanket was way too far back, but there was no way she was getting out to open the trunk from the outside.

Rhonda reached her arm through the gap again and pushed the back of the seat with her free hand for leverage. Her shoulder popped as she stretched, and she gritted her teeth. *Just a little farther.* She could feel the edge of the blanket.

Her fingers scrabbled against the fabric. She was sweating when she finally hooked it with one of her nails. The blanket slipped closer, and she gave it a good yank. The plaid fabric tumbled through the opening, and Rhonda pulled it into her lap, panting.

She climbed back into the driver's seat and wrapped the blanket around her like a burrito, then pulled out her phone and opened Netflix. She needed to drown out the sound of the storm. That whistling was making her even more anxious.

Rhonda scrolled through her list and landed on her comfort show, Gilmore Girls. She pulled the blanket tighter around her, cocooning herself in its warmth, then turned off the engine. It was warm enough, she could last for a while. She had a full tank of gas, but she'd never attempted to spend all night in her car before.

The first episode had just started when, out of nowhere, a loud thud echoed through her car. Rhonda screamed and jumped, her heart slamming against her ribs. Her head whipped toward the window, and she nearly jumped out of her skin when she saw a figure standing there, their face just inches from the glass.

She blinked, then wiped at the condensation, but the figure was already walking around the hood of her car. He was wearing a huge coat and toque, that was all she could make out. Rhonda's pulse quickened, and her fingers fumbled to escape the blanket and find the lock button. Had she locked the doors?

All this time she'd been afraid of getting hit, when really she should've been afraid of murderers. The passenger door swung open, and Rhonda swivelled like a turtle on its back, kicking her tennis shoes up toward the attacker.

The man dropped into the seat and closed the door, his breath fogging around him. He turned, and Rhonda's heart stuttered.

"Is that comfortable?" Jordan asked.

Rhonda dropped her feet, tangling them in the blanket. "What are you—"

"Helping you not die in a snowstorm." He watched her struggle to free herself from her mummification. "That was your plan?"

Rhonda's cheeks flushed. "Yeah." She jutted out her chin. This was her plan, and she was proud of it. She wasn't a damsel in distress. She didn't need anyone to swoop in and save her.

Jordan's jaw tensed. The tip of his nose and the skin just above his cheekbones were pink. "You were going to sleep here? On the side of the highway?"

Rhonda raised her arms as if to say, *what else was I supposed to do?* Jordan glanced away with the hint of an eye roll, and anger bubbled inside her chest. "If you came here to mock me—"

"Get out of the car." Jordan's eyes were dark, his brow furrowed.

Rhonda scoffed and folded her arms over her chest. "No."

Jordan's eyes flicked to her phone, and Rhonda flipped it over in her lap. She'd forgotten the show was still playing. He ran a hand over his face. "You're not staying here all night."

"I can't drive my car on these roads."

"Do you have snow tires?"

She shook her head. "It's October."

"It's Alberta."

She glared at him. "I'm not leaving my car here."

Jordan shifted in the seat, his throat working. "You're not going to leave it on the side of the road. You get in my truck, and I'll drive your car to the exit."

Rhonda's eyes widened. "My car won't even make it up the exit ramp!"

"I guess we'll find out," he snapped. Her mouth hung open as he leaned closer. "Leave your keys, get out of the car, and get in my damn truck."

The air in the car seemed to crystallize. She wanted to slap him. She wanted to grab the collar of his coat and pull him— Rhonda caught herself, her nostrils flaring. "Don't tell me what to do."

Jordan's eyes were fixed on her. Dark. Swallowing her whole. He drew a deep breath and exhaled. "Rhonda. Will you please exit the vehicle and get in my warm truck that has four-wheel drive and *snow tires* and can easily navigate these snowy roads?"

She opened her mouth, then closed it again.

Jordan continued, "I'm going to get your car off the highway at the next exit. We're going to find a place to park it. And then I'm going to take you home so you can have more than potato chips for dinner." He fingered the bag on her lap, and Rhonda flinched.

That did sound nice. As much as she wanted to dig her heels in, she set the bag on the console, then bundled up her blanket and threw it on the back seat. She left her purse with her keys and went to push open her door.

"This side." Jordan motioned to the passenger door. "I don't want you to get hit."

"I—"

Jordan reached down and pulled the bar that allowed him to move his seat back. He clicked it all the way, then took off his boots.

"What are you—?"

Before she could finish the sentence, Jordan reached over and grabbed onto her waist. He pulled her over the console and onto his lap, her legs folding around his thighs. Her hands had somehow found their way inside his coat and lay flat on his chest. She sat there a moment, stunned, straddling him, his hands circling her waist.

He nudged her to turn, and she followed his lead, swivelling until she sat on top of him, her back to his chest.

He brushed her hair from her ear. "Put on the boots."

Rhonda glanced down. "They'll be huge on me."

"Carry your shoes. You can change back once you're through the snow." His voice was low, his breath whispering against the shell of her ear. Jordan's hands grazed her hips, and the underside of her thighs suddenly became seismic sensors. If anything moved or changed on the lower half of Jordan's body, they would know about it.

She nodded, then leaned forward and pulled off her shoes as the first data points rolled in. Jordan was most definitely responding to her moving on his lap. Rhonda shifted more than she had to to get her foot in his boot, and Jordan grunted.

When she did it a second time, he slapped the side of her thigh. "You're a brat."

Rhonda picked up her shoes off the floor and leaned back against his chest, turning her head so her lips nearly grazed his jaw. "I think you like it."

Jordan wrapped a hand over her stomach, gripping on to her as he twisted. It was dark enough, she couldn't see what he was doing, but when he switched hands, his coat was gone and heat seeped into her through his cotton sweatshirt.

Jordan nudged her forward, then draped his coat over her shoulders. It smelled like him. Cool and crisp. She pulled it around her, soaking in the warmth still lingering there from his body.

Jordan grabbed the handle. *Right. Get in the damn truck.* Rhonda pushed open the door and worked to keep his boots on as she stepped out into the storm. The wind bit into her cheeks, and she shivered, gripping the coat like a cloak as she trudged back to his truck.

She got in the passenger side and switched shoes, then slid across the bench to sit in the driver's seat. The truck was so big she felt like a fifteen-year-old again, barely able to see through the windshield.

And then she glanced in the backseat. Poor life choice. The windows were fogged from the cold, and there, along the bottom corner of the back window, were fingerprints. *Her* fingerprints. Or someone else's? He would've cleaned his window from last summer, wouldn't he?

The thought of anyone else being in the backseat with Jordan made her queasy. Thankfully, she didn't have much time to ruminate because her taillights blinked on. A few seconds later, her car started to move. Rhonda's hands shook as she put the truck in gear and followed the lights to the next exit. Jordan drove slowly, but he made it up the exit ramp. She followed him to the right and into an old gas station parking lot.

He stopped next to the building where the ground was still mostly clear. She pulled up next to him, and it took a few seconds to remember he didn't have shoes. Or a coat. Rhonda grabbed his boots from the floor and hopped out of the driver's seat. She took the boots to the side of her car, and Jordan opened the door.

He put them on, but when she tried to give him his coat, he shook his head and motioned for her to return to the truck.

"I need my—"

"I'll get it." Jordan grabbed her purse and the partial bag of chips.

Rhonda retraced her steps and climbed into the passenger side of the toasty cab. Jordan jogged back to the truck and handed her things over before sliding behind the wheel. Rhonda fastened her seatbelt.

Without a word, Jordan started the engine and put the truck in gear. Rhonda knew she should thank him, but the words stuck in her throat. *She would've been fine.* The words felt thin, like watered-down soup, as they trickled through her head. Yes, she would've survived, but this was far better, and realizing that made her nauseous.

The truck rumbled as he drove over the frozen gravel. Rhonda felt an odd sense of guilt leaving her car there in an abandoned lot.

"It'll be fine." Jordan shifted his hands on the wheel as he turned onto the highway, and Rhonda's breath caught in her throat as the truck slid a little before finding its grip.

"Will it?"

Jordan exhaled. "It's not a problem if the wheels slip. It's a problem if you can't recover." He drove slowly, his eyes fixed on the road ahead. The windshield wipers thumped rhythmically, and the heater blasted warm air into the cab. "You need snow tires."

Rhonda pursed her lips. "Well aware."

He glanced over at her, his brow furrowed. "Your tire pressure light was on."

"Yeah. It does that sometimes."

Jordan blew out a breath, and Rhonda turned in her seat. "Are you judging me right now? You didn't have to come out here, I—"

"You were going to get rear-ended and tossed into the ditch. Before or after you froze to death when your gas ran out at three a.m., either or. Take your pick."

"I wasn't going to freeze to death," she muttered.

"Because you're the expert? It's supposed to drop to minus thirty tonight. Everyone thinks they'll be fine until they show up in the ER with black fingers."

Pressure built in her chest like she was hooked up to an air compressor. "Thanks, Dad," she snapped, then sucked in a breath.

"Maybe your dad should've taught you this shit," Jordan barked back.

"Oh, trust me, you and my dad would get along just great. Do you think I'm an idiot for not having snow tires? For not having a winter emergency kit in my car? Perfect. If I ever talk to him again, I'll let him know he has an ally."

Jordan was silent, his hands tight on the steering wheel. Rhonda's pulse pounded in her ears. She wanted to keep going, to spew the vitriol churning inside her, but thankfully she had learned some skills over the past seventeen years. Rule number one: don't keep talking when you're feeling intensely murdery.

"You don't talk to your dad?"

Rhonda turned to him in disbelief. "That's what you got from that?" Jordan nodded once, his eyes trained on the blurring road ahead of them. She stared out the windshield, mesmerized by the swirling snow glaring in the headlights. "No. I haven't talked to him since I was eighteen."

"Are your parents still together?"

Rhonda shook her head. "They were until twelve years ago. Five since they've been officially divorced."

Jordan gave a soft "hmm." They drove in silence for what felt like an eternity, staring at the monochromatic kaleidoscope of snow. "I wasn't judging you." Jordan's voice split the silence, cracking the chill between them and infusing it with everything soft and warm.

Rhonda shivered. "I deserved it. It was stupid not to check the weather."

Jordan made a sound in his throat, and when Rhonda turned to look at him, he pulled at the collar of his shirt as if it had shrunk in the dryer. "I was worried."

Something dropped in Rhonda's gut, like a stone sinking to the bottom of a bucket. If that stone was also connected to all of her internal organs. She tried to say something, but the words stuck in her throat.

She didn't want him to be worried. She didn't want anyone to worry about her. She didn't want to owe anyone status updates. Jordan already knew far too much about her given that he'd seen her underwear, her medical records, and actual tears in her eyes, and now *he was worried about her?*

Damn it.

"Where do you live?"

He'd asked her that question once, and she hadn't answered, instead offering to go get her laptop and meet him at his apartment. Now there wasn't another good option, so she rattled off the address as if she didn't feel like a hand was around her throat, and he typed it into his phone.

The map said twelve minutes, but at their current pace, it was going to be double that. Rhonda curled into herself, working to stave off the panic attack. She should've been fully warmed, but she couldn't feel her toes. Her legs started to ache like someone was separating her calf muscle fibres with a fork.

This was too much. Even though she was sitting in the cab of a truck, she felt like she'd been shoved into a corner with no path back into the middle of the room and no way to spot the exit.

Rhonda reached out and fumbled with the music knob. His radio was tuned to 98.5, but it was at commercial.

Jordan pulled his phone from his pocket, swiped up, and handed it to her. "It's connected to Bluetooth."

She blinked. Staring at his unlocked phone felt almost as intimate as hearing he worried about her. She wanted to throw it back into his lap, but since he'd already seen her wrapped in a picnic blanket for the night, she didn't want him to think she was fully crazy.

Rhonda wet her lips and searched for his music library. She found it at the top right of his screen and tapped, realizing too late that a text message notification had appeared at the exact same moment. Before she could process what was happening, she'd read the last four texts.

CAM

I didn't think Elite took snow days

NATE

Getting soft

CHUBS

There are pills for that, Natters

STEELE

Game's rescheduled. Third week of November.

Rhonda flipped the phone over and pressed it against her thigh.

"What?"

"I—I'm sorry. You got a text, and I accidentally clicked on it."

Jordan readjusted his grip on the wheel. "Who was it from?"

"Your team, I think. Talking about a game being rescheduled. And a guy named Nate's sex life."

Jordan grinned, and there was that almost-dimple. It was more pronounced in the low lighting.

Rhonda flipped the phone back over and swiped back to the home screen. Her finger hovered over the music icon. "Did you have a game tonight?"

Jordan nodded. "It got cancelled."

She nodded but didn't press. "When?"

"Hmm?"

She worked to form words around the constriction in her throat. "When did they cancel it?"

Jordan shrugged. "Before we left the gas station. Why?"

Rhonda's corner turned into a full-on confine. Four walls without any doors or windows. *He'd left Calgary thinking he'd be missing his game.* She tapped on the music app and searched for something, anything, to fill the silence before it swallowed her whole.

She clicked on the first one to pop up, "Birds of a Feather" by Billie Eilish. She'd never heard it before and thought it was a perfect choice until she started listening to the lyrics. Damn it, why was a song with a bird title about undying love? She clicked to the next icon, realizing too late it was Stick Season. Rhonda couldn't type the words "Nickelback" fast enough. She scrolled to "Burn It to the Ground" and hit play, then set Jordan's phone in the cupholder.

He stopped at a red light and shot her a look that confirmed she had not avoided coming off as crazy.

"Sorry. I'm picky about music."

"Tonight? Or in general."

Rhonda moved and got another puff of Jordan-scented air from the inside of his coat. "In general." Her dad loved music. He was always playing classic bands and comparing them to new ones with statements like, "It's the same four chords, do you hear that?" or, "This is the first original thing I've heard since '88."

The memory now felt like a stained glass ornament. Only parts of it would let the light through.

How had she not been able to see then what he was? She'd adored him—idolized him. Even in high school, she thought her mom was crazy for not falling over herself with gratitude for all the things he did for her. It wasn't until she'd been out of the house for a year and had come back for Christmas that the perfect image she'd sculpted for him cracked.

"Is this it?" Jordan pulled to a stop on her street.

Rhonda nodded, staring at the empty driveway. The house wasn't much to look at. It was an older bungalow, likely built in the mid-twentieth century, with weathered red-brick cladding on the lower half, transitioning into painted cream wood siding above. With the snow collecting on its roof, it almost looked charming.

As soon as he put the truck in park, Rhonda grabbed her bag and opened the door. "Thank you," she whispered, then closed it behind her and walked up the driveway. She didn't register that Jordan had turned the engine off until she was putting her key into the lock.

Rhonda heard his footsteps and turned. "What are you doing?"

Jordan paused. "I thought I'd get my coat."

She clamped her mouth shut. Right. With her key still in the lock, she shrugged it off her shoulders. Jordan walked forward and stopped in front of her on the snow covered walkway, and as Rhonda pulled her hands through the sleeves, something inside of her snapped. The pressure in her chest, the ache in her gut—she knew the solution for this. It wasn't more talking.

She shivered, and instead of handing him the coat, she turned her key in the lock and pushed the door open to her dark entryway.

"Rhonda—"

She stepped inside and flicked on a light, leaving the door wide open behind her.

CHAPTER
Seventeen

Jordan

LIGHT POURED from the house onto the snow, outlining Rhonda's footprints in glitter. That look. Her doe-eyes. Her slightly parted lips. He didn't even realize he'd been craving it until she turned back with his coat hanging off her shoulders.

But this time, if he walked through that door, he would be doing it with eyes wide open. He'd figured out her patterns by now. Rhonda didn't run from his apartment because something had gone wrong. She ran because she'd let her guard down.

No names. He understood, now. Everytime she got skittish, it wasn't because he'd missed the vein, it was because he'd pierced it, and she was terrified she was going to bleed out.

But his jeans had been stretched tight since the second she sat on his lap in her car. And she was inviting him in. He could just get his coat.

Jordan stepped toward the door. He could tell her he wasn't going to play this game, and—

Rhonda was topless. Wearing his coat.

Jordan gripped the doorframe, unable to tear his eyes away from her standing a few feet in front of him. Her shirt was draped over the couch. Her shoes were off. And the top button of her pants was undone.

Anything he thought he knew five seconds ago disappeared the second he saw her breasts. *They'd done this before and it was fine, wasn't it?*

He ran a hand over his face. No. That was then. This was now. He'd skipped a game to go looking for her. He'd sent flirty, annoying texts all weekend hoping to get her attention, and she hadn't given it. Which only made him try harder. It was embarrassing as hell.

Jordan stepped inside and closed the door behind him. He didn't try to talk. He knew the rules—understood what this was. Rhonda had been vulnerable tonight. Sex wasn't connection for her, it was control. This was her sitting on his lap and rubbing against him. She wanted to see what she could do. What she could *make him* do.

Right then with her bare skin against the inside of his coat, it was anything.

———

Jordan turned over, dropping his arm across Rhonda's bare back. It was dark outside her bedroom window. Quiet. He wasn't sure when the wind had stopped howling, but the worst of the storm seemed to be over.

She was asleep, her lips parted, and her dark curls splayed out on the pillow. She inhaled and blew out a breath. Jordan swallowed hard and slowly pulled the comforter out from under her. She groaned and curled into a ball, and he covered her with the blankets.

He climbed out of bed and pulled on his clothes, knowing that when he walked back out to his truck, he wouldn't be able to keep his insides from oozing out. He'd done it again. Fallen for someone who only needed him to solve her problems. He was a grown ass man, and he was sneaking out of Rhonda's room like a high schooler who didn't want to get caught by her parents.

Because he couldn't bear the thought of having the inevitable moment of Rhonda waking up and wishing she could hurry out like last time, then realizing she was in her own damn house. He'd make it easy. He always did.

Jordan grabbed his phone and coat, then walked out of the room. He used the bathroom in the hall, then pulled on his boots and stepped out into the snow. Flakes were falling gently now, and windswept dunes covered the yard and driveway.

It was the silence, the peace of early morning, that made him stop next to his truck. He drew in a lungful of biting November air, then swiped open his messages. He found the group with Rhonda and her friends and exited the chat.

———

Jordan walked out of his apartment, freshly showered, as the morning sun made sparkling rainbows over the snow. The plows had already been out, and the roads were clear. He thought about texting Rhonda, offering to help her retrieve her car, then thought better of it. She didn't want him to save her. It went against everything he was, but he put the phone back in his pocket and got in his truck.

The drive to the hospital was a blur, the city waking up around him. Jordan gripped the steering wheel, his stomach already roiling. He was a mess, but he couldn't afford to be. He'd swallow it down and do his job, try not to worry about Steele or Claire or his youth hockey group. Or Rhonda.

As he pulled into the hospital parking lot, the building loomed ahead, its windows reflecting the pale blue sky. He parked and walked through the automatic doors, the scent of antiseptic mixed with coffee and the hum of fluorescent lights greeting him.

The morning shift was already in full swing. Nurses and doctors crossed through the halls, on their own individual flight paths. He spotted Gertie at the nurses' station, her eyes scanning a stack of charts. She looked up and grunted. "You're early."

"Can't win 'em all."

Gertie reached into her pocket and held out two tickets. "For next Monday."

Jordan frowned. "I only needed one."

"Well, your friend will have a tough time using her ticket since the table is only for hospital staff and guests." Gertie gave him a look. "Unless you thought you could get Mallory to add her as his plus one?"

The furrow in his brow deepened. "So, this second ticket—"

"Is for you." Gertie held up a hand as he started to protest. "I swear, if you give me any shit, I'm going to put you on palliative care for the next two weeks." She watched his face, then handed him a clipboard. "Get to work, Wheatfill."

CHAPTER
Eighteen

Jordan

> I have your ticket for next Monday night, the 28th. Six o'clock at the BMO Centre. Percheron Ballroom

RHONDA

> Got it. Should I come pick up the ticket?

> I'll have it. Turns out the table is hospital staff only

Rhonda

> So . . .

> I have to be there

RHONDA

> Don't you have practice?

> You know my practice schedule?

RHONDA

> No, I just heard that your team was there. That you practice after the Snowballs because your rink is under renovation

> Yeah. I had to rearrange some things

RHONDA

> You didn't need to do that . . .

Jordan shoved his phone into his pocket without reading the rest of that message. He wasn't in the mood for her to tell him again how much his efforts were unwanted. Except when they weren't. Except when they were exactly what she wanted, when they were on her timeline. Claire had said the exact same thing about Reviact, and he was sick to hell of it. Would it be so difficult to admit to needing help? To be grateful that someone cared enough to give it?

Yes. For them, it would be. He didn't like comparing Rhonda to his sister, but they did seem to have that in common.

He stepped out of his truck, already yawning, and opened the back door to grab an energy drink. He was going to need caffeine to make it through coaching and then practice. All he wanted to do was get on the ice. To forget the stew of mixed emotions simmering in his gut and toss around a puck.

All day Sunday, he'd wondered if he should bail on the Founder's Event next week. Not just because he'd be missing practice, but because of . . . everything. Ultimately, he couldn't feel good about it. Not because he was doing it for Rhonda. After the other night, the worst thing he could do was see her again when he was trying to disentangle himself.

But somewhere along the line, he'd started to believe in Reviact. He wanted her to meet with Mallory. Claire had actually gone to her appointment and picked up her prescription. He hadn't seen that kind of follow through in years. Add to that the fact that she hadn't called yet, and the faintest glimmer of hope sparked in his chest.

He should've snuffed it out instantly. It hurt too much to keep hoping for something better and watching it fizzle out. But pretending he accepted her situation? That required a regular infusion of fooling himself.

That was the problem with love. He couldn't flick it on or off. It was like herpes. Lying dormant no matter what treatment he used, ready to flair up and make him look like an idiot.

He crossed the snowy parking lot and pulled open the door to the rink. A wave of warm air washed over him as he pushed through the storm doors and wiped his boots on the mat. The familiar smell of the rink filled his nostrils—part rubber, part ice, part machine. He took a deep breath, letting it settle in his lungs. This was his escape. His sanctuary.

He waved at the staff and wound his way down the stairs to the benches and laced up his skates. The scrape of blades, the echo of pucks hitting the boards, the laughter and shouts of the kids warming up—it was a symphony he never got tired of hearing.

He skated out and scanned the rink, mentally taking note of each kid out there. His brow furrowed when he didn't see Ethan. That kid was always there early. Jordan skated back to the bench and grabbed his phone from his coat pocket. No messages. He tapped out a quick text.

Hey. All good?

He waited a moment. If it took longer than thirty seconds for him to respond, he'd start calling hospitals. Phones had become these kids' fifth appendage.

The three little dots blinked on the screen, then disappeared. Finally, a message popped up.

ETHAN

Not feeling well.

Jordan stared at the words. Bullshit. Ethan had shown up in October when he hadn't eaten for twenty-four hours with the stomach flu. He blew out a breath and shoved his phone back in his pocket, then skated to the centre of the rink.

He clapped his hands and started calling out drills. The rest of the kids snapped into action, and Jordan skated over to where Greg was standing against the boards. "Think you can run both groups?" Greg looked up, giving him a questioning look. Jordan nodded toward the stairs. "Something's going on with Ethan."

Greg's eyes widened, then he nodded. "Yeah, sure. Go."

Jordan turned on his skates and made a beeline for the gate. His blades cut a clean path, and he stepped off the ice. It wasn't his job to babysit. But something wasn't sitting right with him about the whole situation. *There was that latent virus, flaring up again.*

He'd never had a coach who gave a shit about his personal life. It was all about performance, stats, and wins. But maybe that was the problem. Maybe if someone had given a damn about players off the ice in his generation, he wouldn't keep collecting players who were struggling to find themselves in their mid-thirties.

Jordan took off his skates, grabbed his coat, climbed the stairs, then pushed through the doors of the rink and crossed the parking lot. He hustled to his truck, his skates slung over his shoulder, and dialed Ethan's mom. When she didn't answer, he tapped out a quick text letting her know he was checking in on him. She responded immediately saying she wasn't home, but he was more than welcome to stop by. Good. He didn't want any weirdness where that was concerned.

He strapped on his seat belt and pulled out of the lot while looking up directions for Ethan's house. It wasn't far. Jordan plugged the address into his maps app and followed the blue line. Ten minutes later, he turned into the neighbourhood and pulled up to the curb in front of their white bungalow. He put the truck in park and sat there a moment, trying to figure out what he was going to say. Maybe if he'd picked up chicken noodle soup or something, he would've had an excuse to show up out of the blue.

Jordan took a deep breath, then opened his truck door and stepped out onto the sidewalk. He walked up the front steps and knocked on the door. After a few moments, he fully expected to have to leave and drive back to the rink empty-handed, but then he heard footsteps on the other side. The door swung open.

Ethan stood there, his eyes widening in surprise. "Coach? What are you doing here?"

Jordan looked him up and down. Totally normal. "Wanted to check in on you." Jordan shoved his hands in his pockets and rocked back on his heels.

"I told you, I'm not feeling well." Ethan stood there, his hand still on the doorknob.

"Yeah, you look like you're on your deathbed." Jordan raised an eyebrow.

Ethan sighed and ran a hand through his hair. "Look. I just . . . I needed a break, okay?"

Jordan nodded slowly, then motioned to the street. "You want to go grab a coffee or something? I'm freezing my ass off out here."

Ethan hesitated, then shrugged. "Sure, I guess."

"Text your mom. Make sure it's okay."

Ethan rolled his eyes. "I'm seventeen."

"Which means I could still go to jail for kidnapping."

Ethan texted her, and Jordan stepped back as he slipped on his shoes and grabbed his coat. "She says it's fine. But she's pissed I missed practice if I feel good enough to go to coffee."

"It's medicinal."

Ethan snorted. They walked to the truck in silence, then drove to the nearest Tim Hortons. The smell of fresh coffee and baked goods greeted them. Jordan ordered a large double-double since he'd left his energy drink at the rink, and Ethan got a maple macchiato. Jordan paid for both, along with a couple of glazed old fashions.

"You kids with your boogie-ass dessert drinks."

"Just because you suffered in the dark ages, doesn't mean we have to." Ethan grabbed a napkin and stir stick.

They found a corner table and sat down. Jordan wrapped his hands around his cup, letting the warmth seep into his skin. He took a sip, then looked up at Ethan. "So. You needed a break."

Ethan shifted in his seat. "Yup."

Jordan leaned back and crossed his arms. "From what?"

Ethan stared at his cup, his jaw clenching. "From everything. From school, from hockey, from life."

Jordan nodded. "I get that. Sometimes it feels like everything's piling up, and you need to step back and catch your breath."

Ethan looked up. "Yeah."

Jordan took another sip of his coffee, then set the cup down. "You know, when I was your age, I had a lot of people telling me what to do. Coaches, teachers, my parents. But hockey was always my escape."

Something flickered across Ethan's eyes. He nodded and took a bite of his donut.

Jordan's ribs cinched as he realized what he had to say next. He didn't like talking about the bridges he'd burned, but he wasn't going to get anywhere with this kid if he didn't give him something.

"When I was your age, I had a friend. Sean. We played hockey together every day and hung out every weekend. Travel teams. Tryouts. We helped each other through a lot of shit."

Ethan nodded, his eyes distant. "Must've been nice."

Jordan exhaled. He was going to have to come right out and say it. "What happened with you and Jace?"

Ethan's face hardened. "Jace isn't my friend."

Jordan raised an eyebrow. "Since when? You were buddies last year."

Ethan scoffed. "Yeah, well, that was before."

"Before what?"

Ethan gripped his cup, the muscles in his forearms tensing. Jordan didn't push. Just sat there, waiting for Ethan to decide if he wanted to share. Finally, the kid took a deep breath. "I don't want to talk about it."

Jordan nodded, taking another sip of coffee. "Sean and I moved out together. We were both entering the draft—"

"NHL?"

Jordan leaned back in his chair. "You don't have to look so surprised."

Ethan laughed. "No, I just—I didn't know you played."

"Because I barely did."

Ethan's brows knit together. He was fully invested now. "But you got drafted?"

"Yep."

"And what about your friend?"

Jordan blew out a breath. "Mm-hmm. Later in the draft than me."

Ethan grinned. "So that's what this story is? You're going to tell me how your friendship got all strained because you were a badass and your friend was jealous?"

Jordan looked straight at Ethan. "No. Around the same time, I slept with his girlfriend."

Ethan's jaw dropped. He stopped fidgeting with his cup.

Jordan paused, letting that piece of information sink in before continuing. "I messed it up. We've never talked since. Then I got injured, and our lives took different paths. Sometimes I wonder—"

"I tried to kiss him." Ethan raked a hand through his hair, then dropped his eyes to the table, his mouth pressing into a hard line.

Jordan's mouth hung open. He blinked. "Tried to kiss . . . Jace?"

Ethan nodded. "We were at a party. It was late, and we were playing cards in the basement." He shook his head. "I don't know, man. We were friends, you know? But then something changed—" He cut himself off and glanced around the restaurant. His pulse pumped fast and hard in his neck.

"Hey." Jordan put out a hand and rested it on his arm. "I don't care whether you're gay or straight. You're safe here, okay?"

The kid looked like a caged rabbit. Slowly, his shoulders started to sag. Ethan's eyes met his for a split second before darting away. "I don't know. I just—I started thinking about things. Things I hadn't thought about before. And then, one night, we were at a party, and . . ." He trailed off, his fingers resuming their nervous dance on the cup sleeve. "I didn't know I was . . . into guys or whatever until six months ago. It was just a mistake."

Jordan nodded, trying to understand. "So, Jace didn't appreciate that."

Ethan nodded, his eyes fixed on the table. "Yeah. I thought he was into me, too. I was wrong. He freaked out."

Jordan leaned back, giving Ethan some space. "Has he told anyone else?"

Ethan shook his head. "I don't think so. None of the other guys have said anything."

Jordan read between the lines. They didn't say anything, but he knew exactly what that looked like in a locker room. Showers. Jace was probably avoiding him. Making sure Ethan wasn't checking him out while he changed. He'd seen it a thousand times. No words needed to be spoken for someone to feel like a pariah.

"Have you told your parents?" Jordan asked. He'd never asked Ethan about his religion, but he knew church was a thing for his family. Ethan only went to fifty-percent of his Sunday games.

Ethan shook his head, then he gave a wry smile. "My parents would be supportive. I just . . . I haven't figured it out yet."

Jordan nodded, his chest tightening. It was possible this kid was more mature than he was. He opened his mouth to speak, then closed it again. He didn't have any experience to draw from. Any advice to give.

"Well, Jace is a dick."

Ethan laughed out loud. "Yeah."

Jordan chewed on his cheek, the image of Rhonda rushing out of his apartment suddenly playing on repeat. "Or he's just scared."

Ethan's smile slipped a bit. "Yeah."

"Probably doesn't know how to handle this any more than you do." Jordan's hands started to sweat.

"Isn't this the part where you tell me what to do?"

Jordan chuckled. "Weren't you listening? You shouldn't ever take advice from me."

Ethan picked up his coffee and lowered his voice, mimicking Jordan in coach mode. "You should talk to your parents and have a heart to heart with Jace instead of skipping practice like a douchebag!"

"Nice." Jordan picked up his coffee and stood. "Maybe you should give the speeches from now on."

"Oh, yeah. I'd be a boss." He stopped by the door. "Wait, who's running practice?"

"Greg."

Ethan's eyes widened. "Jace is gonna be pissed."

"I'll tell him it was your fault."

"Ass. Hole."

Jordan held the door for him. "Better get well soon. Next time you're on the ice, you're doing extra suicides."

Nineteen

RHONDA

RHONDA PASSED exam rooms dotting the long hall and exited to the waiting area. It was only ten forty-five, but it felt like five. Not a good sign for a Monday. At least she had her car back thanks to a rideshare the day before, and now she only had one more stop to make. Medical billing on the admin side of Hilltop Medical. The staff was having issues with rebates not being applied in a timely manner, and that was the last thing she wanted to see when they were barely starting to offer Reviact to patients.

She walked past the pharmacy and glanced up, then paused when she saw a name on the digital prescription board. Claire Wheatfill. She blinked. It wasn't that "Wheatfill" was terribly uncommon, but it wasn't "Jones" or "Smith" either. She stepped forward and scanned the patrons seated in the waiting area. Her eyes landed on a woman in the corner. She had light hair, but her bone structure was unmistakable. Jordan said his sister was on Reviact. There was a chance she'd be at this pharmacy, since it was one of the only ones up north that offered it. If that wasn't her . . . then he had a long-lost doppelganger.

Rhonda hesitated for a moment, then walked forward. "Hey. Are you Jordan's sister?" She gave a smile that was more like a grimace. How weird was it that she was approaching this woman randomly in a pharmacy?

The woman looked up. Her eyes were the same blue as Jordan's. She wore knitted gloves with a flap pulled back, exposing her fingers, and a coat that looked a couple of sizes too big for her. Rhonda's heart clenched, remembering what Jordan had told her in his apartment.

"Hey, yes, Jordan is my brother." Claire's eyes were flighty, moving between the other people in the waiting room and Rhonda's face above her. Rhonda sat down in the chair next to her.

"I'm so sorry. I don't mean to bother you. I just had to say hi. Jordan is . . ." Rhonda hesitated, thinking of the right word. "Well, he's helping me make some contacts at the Rocky Ridge Medical Center where he works."

Claire nodded. "Are you the person who told him about this new medication?"

"Reviact?" Rhonda clarified.

Claire nodded her head. "Yeah. He told me about it. And I did my trial. I'm actually picking up my full monthly prescription right now." A smile flirted with the corner of her lips.

Rhonda grinned. "Oh, that's amazing. Hopefully that means it's been a good thing?"

Claire's teeth scraped along her bottom lip. She lowered her voice. "I don't know how much Jordan has told you, but it's been years since I found anything that helped."

Rhonda nodded. "You're not the only one. I was just talking with the staff here, and there are so many people who struggle coming off their medications for a million different reasons."

Claire let out a puff of air. "Yeah. Well, struggling is a mild word."

Rhonda wanted to reach out and hug her. Instead, she clasped her hands in her lap.

"Listen. I have one more stop to make, and then I was planning to go get lunch. I know you're still waiting for your prescription, but I would love to talk to you more about this—hear your experience. I won't share anything you tell me unless you give permission, but I love hearing patients' experiences. It helps me understand how best to approach hospital administrators."

Claire seemed to sink into herself. "Oh, I can't—"

"My treat. This would be so helpful."

Claire drew a deep breath, then glanced back up at the board. Her name was next. "Okay. That sounds great."

"Perfect. I'll be back in just a second. Meet you back here?" Rhonda waited for Claire to nod then headed toward administration.

She quickly made her way to the offices and jumped in. Since the staff members weren't waiting with bated breath to assist her with every need, it took a moment to get the account numbers and specific issues linked with each patient.

She decided not to tackle it right then and instead saved the information on her tablet to work on later, not wanting to press her luck with Claire still waiting in the lobby.

Fifteen minutes later, Rhonda hustled back and found Claire still seated on the same chair in the pharmacy waiting area, this time with a white paper bag sitting next to her.

Rhonda smiled brightly. "You ready?"

Claire nodded, picked up the bag, and followed her through the sliding glass doors onto the street. There was a Moxie's a block and a half away that, based on Rhonda's web search, had just opened for the day. They walked mostly in silence and found they were among the first customers to arrive.

Rhonda was grateful to sneak in before the lunch rush. She requested a table for two and suggested they sit in a corner booth. That way, as the restaurant started to fill up, it would still feel private.

They sat, and the hostess handed them menus.

"Sorry. I didn't even ask if you like Moxie's." Rhonda slid a menu toward Claire.

"It used to be one of my favorites, but I haven't been here in a long time." Claire ran her finger over the edge of the plastic-covered menu.

Rhonda flipped hers over. "I know they have a lunch deal, but you can get whatever you want. This is on the company card."

"What do you like here?" Claire asked.

"Honestly, I love a big salad. Put some grilled chicken or salmon on there. Keeps me full, but doesn't make me feel like I need a nap at two o'clock."

Claire laughed at that. Rhonda was quiet a moment, giving her time to peruse. When Claire slid her menu to the edge of the table, Rhonda mirrored her and looked up.

"So I know it hasn't been very long, but have you experienced any of the side effects?"

Claire shook her head. "No. I haven't felt sick or had any dizziness or headaches. Well, I guess I should say no more than usual when I'm trying to get sober."

Rhonda worked to keep her face impassive, ensuring there was no flicker of judgment between them. Just like when she'd seen her in the pharmacy, her heartstrings tugged. It wasn't just a patient sitting in front of her. It was Jordan's sister.

Their server appeared and dropped off water. Rhonda opened her paper straw and plunked it in her glass. She'd use it until it got mushy, then abandon it and drink straight from the lip. She was all for saving the planet, but there had to be a better way. "Well, that's really good to hear. Does Jordan know that it's working well for you?"

Claire grimaced. "No. I haven't talked with him yet. I kind of . . ." She glanced down. "Well, I don't want to get his hopes up.

He knows I've picked it up, though." She fingered the paper bag. "He offered to pay for it."

Rhonda's eyes widened, her thoughts spinning. Even with the rebates, a full month prescription was nearly four hundred dollars. She'd talked with Cantra about creating a needs-based payment strategy but hadn't been successful yet.

They had generous rebates, yes, but she hated that patients had to pay that much. She also understood how much went into building a new drug—the testing, the research, all of it was astronomical. She was grateful for innovation, and it also broke her heart a little that it couldn't be accessible to everyone.

Their server stopped by, and Rhonda put a hand on the table. "If I order a pot of tea, will you share it with me?"

Claire nodded.

"Any allergies I need to be aware of?" The server asked.

"Peanuts," they both said in unison.

"And all legumes, including Fenugreek." Claire added.

They laughed, and Rhonda ordered the tea and a chopped salad, adding the grilled chicken. Claire ordered the chicken sandwich with a side salad and a bowl of tomato soup. Their server took the menus and retreated back to his station.

"So how do you know Jordan?" Claire asked.

Rhonda winced internally. Which version of the story did she want to tell? Well, Claire, I found myself at your brother's hotel room and ended up sleeping with him without even asking for his name. Or, I ended up in his urgent care with my face blown up to the size of a watermelon because of a fenugreek allergy while on a date with another man.

"Do you know him from hockey?" Claire asked.

"Yes." That was the simplest explanation. Rhonda smiled. "I'm really good friends with some guys on another hockey team here in Calgary. They play Pucks Deep."

Just then, their server reappeared, incredibly attentive since he had no other tables to work with at the moment. He set down their pot of tea and two mugs. The pot was beautiful, clear glass with loose leaf swirling in steaming hot water, a filter built into the top.

He filled both their mugs, and Rhonda thanked him.

Claire waited until he was a few paces away to lean in. "Which team?"

Rhonda thought about lying but wasn't sure how much Claire knew about the Elite League scene in Calgary. Maybe she was only asking to be polite. "The Snowballs," she answered.

The look on Claire's face told her all she needed to know. Claire was indeed familiar.

"So you don't have a great impression of him then?" Claire picked up her mug, warming her hands.

"I try not to form opinions of people based on third-party information."

Claire snorted. "Isn't that what that entire team does? They heard a couple of stories about Jordan from fifteen years ago and now hold a grudge."

Rhonda considered this. She had heard the stories from fifteen years ago, but there were plenty more where that came from. "I think it might be a little more complicated."

Claire set down her mug and leaned back in the booth. "More complicated for who? I could kick Sean Thompson's ass. Honestly, I could kick both their asses."

The metamorphosis left Rhonda awestruck. Claire transformed from a hesitant, mousy woman into a badass, overprotective sister. She was immediately in.

Rhonda planted her elbows on the table. "Well, I think it's about time I heard everything from your perspective."

Claire shook her head, her eyes still flashing. "Both of them are idiots. Do you know when Jordan and Sean were kids, they were completely inseparable? I'm talking at our house 24/7 or Jordan was over at the Thompsons'. They played on every team together, hung out after practice, did homework together, travelled to tournaments, and always roomed together. If Jordan got an opportunity to advance, he would talk to the coaches until Sean was invited too, and vice versa.

"When they got to college, it was a little more complicated, and I guess I understand that. They were both trying to go pro, and the opportunities were a lot bigger. But they still had each other's backs. And then everything with the draft . . . "

Claire ran a hand through her hair. "Sean had been dating this girl for probably two years. She was nice, but she had this weird fascination with Jordan. She was always flirting with him. Sean hated it, but she pretended it was completely innocent. Told him she was just trying to get under Jordan's skin because Sean loved Jordan more than her. Honestly, it was probably true."

"So what? Jordan just gave in?"

Claire shook her head. "No. He would never do that. I know everybody sees Jordan now as this bruiser, but he has the softest heart of anybody I know. I think he's just had it mashed up so many times. He resents himself for it now instead of wearing it as a badge of honour."

Rhonda blinked, feigning nonchalance, pretending she wasn't inscribing that in her permanent memory.

"Anyway, Sean's girlfriend went to Jordan one night and told him that Sean broke up with her, gave him this whole sob story. She completely took advantage of him."

Rhonda frowned. "I don't understand. Why would that break up a friendship?"

Claire threw up her hands. "Exactly. It shouldn't have. Sean should have ditched her the second he heard the story."

"So why didn't he?" Rhonda asked.

Claire leaned in. "Because he never heard the story."

"What?"

"Yeah. That's why I want to throttle them. It's been over a decade, and they've still never talked about it. Sean was so pissed off, he wouldn't take Jordan's texts. After trying a few times, Jordan just gave up. Neither of them fought for their friendship, which is ridiculous because it was a damn good one.

"Then Jordan went to the NHL, got injured, and came back to Calgary. I honestly don't know all of Sean's story. But now they're in this league with this stupid rivalry."

Rhonda grimaced. "I think it's with the whole team, not just with Jordan."

Claire blew out a breath. "Yeah. Well, that makes sense too. Jordan likes to collect misfits. That's why he still takes my calls."

Rhonda moved her arms off the table as their server appeared with their food. It was a little too fast for comfort, but she was starving, so didn't question it. They ate and continued to chat until Rhonda found a natural opportunity to quell more of her curiosity.

"Is Jordan a relationship guy?" Rhonda focused hard on her salad.

Claire shook her head. "No, he's had a couple of doozies."

"The heart mashing?"

Claire scoffed. "To put it mildly. Jordan is a giver. He gives and gives and gives and never expects anything in return. And that would be fine if he had anyone in his life who was looking out for him." She swirled her spoon in her soup. "I should be that for him. I want to be that for him, but I haven't been able to pull myself together in a long time."

Rhonda took another bite, for the first time in ages dumb-struck. Without meaning to, she blurted, "He saved me in a snowstorm the other day."

Claire glanced up. "What?"

"Yeah. I was driving home from Edmonton, and the snow got so bad I couldn't see anything. I pulled over on the side of the road. He had called me to tell me about this meeting with the doctor at the hospital, and I think I hung up on him. I don't even remember. I was so stressed out. Twenty minutes later, he showed up in his truck, helped me get my car off the road, and drove me home." She left out the end of that story, but a blush rose to her cheeks. She cleared her throat. "Anyway, I guess I see what you're talking about."

Claire dabbed her lips with a napkin. "Yeah. That sounds like my brother. Maybe your team needs to hear stories like that."

They finished their meal, and Rhonda got a few more specifics about Claire's journey with Reviact. She was sober for two weeks, which Claire said she'd accomplished before, but never so painlessly. Rhonda gave Claire her number and asked her to give her an update at the end of the month if she was up for it.

They went their separate ways, but by the time Rhonda got in her car, she couldn't stop her hands from shaking. *That sounded like my brother.* Jordan had gotten her a meeting with Mallory. He'd saved her from a freaking snowstorm. And what had she done in return?

Absolutely nothing.

But what *could* she do in return? Sitting in the front seat of her car, she felt so vulnerable, she wanted to throw up. Doing something in return, saying thank you, would mean admitting that she needed the help.

It would mean accepting that she couldn't do everything on her own. And what Jordan had done for her was so big, so astronomical. How could she ever begin to repay it?

This was why she didn't accept help. She didn't want to be in anyone's debt. But the idea of returning to her house and doing nothing opened up a chasm so deep her eyes nearly welled up.

Rhonda started her car and drove toward Jordan's apartment complex. On the way, she stopped at a Co-op and went in, spending an exorbitant amount of time searching for something to drop off that wouldn't be completely pathetic. Did he like sweets or savory? She didn't even know.

She ended up with a package of brownie bites, some gourmet cheese, olives, and freshly baked sourdough. It was a ridiculous concoction, but it was the only thing she could come up with.

Rhonda drove the rest of the way, not even having to plug it into her maps app. All it took was one time with him, and she had everything memorized.

Before she could second guess herself, she flung herself from the car, grabbed the grocery sack, and strode to the elevator. When she arrived on his floor, she walked down the hall as quietly as possible, set the items down in front of his door, and was about to walk away when a male voice behind her said,

"Hey, Rhonda."

She nearly jumped out of her skin, and in so doing, slammed her hand against Jordan's door. She spun. Darcy stood ahead of her in the hall. Before she could open her mouth, the door behind her swung open.

Twenty

JORDAN

JORDAN OPENED the door and stopped cold, his hand still gripping the handle as if letting go might knock the moment off balance. Rhonda stood in the hall, crouched in a hockey stance, but she faced away from him, staring at something in front of her.

She spun to face him, her lips slightly parted, like she'd frozen mid-breath. Her hair bounced, and one curl looped just shy of her cheekbone, framing a faint freckle he'd never noticed before.

He became acutely aware that he was in sweats and an old T-shirt. *Why was she here?*

His pulse raced as he took a step forward, but Rhonda put out a hand. "Don't—you're going to step on it!" she shouted, and Jordan jumped back. He looked down and saw a pile of . . . food?

He gave Rhonda a questioning glance, then leaned out to see what was hogging her attention. There, leaning against the doorframe of his apartment, was Darcy McClellan. His blond faux hawk a bit mussed, his arms crossed over his chest.

He didn't have to say anything. The smirk on his face was communication enough.

Rhonda straightened. "This is—I was just dropping this off. For a work thing."

Darcy nodded slowly. "Uh-huh." He strode forward, then stopped at the sound of another door clicking open.

"Hey, babe—" A woman with shoulder-length auburn hair ran out into the hall wearing a silk nightie that barely covered her underwear. If she was wearing any.

"Ginger?" Rhonda looked between the two of them. "How long has this been going on?"

Darcy shoved his hands in his pockets. "You're the one bringing bread and cheese."

Rhonda planted a hand on her hip. "You said nothing about the fact that you and Ginger were together when we were at the Dusty Rose. You acted like you were just friends."

"We are friends." Ginger walked up to Darcy and clung to his arm, leaning into his side. "Good friends."

Darcy's neck reddened. "Okay, you two have a nice . . . work chat." He gave a wink that could only be described as sarcastic. As they walked back to the apartment Ginger came out of, Rhonda whirled and dropped her forehead against the wall.

"Shiiiiiit."

Jordan leaned against the wall next to her. "Can I take a guess?"

She nodded, rubbing her skin against paint that was probably applied in the nineties and never wiped down since.

He pulled her back and turned her to face him. "You think he's going to tell the Snowballs."

"Oh he's definitely going to tell the Snowballs."

"But you told him it was a work thing."

Rhonda rolled her eyes. "Yeah, I told him that the first time, too. While I was holding my tights. People don't have work things at each other's apartments."

"Um, we did."

"We had sex after," she hissed.

Jordan tensed, his blood raising a degree at the memory. "It seems he has his own secrets."

Rhonda waved him off. "Nobody's going to care that he and Ginger are a thing. He probably just likes the intrigue of keeping it secret. Like they're role playing every time he goes to the bar."

Jordan nodded, trying to match her end-of-the-world energy. "Right. But they'll all hate you if they found out you knew me."

"Absolutely."

"Because your friends are assholes."

Rhonda groaned. "No, *I'm* the asshole." She slumped and walked back to the entry of his apartment and pointed at the picnic on the ground. "This is a thank you. I didn't know if you liked sugar."

"Doesn't everyone like sugar?" He bent down to pick the food up.

"No." She didn't smile.

Jordan walked the bread and a small jar of fancy olives inside and set them on his kitchen counter, then went back for the rest. "Thank you for what?"

"For helping me. On the road."

Jordan nodded, something white and warm spreading through his chest. "Did you get your car back?"

"Mm-hmm." Rhonda picked up the last few items and handed them to him. Then she swiped her hands together as if she was miming being finished with something. "Okay. So. Thanks." She turned and stalked back down the hall.

Jordan didn't even think to follow her, he was so stunned. He picked up the brownie bites and cheese and barely set them down when his phone chirped.

He found it on the couch, and his stomach clenched when he

saw the name on the screen. Claire. He swiped to answer and held the phone to his ear. "Hey."

"Jordan. Hi." His sister's voice was tired. A door closed, the speaker rubbing against something.

"What's up?" He tried to keep his tone light, but he couldn't shake the feeling of dread that always accompanied a call from his sister. Was he going to have to go pick her up somewhere? PayPal her money?

"I just wanted to say thanks. For this morning."

Jordan leaned back against the counter. What the hell was happening? He blinked and scanned his apartment, making sure he hadn't somehow woken up in an alternate reality this morning. "Okay."

Claire let out a breath. "It's helping. The Reviact."

He took this in while simultaneously scouring the sounds in the background for any hint of where Claire could be at the moment. There was another voice, but it didn't sound like she was in a public place. "That's great."

Her voice was soft. "I'm two weeks sober. I kind of don't want to say it out loud. Don't want to jinx it."

Jordan straightened and started to pace. "Yeah, I get that."

"It feels easier this time."

That tiny ball of glowing hope he'd tried so hard to stamp out flared to life. He drew a deep breath, wishing he could extinguish it. Force it into dormancy until she had at least a year under her belt. Last year at this time, Claire had ended up in the ER. The week before Christmas.

"What do you need?" Jordan stalked to his bedroom, looking for the keys to his truck he'd stashed on his nightstand.

"Oh, nothing. I was just calling," she said. Jordan froze midstep. "Anyway, I have to go, but—" she paused and sucked in a breath. "I can't really make plans, I don't want to . . . you know. Cancel or anything. But I thought I could call closer to Christmas. Maybe we could do brunch or something. If I'm still feeling better."

Jordan blinked. His ears were ringing.

"Jord?"

"Yeah. No, that would be great."

"Okay. Talk soon. Oh, and I applied for a job. It's nothing big, just working at the new Target. But I should know by next week."

Jordan was speechless. The call ended, and he hadn't even said goodbye.

He dropped to the bed and set his phone next to him. Was this some practical joke? He waited for someone to jump out of his washroom and tell him he was on Punk'd.

Rhonda dropped off food. Claire called just to *talk*.

He didn't know what to do with it. Jordan ran his hands through his hair and threw on a baseball cap. He had to go to the rink. He grabbed his hockey bag and stick and then grabbed one of the brownies on his way through the kitchen.

He was going to be early to practice for once.

CHAPTER
Twenty-One

RHONDA

RHONDA PARKED at the curb in front of Tina's house. It was an older split-level, but someone along the way had brought it into the 21st century with a modern, minimalist facelift.

Her hands shook as she fumbled with her keys. She'd been a mess all afternoon, and seeing Darcy and then Jordan took her scrambled insides and threw them in the blender. She rarely *needed* to talk to someone. But if she didn't get this out of her system, she was going to word vomit all over the next solicitor that stopped at her door selling Christmas light installation.

Desperate times.

Darcy, even if he didn't do it intentionally, was going to give this away to the Snowballs. She'd heard them shit talking before games in the past, and the Snowballs were set to play Pucks Deep that week. It was too good. If Darcy could fuel the fire before a rivalry game, he sure as hell would.

And this would fuel the fire.

Rhonda strode up the sidewalk and knocked before she could second guess herself.

Tina opened the door, and her eyes lit up. "Girl!" She jumped forward and wrapped Rhonda in her arms, getting her bare feet wet on the snow-soaked welcome mat. She stepped back and waved her in, leaving dirty footprints on the wood floor in the entry.

Tears pricked at the corners of her eyes as she followed Tina into the kitchen. She gripped her purse strap tighter.

"Anne! The prodigal has returned!" Tina shouted.

Rhonda laughed, but it came out sounding more like a dying seal. She rubbed her hands together, and only then noticed they were shaking. She shoved them in her coat pockets.

She loved Anne and Tina's style. They'd been roommates for years, and their preferences had blended into one cozy, modern, vintage conglomeration. A funky lamp with a stained glass shade sat on the side table, and the sofa was covered in colourful throw pillows and a patchwork quilt. Rhonda wanted them to adopt her. For real.

Anne stood at the island with her laptop, and she slammed it shut as Rhonda walked in.

"I didn't mean to interrupt." Rhonda sat on a stool at the counter.

"Are you kidding? Anne's always looking for a chance to ditch work." Tina reached into a cupboard for glasses.

Rhonda grinned. "You kind of sound like an old married couple."

Tina filled the glasses with water. "Whatever. I see Anne about as much as I see you these days."

"Ah. Time with Gary?" Rhonda waggled an eyebrow.

Anne scoffed. "I'm gone, like, two nights a week."

"And he stays over. I did *not* need to know what brand of boxers he wears."

Anne laughed out loud. "I thought you were at work!"

Rhonda's throat tightened. The pricking sensation at the door turned into full-on burning, like she was huffing onion. She looked from Anne to Tina, her stomach knotting. Her brain screamed at her to shut it down. To shove everything back into the box and slap a lid on it.

"It's Jordan," she blurted.

Anne frowned.

Tina set the glasses down on the counter in front of them. "Do we know a Jordan?"

"Medicine Hat Guy. Parking Lot Guy. It's Jordan Wheatfill. He's the—"

"Captain of Pucks Deep!?" Anne's voice lifted an octave at the end of that sentence.

"Wait, Hat Guy and Parking Lot Guy are the same guy?" Tina demanded.

Rhonda groaned and dropped her head over her folded arms. She nodded, her forehead rubbing over her sleeves. "And now he's also His Apartment Guy. And My House Guy—"

"Shut the front door. You've been seeing him?" Tina pulled up a stool, her voice hushed even though they were the only people in the house.

"Wait, is he—oh my hell, he's Text Chain Guy. Rhonda, is he—?"

"YES." Rhonda wiped her eyes and forced her head up. "I thought I was texting Jenna, but I saved his name in my phone as 'J' and—"

"You saved his *phone number?*" Tina stared at her with wide eyes.

"It wasn't like that! He works at Rocky Ridge, and I needed to get an 'in' with the doctor there, so when he gave me his number at Dusty Rose—"

"Okay, stop!" Anne stood up and walked to the fridge. She pulled out half a pumpkin pie and a canister of whipped cream. She set the pie on the island and motioned for Tina to get plates, then flipped off the cap on the cream and held it up. "Open."

Rhonda tipped her head back, and almost choked with

laughter as Anne pressed the nozzle, filling her mouth with fluffy cream. She blinked back tears and tried to swallow while Tina dished up pie on white plates with roosters on them and the words, "Nice Cock."

"Gift exchange?" Rhonda asked.

Tina laughed. "Too bad you missed it."

Rhonda had missed the team white elephant the year before, but this year she was ready. The pair of boxers that said, "I licked it so it's mine" sat in the back of her closet.

Anne passed out forks and added a dollop of whipped cream to each piece of pie, then took a bite. "Okay. Start from the beginning."

So she did. Rhonda told them about how she'd thought Jordan was from Grande Prairie, which they already knew, but then she saw him that night in the bar and found out he was on Pucks Deep. She told them how he slipped her his number on a napkin, then about her allergic reaction and seeing him at urgent care, and on and on until she finally landed with her taking the weirdest charcuterie collection to his doorstep.

When she was finished, Anne licked her fork and shot Tina a look.

Tina looked very seriously at Rhonda. "You broke your rules."

Rhonda took another bite of pie. Both of their pieces were gone, but she'd been blabbing the whole time. "Yeah."

"You *like* him."

Rhonda shoved another bite in her mouth, and her eyes welled with tears. "Yeah."

Anne got a look on her face like the rabbit in Bambi. All heart eyes and thumping foot. "You can't stop thinking about him."

Rhonda groaned and took a drink of water. "I need to make it stop!" She set her glass down and pulled at her shirt. "It's like this burning in my chest, and I feel too hot, and then I'm constantly shaking, and I feel sick—like really sick—and—"

"Holy shit. You're falling for him. Hard." Tina whispered.

That's when Rhonda started to cry. Big, fat tears rolled onto her cheeks, and Anne grabbed onto her, pulling her face straight down to her boobs.

Rhonda didn't care. She sobbed into her bosom like a five-year-old, letting Anne stroke her hair. "I think I'm dying!" She knew what all of this must look like to her emotionally stable, relationship capable friends, but death felt like the most real possibility at the moment.

She couldn't think straight. Didn't care about anything like she used to. Her thoughts ignored any of the important things in her life, instead orbiting anything Jordan related she could grasp onto.

"I think I'm depressed. Or maybe I have an anxiety disorder?" She pulled her head up, her face streaked with tears. "Maybe I just need to get on some medication or—"

"No!" Anne shook her shoulders. "This is normal, okay? This is what all of us feel like *all the time!*"

"What is it Brett always says?" Tina snapped her fingers. "That sober acronym . . ."

"Oh yeah! 'Son Of a Bitch, Everything's Real.'" Anne laughed. "Yes, that's exactly it." Her eyes snapped back to Rhonda. "You're getting sober."

Rhonda blinked. Sure, she drank socially, but she wasn't out of control. "I don't have a drinking problem."

Anne motioned for her to take another bite of pie while Tina handed her a tissue to wipe her eyes. "No, babe. You have a control problem."

Rhonda chewed, the warm spices diffusing over her tongue. "What?"

Tina gave a hesitant smile. "You've been white knuckling for a long time."

"I don't get it." Rhonda looked between the two of them. Wasn't being in charge of your life a good thing? "Get it under control" was a literal life success strategy.

"Besides this, when was the last time you told somebody—anybody—how you really felt about something?" Tina asked.

Rhonda frowned. "I tell you guys what I think all the time."

"Yeah, what you think. But what about how you feel?" Anne let that settle in a moment. "You talk about your work, about the people you meet, the asshole doctors. We joke about it, we laugh, but I have no idea what it actually feels like for you. Do you ever feel scared? Lonely when you're on those trips by yourself?"

Rhonda opened her mouth, then closed it again. Yes. She felt those things. But that wasn't something she would ever say out loud.

Tina rested her elbows on the counter. "Or when you talk about the guys you sleep with. You have the best stories, hilarious. But what about when you walk out the door? What about when you were sitting at Country and Jenna's wedding? You didn't say a word about that—"

"I was happy for them," Rhonda interjected.

"Yeah, I know, but you also got completely hammered after the reception." Anne held out the whipped cream, but Rhonda shook her head.

"Okay." Rhonda's head was spinning. "Okay," she repeated. "So what you're saying is . . . people talk about those things."

"Yes." Anne nodded her head.

"But I've never talked about those things." Her hands were clammy. She set her fork down next to her plate.

"Right, because it makes you uncomfortable. So we usually . . ." Tina shrugged and looked at Anne.

Rhonda looked between the two of them. "You talk about that? But just not with me?"

They nodded in unison. "But not because we don't want to," Tina said.

Rhonda exhaled. "Because I don't want to."

"Exactly." Anne gave an apologetic smile. "But it's not a bad thing—"

"It sounds like a bad thing." Rhonda pushed up from her

stool. "I need to lie down." She stalked into the living room. Anne and Tina followed, sitting in the chairs across from the couch as she plopped down and lay back on the pillows.

Rhonda felt like she was drowning, swirling around in a cesspool of emotion that had never made it past the floodgates. At least, not for a very long time. "I'm a bad friend."

"No. Never," Anne said vehemently.

Rhonda stared at the ceiling, her thoughts fragmenting, spinning.

"Feelings are a good thing." Tina leaned back in her chair.

Rhonda turned her head. "How? All this feels like is a liability."

Anne frowned. "With us?"

Rhonda ran a hand through her hair. "With everyone! He's Jordan freaking Wheatfill! You know exactly how everyone on the Snowballs would react."

Tina made a face, and Anne smacked her leg. "What? She's not wrong."

"Okay, fair, but that's not really the point." Anne turned back to Rhonda. "Let's worry about that later. Why does this feel like a liability, besides the fact that he's Jordan freaking Wheatfill."

Rhonda considered this. "Everything in here," she motioned at her midsection, "is making me crazy. It's not like I don't have feelings. I just don't let them get out of control." She twisted a curl through her fingers. "I've always been able to shut them down. Especially with men. If I ever feel more than just that tingle of excitement, I think about all the ways it could go wrong, and poof. It's gone."

Tina blinked. "So you're sabotaging."

"Protecting is a better word, I think?" Rhonda grinned sheepishly. Her throat tightened. This was when she'd normally crack a joke. Talk about some guy who hit on her at a luncheon. Instead she drew a shaky breath and said, "I don't think I trust myself."

Tina leaned in. "Please tell me we're going to talk about your daddy issues."

Rhonda scoffed. "How the hell—?"

"Oh, c'mon! Anytime he comes up, you bolt so fast—"

"I don't bolt!"

Tina laughed. "You're like 'Squirrel!' And don't get me wrong, I love the squirrel stories, they're usually your best."

Rhonda shot up on the couch. "So all this time, you guys have been looking at me knowing I'm a trash fire, and you never said anything?"

"BABE." Tina pointed out at the patio. "We tried, if you remember? That whole relationship conversation?"

Anne shifted uncomfortably. "It didn't go over well."

Rhonda swallowed. Hard. "Okay." She nodded. That was fair. She had gotten sulky. And told them they were trying to control her life and make her fit their relationship mould. "Okay."

Tina motioned for her to continue. "Daddy issues. Please."

Rhonda snorted. "Fine!" She ran her hands over her knees, staring at the coffee table. "I thought he was a saint. Like, a literal hero, you know? He always solved everything. Fixed everything. But then I came home for Christmas one year, and . . . It was like my rose coloured glasses were smashed. All those things he did, the compliments, the stepping in to solve things, they were just ways to get what he wanted."

Anne's eyes softened. "Rhonda, that's . . . I'm so sorry."

Tina nodded. "That's a lot to unpack."

Rhonda's fingers dug into the couch cushion. "I don't know how to explain it. He'd buy Mom flowers, but only if she did something he liked. He'd take us out to dinner, but only if we all acted perfect in public. It wasn't about us, it was about him." Rhonda's voice cracked. "I thought I was so smart. So aware. But I missed it. All those years, I missed it."

Tina shook her head. "You weren't supposed to see it. He was your dad. That's on him."

"Yeah, but it doesn't make me any better at seeing reality." She grabbed a pillow and held it to her chest. "I'm terrified that I'm going to make the same mistake my mom made. That I'm going to be used. That I already am being used."

"So you sleep with people," Tina said, matter-of-factly, and a switch flipped in Rhonda's head.

Mother of pearl. SO SHE SLEPT WITH PEOPLE. That was exactly it. Use them before they could use her. Get what she wanted so she didn't have to wonder whether there would be a cost.

"Holy shit." Rhonda studied the wood grain of the table like it was a commissions statement. "I think I need to go." She stood up, her head spinning a little.

"Are you okay?" Tina asked, at the same time Anne squeaked, "Do you hate us?"

Rhonda laughed. "Yes, and no." She rounded the table and pulled both of them into a hug. "Thank you." She extracted herself and strode to the entry to put on her shoes. "Seriously, thank you."

———

Rhonda stepped out of her car, keys jangling in her hand as she locked the doors. She hesitated in the parking lot, unwilling to walk into the Ice Centre just yet. She'd spent hours over the past few days on the phone with her mom. Not talking about bills or work. Not talking about anything except for her growing up and the way her mom had dealt with her broken marriage.

Rhonda wanted to know everything. How her mom had fallen for her father in the first place and, most importantly, why she stayed.

Since that moment in Anne and Tina's apartment, everything

in her life looked different. Some of it less shiny. Some of it brighter than it had been in years.

But that didn't mean she knew what to do with it.

Rhonda drew a steadying breath and started toward the entrance, her boots crunching on the packed snow. The nervous energy that had been plaguing her all week hummed like static in her veins. Admitting to Tina and Anne that she had feelings for Jordan had shaken her like a snow globe and nothing inside her had settled.

She'd lived her whole life navigating casual relationships, and this? Whatever the hell this aching, collapsing, burning feeling was whenever she thought about Jordan? This was uncharted territory.

The doors to the Ice Centre swung open, and a blast of warm air hit her as she entered. She walked through the entry and into the stands, the roar of the crowd washing over her like a wave.

She scanned the sea of baby blue jerseys until she spotted Kelty's jet-black hair and Jenna's good-luck toque. Rhonda descended the stairs and scooted past other fans toward their group. Melissa was already there, and the two of them screamed like school girls, bouncing and hugging each other.

She grabbed Jenna next. "Are you okay?"

Jenna nodded, a sadness sitting behind her eyes. "It'll happen. When it's right." Her face lit up. "Did I tell you? Tyler has a lawyer friend. She's coming to Calgary for some work thing, and she's meeting with us. She's done adoption work before."

"That's amazing. You're a warrior." Rhonda gave her one more hug, then sat in an open seat on the other side of her before people got pissed off that she was blocking their view.

She got a little choked up at Amaya and Bailey sitting with Aelin with their "Go, Daddy!" sign. It was adorable, but that plus seeing Jenna was too much.

It was like a valve had been opened on Monday, and she couldn't shut it off. A constant flood of emotions wreaked havoc on her system at all hours of the day. She probably wasn't fit for human interaction at the moment.

Her mom had been nineteen when she met her dad. She'd only been in one other relationship.

Rhonda cheered as the Snowballs took the ice, her claps half-hearted compared to the enthusiasm around her. Her stomach churned as she glanced down the row. Jenna, Anne, Emma, and Penny were all decked out in Snowballs jerseys, their energy infectious.

Her dad showered her in gifts and never let her give anything in return.

Rhonda's eyes migrated to the opposite side of the ice. Jordan Wheatfill, with the "C" on his jersey. The guy the entire Snowballs fan section loved to hate. He skated out with long, deliberate strides, his presence commanding. He'd leaned down and picked up the gifts she brought. He hadn't told her she couldn't bring him something. He'd let her say thank you.

Jordan skated into position for a face-off with Sean, his eyes locked on the puck. Rhonda's breath caught in her throat as she watched his muscles tense, his stick poised. The referee dropped the puck, and in an instant, Jordan snapped it back to his defenceman.

Rhonda glanced at Anne and Tina, trying to play it cool, but by the glints in their eyes, they knew exactly what was going on in her head. She shoved a handful of popcorn into her mouth, hoping the crunch would drown out the sound of her pulse thudding in her ears.

Her mom didn't want to have kids right away, and her dad told her she wouldn't get pregnant if they used condoms. He said he knew her cycle, and she believed him.

Rhonda had an education. She knew her own body. She'd pick up on a red flag like that, wouldn't she?

"Nice pass!" Melissa yelled, and Rhonda nodded, her mouth too full to respond. As she swallowed, she kept her eyes on

Jordan. He skated hard, weaving through defenders like they were practice pylons.

Her breath hitched as he approached the blue line and wound up for a slapshot. The puck soared through the air, and Rhonda's heart leapt into her throat. The goalie deflected it with his pads, but Jordan was right there for the rebound. He flicked it back, and the puck ricocheted off the post.

"Aww, what was that!" Penny yelled as Jordan knocked someone into the boards. Rhonda forgot to breathe.

"That was a nice save," Tina said.

"Jordan is playing dirty though," Jenna noted with a frown. Every muscle in Rhonda's body tensed.

Aelin leaned forward. "Who's Jordan?"

Jenna pointed. "Captain of Pucks Deep. He's always taking cheap shots behind the ref's back."

Rhonda glanced at Jenna, her face neutral. "He's just doing what everyone else out there is doing." She shrugged like she didn't have an opinion one way or another. "Trying to get under their skin."

Jenna shot her a confused look. Rhonda reached for more of her popcorn, and when Brett scuffled in the neutral zone she yelled, "Did you see that hit? Our boys aren't messing around tonight!" Hoping her voice was loud enough to deflect any suspicion.

The game intensified, and the insults hurled at Jordan from her friends cut deeper than she expected. She swallowed hard, cheering when she was supposed to and laughing when the others did, but every comment about Jordan playing dirty felt personal.

A few minutes into the second period, the tension between Jordan and Country that had been simmering under the surface finally boiled over. Jordan jostled with Country near the boards, their sticks clattering together. She barely registered the puck soaring down the ice. The two men exchanged heated words, their faces inches apart, and then it happened.

Jordan dropped his gloves, and Country did the same. Rhonda's breath caught in her throat as the two men lunged at each other. They grabbed onto each other's jerseys, fists flying.

The crowd erupted, but Jenna's reaction was immediate. "What the hell are they doing?" She jumped to her feet, her hands clenching into fists at her sides.

Rhonda's heart jolted in her chest as Jordan and Country grappled with each other. Jordan landed a solid punch to Country's jaw, and Rhonda winced. Country retaliated with a blow to Jordan's midsection.

"Get off him!" Jenna stood up and looked like she was about to jump over the boards.

Her dad never did anything he wanted and always made sure to blame her mother for it.

Jordan did what he wanted. He coached. He played hockey. He went out with his friends.

The referees skated over, trying to separate the two men. It was like watching a car crash in slow motion. She knew she should look away, but she couldn't. Every punch, every shove felt like a physical blow to her own body.

Had she enjoyed this before? How could Jenna watch this night after night, knowing the man she lov—

Rhonda stopped that thought short, a lump forming in her throat. What had Tina said? Falling hard. *Love.*

No, not that. It couldn't be that.

Finally, the referees managed to pull them apart. Jordan and Country were both breathing heavily, their faces flushed, blood smeared on their lips and jerseys.

"Unbelievable," Jenna muttered, shaking her head. She folded her arms over her chest, her eyes narrowing as she watched them skate off to their respective benches.

Rhonda's hands were trembling, and she shoved them into her pockets. She tried to join in as her friends started cheering for the Snowballs again, but her voice faltered. She couldn't look at Anne and Tina. She couldn't look at anyone.

The score was two to two as the third period wound down and the Snowballs mounted one final offensive push. They passed the puck with precision, weaving through Pucks Deep's defence. Her heart raced as the puck found its way to Sean. He wound up and took a slapshot, the puck rocketing toward the net.

Time seemed to slow as the puck flew through the air, and then it was past the goalie, hitting the back of the net with a satisfying thud. The arena exploded with cheers, and Rhonda jumped to her feet with everyone else.

When the final buzzer sounded, she tried to be happy. She tried to match the energy of her friends. She faked it all the way out of the arena and while they waited at the top of the stairs, her legs buzzing. She'd tried to leave twice already, but kept being pulled into conversations.

She shifted her weight from one foot to the other, biting her lip as she watched the first players ascend, and she knew it was him before she saw his face. Her breath caught in her throat.

Jordan.

Her heart stopped. He had a cut across his left eye, a thin line of dried blood. His hair was damp, just like the first time she'd seen him behind that hotel room door. Rhonda's fingers twitched, and she fought the urge to rush to the stairs and check if he was okay.

That ache inside her grew until it choked off her air. And then the Snowballs appeared. Aelin and the girls ran to Ryan, and the fans erupted in celebration.

Jordan walked past, his eyes flicking up for the briefest moment.

Her hands twitched, but she stood frozen to the concrete floor. And then he was gone, absorbed into the crowd with the other players.

And Rhonda added a new attribute to her wildly expanding sense of self.

Cowardice.

CHAPTER
Twenty~Two

MONDAY NIGHT, Rhonda stepped out of the rideshare and into a puddle of slush. She was glad she hadn't taken her own car. The roads were slick with the remnants of snow that was now solidifying since the sun had gone down. She pulled her coat around her shoulders, wishing she'd worn wool pants. She smoothed down her sleek black dress, the hemline brushing just above her knees. Professional, yet sexy, as usual.

She walked through the doors of the event centre and followed signs for the Founder's Event. When she arrived outside the ballroom, Rhonda's breath caught in her throat. Even glimpsing it through the arched doors, it was a sea of opulence. Crystal chandeliers sparkled overhead, glinting off crystal glassware and pristine white plates. The hum of conversation blended with the delicate strains of a string quartet.

Guests milled about in the entry hall in designer gowns and sharp suits, sipping champagne from fluted glasses. Towering floral arrangements punctuated the space, their blooms so perfect their existence seemed impossible for Calgary in November. Rhonda's eyes scanned the space, the air thick with the scent of expensive perfume and cologne. She caught a glimpse of her reflection in the mirror behind one of the pop-up bars. *One of these things is not like the others.*

As she turned to find the Will-Call or check-in desk, she spotted Jordan across the crowd. Her breath hitched. He was wearing a tailored dark suit that hugged his broad shoulders and lean frame. He was clean-shaven. His hair, wavy and sleek. It was like seeing a favourite piece of art only to realize that the versions she'd admired before were knock-offs.

Rhonda's stomach did an involuntary flip. She was back in her entryway, tearing off her top and posing for him in his coat. Her cheeks flamed.

Jordan was gone when she woke up Saturday morning. She'd known he would be. That look he'd given her on her front step wasn't one of excitement or desire. It was pain. Self-loathing. And still, she'd let him walk through the door.

And then she'd let him walk past her at the Ice Centre without even acknowledging him. No charcuterie board could make up for that.

For a moment, she wondered if she should turn around and walk right back outside. Then she remembered her texts with Derek that morning. How thrilled he'd been that she'd secured an audience with Dr. Mallory for the first time in years.

As much as she wanted to pretend that praise didn't matter, that it was all about what was best for patients, it absolutely did. She'd worked her ass off for years to prove she was worthy of a promotion. How many misogynistic comments or dismissals had she bounced back from? How many times had she been looked over or rejected? Even by her own people at Cantra?

No. She had to go through with this meeting, even if it meant sitting next to glow-up Jordan and facing the terrifying reality that she was a little bit dead inside.

Rhonda inhaled a steadying breath and strode across the hall.

Jordan waited next to the official entrance to the ballroom, and she couldn't help but notice the eyes of a few women lingering on him. He had that whole rugged-with-a-touch-of-sophistication thing going for him. Plus, he was at least twenty years younger than any other man in the immediate vicinity.

Jordan turned, and his eyes locked with hers. Was that a flush creeping up his neck, or was it just the warm lighting?

"Hey, sorry I'm a bit late." Rhonda gave him a smile, hoping it came off as casual.

Jordan cleared his throat. "No problem. I just got here myself." He lifted a hand, then thought better of it. "The coat check is there."

Rhonda nodded, her stomach souring. "Right. Thanks." She walked over and handed the woman behind the table her coat in exchange for a ticket, grateful there wasn't any line. When she reappeared at Jordan's side, he held up two tickets.

"Hope it's okay. I got these already."

Rhonda nodded, her brow pinching. "Of course." He hadn't smiled at her. More than that, apart from the moment she'd greeted him, he wasn't making eye contact. It made her feel woozy. Off-centred.

She tried not to stare at the way his suit jacket clung to his shoulders or how he had one hand casually slipped into his pocket. He looked confident. Strong. Without realizing it, she'd planned on him being her ally, but right now, he felt like a paid escort.

How had Jordan gotten these tickets? She knew how much a table at one of these events cost, and she hadn't even thought to ask.

They wove through groups of people, Jordan nodding and exchanging pleasantries with a few familiar faces. Rhonda's heels snagged in the industrial carpet as she tried to keep up. The tables were set with precision, each one a tableau of intricate centrepieces, gleaming silverware, and name cards written in elegant script.

Finally, Jordan stopped at their table. It was tucked toward the edge of the room. Not quite in the thick of things but not banished to the outskirts, either. Perfect.

As they approached, Rhonda scanned the table's other occupants. She recognized a few of them from her visits to various hospitals around Calgary. One of the women, Doctor Smithson, was a stern-looking woman with her hair pulled into a tight bun and a pair of glasses balanced on the bridge of her nose. She didn't realize she'd moved to Rocky Ridge and felt like an idiot for not keeping better tabs.

She recognized Doctor Mallory immediately. He had salt-and-pepper hair and a neatly trimmed beard, and he was looking at them with either intrigue or pure disgust. "I didn't realize you'd changed your name to Gertie."

Jordan picked up the name card. "She wasn't available tonight, but you can call me that if it makes you more comfortable."

The other doctors chuckled, and Rhonda tried not to panic. Dr. Mallory didn't know they were coming.

Jordan motioned to Rhonda. "This is Rhonda, my plus one."

Plus one. The words stung like a slap, even though she had no right to expect he'd call her anything else. She gave a small wave and looped her purse over the back of the chair.

"We met a few years ago, didn't we?" Dr. Smithson leaned forward.

Rhonda nodded. "Yes, you were over at Hilltop."

Dr. Smithson smiled, pleased she'd remembered. "Are you still with Cantra?"

Rhonda nodded. "I am."

Dr. Mallory visibly stiffened. His eyes flicked to Jordan, but Jordan was turned, waving to an elderly woman at a neighboring table with a brunette bob. Rhonda suddenly felt like she'd swallowed a handful of gravel.

Jordan turned, then leaned back in his chair as a server approached to fill their water glasses and offer them a wine list.

The rest of the doctors introduced themselves to her. It was obvious Jordan already knew them, and they easily jumped into conversation about the hospital. Jordan ribbed them about their various quirks, and they preened at the attention.

Jordan was smooth. Funny. Rhonda smiled and added in a sentence here or there, but couldn't take control like she usually did. She didn't want to. From the second she'd seen him across the hall, all the energy she brought to events had been sucked out of her. She was like a white dwarf, an impotent core left behind to orbit any other object with greater mass.

She tried to be interesting when their appetizers arrived and succeeded at pulling out a few comments about the best wings in Calgary. Then, she asked questions about their various professional struggles and goals. She'd hoped to bring that back around to her own goals with Reviact, but then the lights dimmed, and the hum of conversation dissolved into expectant silence.

A microphone crackled to life, and a well-dressed man in his sixties stepped onto the stage at the front of the ballroom. "Good evening, ladies and gentlemen," he began, his voice resonating through the room. "I'm Dr. Andrew Keller, and it's my privilege to welcome you to the annual Calgary Founder's Event. Tonight, we celebrate the remarkable strides we've made in cancer research and treatment, and we look forward to the future with hope and determination."

Applause sounded through the room. Rhonda tried to focus on the speaker, but her eyes kept drifting to Dr. Mallory, who nodded thoughtfully, his fingers tapping rhythmically on the tablecloth.

Dr. Keller continued, introducing a series of speakers who shared stories of breakthrough treatments and heart-wrenching patient testimonials. Each anecdote was punctuated by the soft clink of silverware as servers began to bring out the second course of their meal.

The aroma of seared scallops and tender filet mignon wafted

through the air, and Rhonda's stomach growled in response. She reached for her fork, and then her attention was pulled back to the stage as a young woman stepped up to the podium.

"Good evening, everyone. My name is Sarah, and I'm here to share my story as a survivor of stage three breast cancer."

Rhonda's heart clenched. Stories like this never failed to hit her in the gut, which of course was the point. But she couldn't handle another infusion of any kind of emotion at the moment.

Dr. Smithson leaned in. "Isn't it incredible what they're able to do now with targeted therapies?"

Rhonda glanced up as she cut into her scallop. "I've been reading about some new advancements in immunotherapy."

"Mmm." Dr. Smithson focused on her plate. "It's exciting. To be able to tailor treatments to individual genetic profiles."

Rhonda nodded, relief rushing through her. "I agree. I've been educating doctors around the province on a new addiction treatment drug. I know it's working well, but I can't imagine how much more effective it would be if it were individually targeted."

The doctor across from her, thin and wiry with a slightly wrinkled white shirt, looked up from his plate. "Addiction medicine is a complex field."

"Absolutely." She took a sip from her water glass and drew a deep breath. "That's why it's so exciting to see real results."

Dr. Mallory's eyes flicked to her, and Rhonda's heart skipped a beat. He held the key to getting Reviact into Rocky Ridge, and she wasn't about to miss her opportunity. "What addiction services do you offer at Rocky Ridge?"

Dr. Mallory leaned back in his chair, folding his hands neatly in his lap, his expression measured and deliberate. "At Rocky Ridge, we pride ourselves on a comprehensive, multidisciplinary approach to addiction treatment," he began, his tone as crisp as the white coat hanging in his office. "Our services range from counseling and outpatient programs to medically-assisted detoxification and long-term recovery planning. We're thorough, because we need to be. Addiction treatment is an area where lives are at stake, and every decision carries weight."

Rhonda nodded, her face open and attentive, but inside, she braced herself. This was the kind of conversation that could either soar or crash.

Dr. Mallory's gaze sharpened. "That's exactly why we're cautious about new medications entering our formulary. It's not just about the numbers on a trial sheet or a slick presentation—no offence." His lips twitched in something resembling a smile, though it didn't reach his eyes. "It's about the real-world impact. The long-term outcomes. How the drug performs when faced with the complexities of actual patient care."

Rhonda resisted the urge to shift in her seat, keeping her smile steady. "Of course, Dr. Mallory. That's precisely why Reviact is such a game-changer. It's been thoroughly tested not just for efficacy but for safety. Its mechanism of action allows it to—"

He held up a hand, cutting her off. "I've read the literature. And while the initial data is promising, we've seen promising data before. The trouble comes later. Unintended side effects. Adherence issues. Patient affordability. We don't gamble when it comes to these matters. Our process is deliberate for a reason."

Rhonda took another sip of water, keeping her breathing steady even as her nerves coiled tighter. "I completely under-stand. That's why I work with medical centres. Not just to talk numbers, but to work with your team to address any concerns. Reviact has shown incredible results, especially in patients who've struggled with adherence in the past. I'd be happy to arrange a peer-to-peer consultation with prescribing physicians who've had success with it. Perhaps that could help alleviate some of the doubts?"

Dr. Mallory studied her for a long moment, his gaze inscrutable. "Could you pass the butter?"

Rhonda nodded, even as her stomach churned with frustration. She picked up the butter dish and passed it to Jordan, who handed it to Dr. Mallory.

And that was that. Her one chance. Blown.

Thankfully, she didn't have to stew on it for more than a few seconds. The woman who'd been speaking earlier said something compelling, and everyone in the room turned their attention forward. Rhonda had never been grateful for a tear-jerking story before, but there was a first for everything.

"You okay?" Jordan whispered as he turned his chair so he could watch without craning his neck.

She nodded, but didn't turn to look at him. After a brief introduction, the auctioneer took over. He was an older man with a booming voice and a flair for drama. He started with jokes and instructions that sent ripples of laughter through the room, then began with a series of lavish items that made Rhonda's head spin.

A private wine tour in Napa Valley. A diamond necklace from a renowned local jeweller. A week-long stay in a villa on the Amalfi Coast. The bids flew fast and furious, paddles shooting up like popcorn kernels in a hot pan.

Rhonda watched, her heart racing as she tried to calculate the zeros behind each number. "Twenty thousand," the auctioneer called out for the wine tour. "Going once, going twice—" It felt like they'd all been handed a stack of Monopoly money.

She turned her attention back to Dr. Mallory, who watched the proceedings with calculated interest. Rhonda needed to make an impression, but how? She couldn't outbid these people. Her salary was respectable, but it wasn't even in the same stratosphere as the numbers being thrown around.

The auctioneer introduced the next item, and Rhonda's ears perked up. "Our next item is a weekend getaway at the prestigious Canmore Cascade, a boutique hotel nestled in the heart of the Rocky Mountains. This package includes a two-night stay in a deluxe suite, breakfast in bed, all meals included at their Michelin-starred restaurant, and a couples massage. December twentieth, right before Christmas, folks. And I'm sure you'd be able to swap dates—is that correct?" He looked to the administrators at a table off to the side. They nodded, and he laughed. "Right-0, so let's get this one off to a good start, shall we?"

Rhonda's eyes flicked to Dr. Mallory, who leaned forward ever so slightly. His paddle was still on the table, but the wheels turned in his head. This was it. This was her chance.

"Let's start the bidding at two thousand," the auctioneer announced.

Rhonda took a deep breath. She'd never been one to shy away from a challenge, and tonight was no different. She raised her paddle, her hand steady.

"Two thousand, thank you, ma'am. Do I hear three?"

Dr. Mallory raised his paddle. Rhonda's pulse quickened.

"Three thousand, thank you, sir. Do I hear four?"

Rhonda was going to throw up. She raised her paddle again.

"Four thousand, wow, sir, are you going to let her steal that from you? Do I hear five?"

Dr. Mallory's paddle went up with a flick of his wrist.

"Five thousand, thank you, sir. What do you think, little lady? Do you want it for six?"

Damn it. She couldn't hear over the pounding of her pulse.

Jordan put a hand on her knee. "Rhonda—"

She brushed it off and raised her paddle. "Six thousand, thank you, ma'am. Do I hear seven?"

Dr. Mallory raised his paddle, and Rhonda's stomach twisted. *What was she doing?* She didn't have seven thousand dollars to throw around. But she also couldn't back down now. Mallory thought he could shut out the rest of the world and keep his hospital in the dark ages. The way he looked at her, like she was a nuisance, made her want to slap him. Instead she raised her paddle.

"Seven thousand, wonderful! Do I hear eight? Think of all the good this will do, and imagine eating a perfectly seared steak—"

Dr. Mallory raised his paddle, and Rhonda started to see

stars. She couldn't go any higher or she'd have to take out a second mortgage. The auctioneer looked at her expectantly, but she shook her head.

"How about eighty-five hundred?" He walked up the aisle, but Rhonda kept her paddle on the table.

"Going once, going twice—"

"Ten thousand."

Rhonda turned to stare at Jordan. He held up his paddle, his face stone-cold.

The auctioneer grinned. "Ten thousand, going once—"

Dr. Mallory frowned, then put his paddle down.

"Going twice . . . and sold to the gentleman next to the lovely lady in the corner!"

Applause filled the room, but Rhonda's ears were ringing. She pushed back from the table and strode toward the washroom. The applause from the room turned into a muffled hum as she slipped past the double doors.

She drew a deep breath, then another, trying to tamp down the turmoil roiling inside. She couldn't splash her face with water and make her mascara run, so this would have to do. After her breathing returned to normal, she pushed back into the hall.

Jordan stood there, leaning against the wall. He looked so handsome, and that fact was like lighter fuel dumped over the coals that were still simmering from when she'd stood up and left the dining room.

She wanted to run. She wanted to sneak past and go back to her table, and that thought took her right back in the Ice Centre. Watching him disappear into the crowd. She wasn't going to take the easy way out this time.

Rhonda stepped forward, the pressure in her head still making it feel like her eyes were sunburned, but at least tears were no longer threatening to spill over.

Jordan looked up. "Hey." He pushed off the wall and walked toward her.

Rhonda stopped. "I think they're serving dessert."

"Did I do something in there?" Jordan asked, completely ignoring her statement. His expression was hard, as if daring her to say anything critical.

Rhonda felt like a tea kettle, sealed up with only one tiny airway, about to burst. "I didn't need to win that," she worked to keep her voice calm.

"I know. I just thought—"

"Jordan, you have to stop doing this," she said. His eyes hardened. "I know I asked for your help to meet with Doctor Mallory, and I appreciate you giving me this opportunity."

"I'm feeling very appreciated right now."

"Don't do that."

"Don't do what? I bent over backward—"

"You didn't have to do that!"

Jordan scoffed. "Right. Because what I want doesn't matter. I'm just your call boy."

Rhonda leaned in. "I was very clear the first time I met you."

"And what about the second time or the third? You're the one who texted me. Remember?"

Rhonda opened her mouth, then snapped it shut.

Jordan clenched his jaw. "I didn't mean to have feelings for you. Okay? I fought like hell not to have feelings for you. And I get that you don't feel the same way about me, but—"

"I don't know how to do this!" Rhonda sucked in a breath, clapping a hand to her chest like she was Céline Dion.

Jordan stopped, his eyes burning into hers. His throat worked, and then he asked, "You don't know how to do what?"

Rhonda grabbed his arm and pulled him to the side wall where they wouldn't be in the way. "This! Where you're doing nice things for me, and—" She let out an exasperated sigh. "I can't be in your debt."

"You're not in my debt."

"You just spent ten grand—"

"That was my choice."

"I understand. But if I wouldn't have been here, you never would have made that choice."

He raised an eyebrow. "How do you know that?"

She gave him a look, then tried to steady her breathing. "You're doing these things for me, and it makes me feel—"

"Good?"

She watched him, her body tearing itself apart from the inside out. This was it. Fight or flight. "No. It makes me terrified."

Jordan frowned. "I don't understand."

"In my experience, whenever anybody does something nice, it's because they want to hang it over your head or they want something from you. Something you don't always want to give."

"So you don't let people do things for you?"

"No. I don't. I take care of myself."

"That's . . . sad."

Rhonda swallowed hard. "It's safe." She squeezed her eyes shut and turned to flatten her back against the wall, forcing her lungs to expand. The light in the hall seemed to tunnel around her as she blinked.

"Do you need to sit down?" Jordan's fingers grazed her elbow.

Rhonda squeezed her arms around herself, wishing she had her wrap. Jordan took off his suit jacket and pulled her from the wall just far enough that he could sweep it over her shoulders.

She looked up at him. The shivery feeling she'd had all week came back in full force. It made her teeth start to chatter and her knees begin to knock. Whatever she'd felt in her stomach sitting across from Claire at Moxie's had grown to ten times the size without her recognizing it.

And right then, looking into the deep blue of Jordan's eyes, she could no longer hold it in. "I think . . . I want to know your name." The words spilled out of her, and she gasped like she'd just been exorcised.

It was the truth. Her most intimate truth. And she'd just spoken it in front of Jordan Wheatfill.

She could think of a thousand reasons why Jordan would be so damn intriguing when compared to other men she'd been with. He was funny, which meant he was smart. He was confident, bordering on cocky, which always drove her insane for probably some very messed up psycho-evolutionary reason. He took care of himself, worked his body hard, and bordered on dangerous. Add in the fact that he was quite literally the forbidden fruit, and it all added up on paper.

But none of those reasons were at the forefront of her mind because they couldn't squeeze in past the two that sat front and center.

First, Jordan was kind. She'd seen it in action, and that didn't compute with his bad boy reputation.

Second, he didn't need her just as much as she didn't need him.

And yet she wanted him.

Badly.

Neither of those things made logical sense, and her brain couldn't stop obsessing over the solution to that puzzle.

Jordan wet his lips, and his eyes narrowed. He stood there, staring at her.

"What are you doing?" Rhonda asked.

"I'm making sure your pupillary dilation is the same in both eyes."

"Jordan—"

"Okay. So you do know my name."

She couldn't help her exhausted grin as she dropped her head back against the wall. "I meant . . . I want to know *your name.*" It was the same thing she already said, but she couldn't think of any other way to explain it. Not without dying of embarrassment and shame. She levelled her gaze at him again and watched as his eyes flared with understanding.

He let out a soft "hmm" and she knew he got it. That night at his hotel. *No names.*

Then the wave hit her. Heat. Want. Not that she hadn't been noticing him all night, but everything about him seemed to sharpen in that moment. His almost dimple, the nick in his eyebrow, the way his shirt sat slightly askew after he pulled his jacket off.

Maybe that was the problem. She just needed to blow off some steam.

Rhonda looked closer and noticed the pattern on his tie that she'd thought was diagonal stripes were actually tiny roses smooshed together. She reached out and threaded the silk between her fingers. "Can we just get out of here?" Her voice was low, and only after a moment of silence did she allow her eyes to wander up over his collar, the swell of his Adam's apple, his jaw and cheekbones.

Jordan exhaled, his nostrils flaring. "No."

Rhonda blinked as a flash of ice hit her hands. "Oh. Okay." She started to disentangle his tie from her fingers when Jordan's hand slid inside his jacket and curled around her waist.

"If you want to know my name, then I'm not going home with you." His lips were so close, they brushed her cheekbone.

The waves crashed stronger. She needed him to come home with her. It was like she was sitting at the symphony waiting for them to play the final chords, but the conductor wouldn't lower his damn baton.

"But—"

"My first rule is you don't get to tell me when I'm allowed to be nice to you," he said. Rhonda's breath caught in her throat, but Jordan was already talking again. "Rule number two, no sex."

Rhonda's jaw dropped, and she pushed him back. "What are you—"

"You don't think I see what's happening here? You don't think I know how this goes?" He scrubbed a hand over his jaw and leaned in again. "I've been that guy, Rhonda. The guy who is perfect for the night, but who nobody wants to take home to their parents."

"I never said—"

"You didn't have to. You took one look at me in that hotel room, and you knew that's what I was."

"You didn't tell me to leave."

He blew out a breath. "Exactly. Maybe I don't know how to do this either." His hands tightened like a belt on her waist. "But I know it's not the way I've been doing it."

Rhonda breathed him in. She wrapped her hand around his tie and tugged, pulling just hard enough that he grunted. "So what do we do?"

"The opposite."

"Which is?"

"I'm going to walk out that door after cashing out. And you're going to decide whether to stay and endure more miserable talk with hospital administration. And then you're going to go back to your place. Alone." Jordan's palm found the edge of her opposite hip, and the pressure made her arch involuntarily.

"And then what?" Her breath came in short gasps, the heat from his body soaking into her like sunshine.

"And then you can text me."

"I can text you."

"Yeah. I've got an early shift tomorrow, so I might not even respond. I don't know. I guess we'll see."

His words were both oxygen over coals and a bucket of cold water. So damn cocky. "The opposite sounds shitty."

Jordan laughed, his breath whispering over her neck. "I'll see you soon." He pulled back, forcing her to let go of his tie, then slowly pulled his jacket off her shoulders. He gave her one last look and turned toward the tables at the exit.

Just as she was about to peel herself off the wall, Jordan turned. He looked her up and down, a muscle in his jaw jumping. "You know, you could use that energy for something."

"Oh, I will." Rhonda snapped, and Jordan smirked.

"I meant before you get home and take off that little black dress." His eyes drifted, and heat flashed over Rhonda's thighs. He cleared his throat and straightened his tie. "You don't have anything to lose with Rocky Ridge." He smiled, then continued on his path to the exit.

Rhonda made a beeline back to the washrooms. She grabbed two paper towels and wet them with cold water, then pressed them to her neck and shoulders. After her breathing slowed, she washed her hands twice and stared at herself in the mirror. *You have nothing to lose with Rocky Ridge.*

She chewed on Jordan's words. What would she say to Doctor Mallory? If she didn't give a damn whether he let her into his hospital or not?

Jordan was right. After tonight, it didn't seem like she was any closer to convincing him.

Rhonda straightened and dried her hands. She walked back into the ballroom and for the first time in a week felt solid on her own feet. She wound through the tables until she found her seat.

Doctor Hughes leaned over. "I'm sorry. Jordan said he had to go. Said he has an early shift in the morning."

Rhonda nodded and picked up her purse and wrap. She fumbled inside her bag for her coat check ticket, then swivelled in her seat. The auction was still going on, but nobody at her table was obviously bidding, their paddles sitting flat on the table next to them.

Rhonda lifted her chin, her tone steady and composed. "Dr. Mallory, I understand the importance of exercising caution when considering new pharmaceuticals—especially when patient costs and institutional risks are at stake. I also understand that not every new drug lives up to its initial promise over time. But the decisions you make directly impact thousands of patients across the Calgary area, and those decisions carry profound weight."

She paused, drawing a measured breath before continuing. "There are people out there suffering needlessly who could benefit from this treatment. I fully respect the significance of your position and the responsibility it entails. By all means, share the available information with your patients and present them with the pros and cons. But refusing to explore a promising pharmaceutical outright because of the possibility of being wrong isn't prudence—it's stagnation."

Dr. Mallory blinked, clearly taken off guard, but she didn't give him a moment to interject. "You've said you've reviewed the research, and perhaps you have. But I've yet to encounter another treatment option for addiction that demonstrates this level of efficacy. If there's a superior alternative in your hospital's formulary, I'd love to hear about it. Otherwise, patients leaving your operating rooms every day are struggling with opioid addiction, and this represents a chance to help them."

Her voice softened, but her resolve remained firm. "Sure, some patients may decide not to pursue this option due to cost, just as many patients decline elective surgeries. But we still provide them with the information to make an informed choice. I'll send the research to your email for a third and final time. Whether you review it and respond is up to you, but this is the last time I'll be reaching out."

Rhonda scanned the table. "It was lovely meeting all of you. I hope you have a wonderful holiday season." She scooped her bag and wrap into her arms and strode out into the hall.

JORDAN

JORDAN HAD BEEN all confidence on Monday night. Something about the way Rhonda had been desperate for him in the hall at the Founder's Event made him feel powerful. In control.

But Tuesday morning, he'd woken up in a cold sweat. Rhonda hadn't texted him. Not that he'd expected her to.

But he'd kind of expected her to.

Maybe he'd pushed too far? Made too many demands?

He rolled out of bed and jumped in the shower. He only had five minutes if he wanted time to make eggs for breakfast, but he wanted to stand there for an hour.

He'd come home on cloud nine, high on the euphoria of feeling a genuine connection. But he'd been in this exact place before. Sonya had a thousand moments of vulnerability, and then she sealed back up like a lockbox.

That was almost worse. If she never would have opened up, he never would have been able to convince himself to stay hooked. The constant whiplash had almost destroyed him. The only reason he could still be in contact with Claire was because he wasn't in a romantic relationship with her.

Everything he'd said to Rhonda was true. He didn't want to be that guy. Not with her. He couldn't put his finger on why it felt different, but it was.

Rhonda was pure energy. Her mind went places his didn't. When he was with her, it was like the record he'd been listening to had been flipped over to secret, alternate tracks.

He'd never been with a woman who was so intuitively herself. She knew what she wanted, not only sexually, but in every aspect of her life. It was like a drug to him. Not having to guess, watching her dive into her own pleasure and grab her goals by the balls.

That was why he'd never gotten Medicine Hat out of his head. Why he'd tripped over himself to get her out to the parking lot in Okotoks. Why he'd given her his number on a napkin.

Jordan got out, dried himself off, then put on his scrubs and walked into the kitchen. He heated up olive oil, cracked two eggs in the pan, and then scrambled them. He shouldn't have gone to the event.

He'd been in such a logical headspace for the past week. Then Rhonda had shown up at his door, and he'd had to endure her wearing his jacket and looking up at him with her dark eyes, saying things like, "I want to know your name."

He was cooked.

Jordan ate before the eggs had fully cooled off and burned the inside of his mouth. He hurriedly brushed his teeth, threw on his coat, and hoped his erection would fade by the time he got to the lobby.

He rode the elevator down to the street and scraped off his windshield. The streets were clear, and he arrived at the hospital with just enough time to grab a coffee. His morning rounds went quickly, which he was grateful for since he had a shift at urgent care later that night.

He tried to double-stack them, especially on weeks when he had tournaments and had to be gone all weekend. This weekend, they were driving down to Lethbridge for an eight-bracket round robin. They'd play some of Alberta's favorites, but there were at least four teams from British Columbia as well.

It was a perfect way to get tuned up before the Christmas invitational. He was about to take his lunch when his phone buzzed in his pocket. He pulled it out, and when he saw Rhonda's name on the display, he paused before swiping up.

He wasn't sure he was ready to see it, but his curiosity got the better of him.

RHONDA

Hey. How's your day going?

Jordan pursed his lips and drew a deep breath.

"Wheatfill, stop slacking." Gertie came around the corner, giving his phone the whole eyeball. Jordan turned the screen to her.

"Gertie, what am I supposed to say to this?"

She scoffed. "That depends."

"On what?"

"On whether you like her."

Jordan grinned. He was about to ask her how she knew it was a woman until he realized that Rhonda's name was at the top of the text thread. "I was about to take my lunch, by the way."

Gertie waved him off, reaching for the stack of Post-its.

"What would you say if I did like her?" he asked.

"That's easy. You tell her it would be better if she were here."

Jordan laughed. "I can't say that yet."

"Why not? What are you waiting for?"

Jordan pondered this for a moment. If Rhonda was his drug, it wouldn't be long until he was desperate for another hit. "I don't know. To know if it's safe."

Gertie scoffed. "Safe? Love is never safe. If it was, it wouldn't be so good."

Jordan's grin widened. "You've been married for thirty years."

Gertie turned to look at him with her eyebrows raised. "You don't think it's terrifying every single damn day? Love is never safe. After a week, after a month, after a year, after thirty years. You have to keep offering up your beating heart and hope that the person you hand it to is gonna wake up wanting it in the morning." She turned back to the desk and hunched over. "So I'll ask this one more time, asshat. What are you waiting for?"

She finished writing her Post-it note and stuck it to the edge of the desk. *No pudding. Room 278.*

Jordan didn't even want to ask. "And what if she doesn't want it?" He folded his arms over his chest.

Gertie blew out a breath. "Oh, honey. Heartbreak is so much easier than love. Because you don't get a choice in the matter. You just have to endure it." She took a step closer. "You're standing here, aren't you? Means you already know how to survive that. You either choose love or it chooses for you." She patted him on the arm. "That cheesecake wasn't great, by the way." She stalked past him. "How was the small talk?"

Jordan snorted. "I didn't even stay for dessert."

Gertie laughed out loud, grabbed her clipboard, and walked back down the hall.

Jordan turned his phone over and started to type.

It would be better if you were here.

RHONDA

See, you said no sex, but then you send something like that.

How are you?

RHONDA

I wanted to text you last night

Why didn't you?

RHONDA

Too busy panicking about what I said to Mallory

Damn it. I left too soon

RHONDA

I'm sorry if you get fired

Double damn it

RHONDA

You were right. I don't have anything to lose

I'm usually right

Can you still make your sales goals without it?

RHONDA

Doubtful

I'm sorry

RHONDA

I don't know. I suddenly don't care as much as I did a month ago

Jordan stared at that message, his heart picking up speed. He stalked out of the nursing station and leaned against the wall. *This was hot.* This was so damn hot, he regretted everything he said the night before.

That's me. I'm a bad influence

RHONDA

That's what the Snowballs keep telling me

RHONDA

RHONDA

So now what?

You're bored of texting already?

RHONDA

So bored

I have a double shift tonight, but what about lunch tomorrow?

RHONDA

I have a work lunch in Airdrie. After?

No. I have coaching, then practice, and then a night shift

Rhonda

> Overachiever

> Thursday?

Rhonda

> I leave Thursday to go down to Fort McMurray.
> I have meetings there until Friday evening, but
> then I'm home on the weekend

> I leave Friday to go down to Lethbridge for a
> tournament

Rhonda

> 💀

Jordan hesitated. Then he held is breath and typed:

> You could stay

The three dots appeared, then disappeared. Jordan wondered if he was experiencing a cardiac event.

Rhonda

> What do you mean?

> Fort Mac is only 30 min from Lethbridge. You could come to the game after your meeting

> If you want

He typed and re-typed different versions of "But you don't have to" until Rhonda's message came through.

RHONDA

> Okay

> Okay as in yes?

RHONDA

> Okay as in I'll consider it

> What's there to consider?

RHONDA

> The fact that I'll be on vacation and won't be able to have sex?

> You can have sex, just not with me

Rhonda

See you Friday

Rhonda

I'm packing all black lace

Brat

———

Chubs' house was the epitome of suburban living in Northeast Calgary, with its long, straight street and neatly manicured lawns. The quiet was disrupted by the rumble of engines as his teammates pulled up and parked their vehicles, then grabbed their gear and hauled it to the driveway, ready to load it into the passenger van he'd rented to take to Lethbridge. They'd driven separately before, but it was always more fun to get rowdy.

Jordan pulled up next to the group and parked, pretending to tip a chauffeur hat. He got out and opened the storage compartment at the back of the bus, then climbed back in the driver's seat.

The guys piled in, and Chubs' brother Mike climbed in last. He used to travel with the team for every tourney, but then he went and got married. Now he had two toddlers and they rarely saw him on the weekends.

Jordan fist-bumped him over the seat, waited a second for everyone to get settled, then pulled away from the curb.

"Jord, your eye still looks like shit," Cam called from a few rows back.

Jordan smirked. "Thanks, bud. Appreciate you."

Steele leaned over the seat. "I wondered if Country mentioned you on his latest YouTube stream. Haven't watched it yet."

Jordan glanced in the rearview. "Let me know if I'm famous."

Chubs opened a bag of chips. "Speaking of famous, I set the new squat record at the gym last night. Seems that piqued Ellie's interest." He lifted his arm and flexed.

"Can't deny a man who locks in on leg day." Wyatt nodded in approval.

Jordan laughed. Van talk was just as good as locker room talk. Maybe better. After sitting around the table across from the doctors on the board at Rocky Ridge, he'd briefly questioned his life choices. Here he was in his thirties still laughing at jokes about ball sacks.

At work, he put on a mature face, and that part of him did exist. The part that took life seriously, that thought about life goals, taxes, and retirement. But the idea of eating the same thing for breakfast every day and tracking his HDL intake felt like a death sentence. Maybe he wouldn't ever have to be the guy that sat at a table he sponsored with a sour expression on his face. Maybe he'd be the one copping a feel on his wife beneath the tablecloth.

Wife. That thought brought his train of thought to a screeching halt. Had that word even once crossed his mind in the past ten years? It had been there in his early twenties. After everything went down with Lisa and Sean, it had taken him a while to bounce back. But when he did, he'd been positive he wanted someone permanently in his life. After Sonya, he was dead set against it.

". . . already texting me. Said I was 'unexpectedly charming.'" Chubs was still on his leg day story, then. Jordan reached for his water bottle.

Mike laughed, shaking his head. "That means she expected you to be a complete disaster, bud. Low bar."

"You're one to talk." Chubs shot back. "Bet you've forgotten what a first date even feels like."

Mike grinned, unbothered, and leaned forward. "Yeah, well, while you're out here fumbling through Tinder and doing squats for attention, I'm at home with a wife who knows how to make lasagna better than your mom."

Cam snorted. "Food flex. Shit's getting real."

Jordan chuckled. He was in a damn good mood, and there was one reason for that. He glanced down at his phone, but there weren't any new notifications from Rhonda. She was probably busy schmoozing doctors.

Plenty from Ethan, though. They'd been texting for the past couple of days. He'd shown up for practice the day before, which was a step in the right direction. Finally, as of last night, he'd convinced him to at least think about talking to his parents and reaching out to Jace's. He of all people understood what it looked like to avoid the tough conversations.

His phone screen lit up, and he grinned. Think of the devil.

RHONDA

> Should be at the rink by about eight thirty. Nine
> if I suck at my job

Jordan glanced over at Steele in the passenger seat. He couldn't ask him to type a message out for him. Instead he waited until they were at a red light, then tapped out a quick response.

RHONDA

He laughed and set his phone back in the cupholder. By the time they left the city limits, the van interior transformed into a makeshift convenience store, the guys breaking out snacks like they'd been starved for Red #7. Bags of gummy bears, chips, and cans of soda were passed around. Steele, true to form, had a protein shake and a bag of almonds. He made sure to hand out judgemental looks like religious pamphlets.

Someone connected their phone to the Bluetooth, and soon enough, the van was pulsing with an early 2000s playlist. He didn't know he needed every lyric to "Work It" by Missy Elliott dragged from his brain, but there it was.

They pulled into the hotel parking lot, and the team unloaded, eager to check in and rest up for a few hours before round one in the tourney. Jordan grabbed his bag from the luggage compartment and followed the line of guys through the sliding doors and up to the front desk.

Steele checked in for them, then turned and handed Jordan his key. "I feel honoured."

Jordan took the card. "I need your ugly mug to keep me on the straight and narrow."

Steele snorted. "I don't need to be in the room to know what you're up to, bud."

They left the others and headed to the fifth floor. Jordan

tossed his bag in front of the bed and used the washroom, then dropped onto the mattress and stretched out.

"Thanks for driving." Steele plugged in his phone charger.

"No worries, bud." He stacked another pillow behind his back. "Hey, you doing okay?"

Steele nodded. "I'm heading out to Toronto for Christmas. It'll be good to see the fam."

Jordan gave him a look. "You're not missing Christmas dinner, though."

He laughed. "Nope. I leave on the twenty-first."

"Good. Glad I don't have to cut your ass." Steele had a bit of a community at the shop where he worked, but Jordan wasn't sure he'd really put down roots. He'd come to Calgary with a girl he'd been dating, and when that hadn't worked out, he'd been waiting for the day Steele told him he was heading back east. He didn't want to lose him. He was a good guy and an even better winger.

They relaxed in silence until four o'clock. Steele looked up from the floor where he'd been arranging his gear. "I'm gonna grab something to eat. You coming?"

Jordan glanced up from his phone and spotted two socks draped over the chair, one purple and one green. "Do they always have to be those colours?"

Steele shook his head. "Nope. Just mismatched."

Jordan sat and threw his legs off the bed. "Ever missed a game?"

"Yep. And regretted it."

Jordan grabbed his wallet, and they headed down to the lobby. He didn't have an obvious superstition like many of the other guys, but he did have a pregame ritual. He put his skates on first because when he was first going pro, he'd accidentally created a Pavlovian response. Skates equaled pre-game dump. It was annoying to take off his gear. Skates, toilet, then gear. Worked every time.

They found a restaurant nearby and ordered spaghetti. They

didn't have a lot of time and easy carbs were the best thing before a game. By the time they got back to the lobby, Nate and Mike were already sitting on the couch.

Nate held up a hand. "You two need to hurry the hell up."

Steele flipped him off on the way to the elevator.

They didn't have far to drive to get to the rink, and by the time they pulled into the parking lot, the chatter had started to die down. Jordan grabbed his gear from the back and followed the rest of the team inside the building.

In the locker room, their laughter and easy conversation gave way to the sounds of bags being unzipped and sticks clattering against the benches. Everyone had an earbud in, listening to whatever got their blood flowing.

Jordan followed his ritual to a T, and just as he pulled on his jersey over his pads, Mike clapped his hands together.

"Alright, boys, let's focus up." He stepped into the centre of the room. Jordan loved when he came along to games if only so he didn't have to do the pep talk.

When they were mostly circled up, Mike continued, "We've got Puck Me from Stirling, and while I've heard they've had some struggles with flow this season, don't for a second underestimate their centre . . ."

Mike dove into specific strategies and pulled out a whiteboard. Jordan looked around the room. His time in the NHL might have been cut short, but he wouldn't trade playing Elite League for anything. How lucky was he that in his thirties he could still get out on the ice and compete? It wasn't a million dollar paycheck, but that couple thousand bucks at the end of the season felt just as good as a contract celly.

Mike continued, outlining their strategy for the first period. Jordan tried to focus on his words, but his thoughts kept drifting. The words "Rhonda's coming" played on ticker tape on repeat in his head, and his skin buzzed like he'd just chugged Pre-Workout.

They huddled and cheered, then walked out to the bench.

Jordan took a few laps around their side of the ice, but that was it. He didn't like doing an extensive warm up before the whistle blew.

The game against Puck Me from Stirling started out intense, but by the end of the second period, their energy began to wane. Jordan and his teammates took advantage, and by the time they entered the third, the score was four to one.

He came off the ice with fifteen minutes on the clock, and that's when he found her. Rhonda walked down the steps to the centre section of the stands. Her hair was pulled back, and she had on a dark blue toque. She wore a puffy white jacket, and her cheeks were flushed from the cold. She sat, then looked up and scanned the ice. He waited for her to make it to their bench, and when she did, his pulse quickened.

A couple of minutes later, Jordan jumped back onto the ice, infused with new energy. He joined the line change and took up his position. The puck was in their defensive zone, and Cam and Nate worked to clear it.

The seconds bled away, and Jordan's adrenaline spiked as they entered the final minute of play. He knew they had the win in the bag, but he wanted to put an exclamation point on it. Point differential could influence their seeding in later rounds.

With thirty seconds left, Steele intercepted a pass and sent a clapper up the ice. Jordan was already in motion, and he caught the puck on his stick. He skated past the blue line, then cut left to avoid a defenceman.

Jordan faked a shot, then pulled the puck back and slipped it between his legs. The goalie bit on the fake, and Jordan lifted the puck top shelf. It hit the netting with a satisfying thud, and the crowd erupted as much as they could for an out of town team.

His teammates swarmed him, slapping his back and helmet, but he was looking up into the stands. There she was, on her feet, her hands clapping above her head. He hadn't realized until that moment how much he'd ached to see her cheering in their game against the Snowballs. He knew she couldn't, but damn if he didn't want her to.

Jordan skated back to the bench as the final seconds ticked away and the buzzer sounded. They lined up for their handshakes, then retreated to the locker room. When Jordan arrived after thanking the refs, the air was already thick with steam from the showers.

Jordan hurried to his locker.

"You in a rush there, Wheatfill?" Cam hollered from the other end of the bench. Jordan ignored him, stripping down to his compression shorts and grabbing his towel. He marched past Steele, who was grinning like a Cheshire cat.

"I know that look!" Steele called out, and Jordan flipped him the bird as he disappeared into the shower.

The water was scalding. Better than the lukewarm water at their home base. He let the heat seep into his muscles, washing away the adrenaline and lactic acid buildup. He soaped up, rinsed, and was back in the locker room in record time.

Jordan ignored the looks and quickly towelled off, then reached for his clothes. He pulled on his jeans and shirt, then tossed the keys to the van to Cam.

"Cap's got a girl." Chubs waggled an eyebrow.

"Not just a girl. A Southern Alberta girl," Wyatt held up the keys and jangled them.

"Southern Alberta girls are tough as nails," Steele grinned.

"They'll change a tire on a gravel road and still make it to puck drop," Nate quipped.

Mike laughed. "They'll walk three miles in the snow just to tell you you're wrong. Ask me how I know that."

The guys laughed, and Steele bumped Jordan's shoulder. "You gonna join us after whatever this is?"

Jordan chuckled. "If you find something open past ten in Lethbridge, I'll be impressed." He nodded to the team. "Great work out there." He turned back to Steele. "Keep me posted. I'll be back after dinner."

Nate whistled, and Jordan pushed through the door to hoots and hollers. He wound his way back up to the main entryway and didn't see Rhonda at first. He frowned, his eyes darting from face to face, until he found that white puffy coat.

Rhonda turned her head and spotted him, a smile spreading across her face. Jordan's stomach flipped. They walked toward each other, avoiding the other players and fans milling about, and then they were finally standing in front of each other.

"Hey," he started, but before he could say anything else, Rhonda was on him. She didn't waste time with pleasantries. She wrapped an arm around his neck and pulled him down, her lips pressing against his.

Jordan's eyes widened in surprise, but it only lasted a second. He melted into her, his hand sliding up to cradle her jaw. She tasted like snowflakes. Cool and crisp. It might've had a little to do with the Wintergreen gum she was chewing.

He pulled back, breathing hard, a laugh rumbling in his chest. "Well, hello to you, too."

Rhonda grinned, her cheeks flushed. "Sorry, I was just—"

"Don't apologize." Jordan took her in.

She bit her bottom lip, her breath still coming in little puffs. "Okay, well. Hello." She stepped back, adjusting her toque.

Jordan worked to draw a full breath, but his body wasn't cooperating. "You hungry?" he asked.

Rhonda shifted on her feet. "Are you asking me on a date, Wheatfill?"

Jordan grinned. "That depends. Do you have your car?"

Twenty-Four

RHONDA

RHONDA'S PULSE pounded in her ears as she got in her car. After all the crap Jordan had given her about not having snow tires, she didn't especially look forward to him noticing all the other maintenance issues she'd been ignoring.

"Where are we going?" she asked, glancing over and catching his eyes on her.

"Not far." Jordan had his phone out, looking at a map. "Just turn right out of this parking lot.

She nodded, her heart rushing like a white noise machine. "I saw your goal."

Jordan turned to her, that dimple so close to forming, she wanted to reach over and press her finger into his cheek. "I know."

She rolled her eyes and stopped at a red light. Jordan gave her the last few directions, and within a few minutes, she pulled into a small parking lot.

The restaurant was a converted house, its windows glowing

with warm, inviting light. Rhonda opened her door and stepped out, her boots crunching on gravel. Jordan walked ahead of her, and she shamelessly ran her eyes over his backside.

Jordan opened the door, and as she walked in, his hand brushed her lower back. She barely felt it because of her coat, but electricity still shot from her belly button to her toes.

The restaurant was small and intimate, the tables dressed in white linens with a flickering candle on each one. The aroma of herbs and fresh bread filled the air, making her mouth water.

A hostess greeted them and led them to a table near the back. Rhonda slid into her chair and reached for the menu.

Jordan cleared his throat. "What are you in the mood for?"

Rhonda couldn't focus on the words in front of her. If their server hadn't approached with a silver pitcher of water, she would've told him exactly the menu she had rolling through her head.

Rhonda looked up as the waiter approached. "What do you recommend?"

"Do you eat red meat?" he asked. Rhonda nodded. "Then I'd do the New York strip, it comes with a bed of mashed sweet potato and fennel, or the house specialty, our bourbon braised meatloaf."

Rhonda hummed in her throat and dropped the menu. "Meatloaf it is."

Jordan grinned. "You don't have to think about it?" She shook her head, and he set his menu on top of hers. "Then I'll do the steak."

Their server beamed. "I'll get that in for you."

Jordan leaned back in his seat, his eyes never leaving hers. "So, where should we start?"

Rhonda's clothes suddenly felt two sizes too small. She could think of a hundred ways to answer that with a smart-ass comment, but that wasn't what he wanted. It wasn't what she wanted, either. Theoretically.

She took a sip of water to buy herself some time. The cool

liquid did nothing to calm the heat that was climbing up her neck. "Umm, well, I work." She set the glass down and ran a finger along the condensation on the outside. "But you already know that." She winced.

Jordan raised an eyebrow. "That looked painful."

"Like passing a kidney stone."

"Have you passed one before?"

She nodded. "Once."

"Nice, so you have a shredded urethra. Now we can talk about anything."

Rhonda laughed. "Hemorrhoids?"

"Oh, so many." He leaned forward, resting his arm on the table. "Where'd you grow up?" Jordan's eyes flicked to her shoulders. "Don't do that."

"What?"

"Start to fold into yourself."

Rhonda paused, becoming hyperaware of her own body. "I don't know if I can help it."

"Just a city. You don't have to tell me more than that."

She wet her lips. "Kamloops. Until I was twelve, then we moved to Calgary."

"Is your family still around?"

Rhonda shook her head. "My mom's back in Kamloops."

Jordan scrubbed a hand over his jaw. "Siblings?"

She held up one finger. "Sister."

Jordan nodded. "You're the oldest?"

"Yep. You?"

He nodded again, then reached out and twisted his water glass. "My parents and sister are still here in Calgary. I grew up in Okotoks."

Rhonda fingered the cloth napkin on her left. She wanted to ask him more about his family and everything Claire told her about Sean but realized she hadn't even told Jordan the two of them had met.

"I had lunch with your sister last week," she said, and

Jordan's eyes widened. She hurried on to explain. "I was at Hilltop, and she was there at the pharmacy waiting for her prescription. I saw her name on the board, and she was obviously related to you, so I said hi."

He watched her, his brow pinching. "Wow, okay."

"I'm sorry I didn't say anything. That was—well, it was before the Founder's Dinner." *Before I broke down in your apartment complex parking lot and found out via my friends that I was emotionally stunted.* "I guess she never said anything to you?"

He shook his head. "No."

"I don't see why she would. I didn't let on that we were anything but work colleagues."

Jordan gave a wry smile. "Oh, she definitely would've mentioned it if she thought we only worked together." It was Rhonda's turn to look confused. Jordan glanced up and met her eyes. "She'd zip it if she was worried she was going to scare me off."

Rhonda tried to ignore the meaning of that statement. Or what looking into Jordan's eyes did to her. Was this what taking a pact of celibacy did to a person? Everything about him suddenly became an aphrodisiac? She picked up her water and took a sip. "Well, it was a lovely conversation."

"About?" He raised an eyebrow.

"Reviact." She paused, letting him squirm for a second. "And your early hockey career." Jordan looked more uncomfortable than her for the first time ever. "Why didn't you ever tell anyone what happened with what's her face? Sean's girlfriend?"

"Claire told you about that?"

"She did." Rhonda set her glass back on the table. She wanted to press him, then recognized the hypocrisy. She'd barely been able to give him the name of the city where she grew up.

"Back then I figured if my best friend didn't know me well enough to ask questions instead of assuming I'd do something like that, then it wasn't worth my energy." Jordan's jaw was tense.

"Yeah." Rhonda nodded, something twisting in her gut. Did anyone know her well enough to ask questions?

Their food arrived with a flourish, the sizzle of Jordan's steak and the savory aroma of her meatloaf. Rhonda took a moment to appreciate the presentation, the vibrant colours of the vegetables and sauces.

They thanked their server, then Rhonda turned to Jordan. "The Snowballs players are good people." That was the best she could do. She wasn't going to tell him to have a heart-to-heart with Sean, but it was true. She'd seen them take care of each other, welcoming everyone in with open arms. But she supposed everyone had their blind spots.

Jordan grunted and picked up his fork and steak knife. "So are my players."

Rhonda ignored the fluttering in her stomach and asked the questions on the tip of her tongue. *If he wanted real, this was real.* "What happened with the fight in the parking lot? I heard someone on your team sent someone to the hospital. I've heard about so many fights between your two teams, and honestly . . ."

Jordan took a bite of steak. "Honestly, what?"

Rhonda took a moment, her fork hovering over her plate. "Honestly, you don't seem like that guy."

Jordan chewed and swallowed, then took a drink from his water glass. "There are a lot of guys in this sport who are angry. They put their heart and souls into hockey, and then got dumped on their asses." He shrugged. "I used to be one of them."

Rhonda nodded. "You're not anymore?"

He cut off another piece of meat. "I'm not a saint."

"Obviously." She grinned, taking a bit of each part of the meal in front of her onto the tines of her fork.

The corner of Jordan's mouth quirked. "I'm not angry any more. But some of the guys I recruit are still figuring it out."

Rhonda finished chewing. "Your sister said you collect misfits."

Emotions flickered through his expression, but never settled. "It's probably true."

"Does that mean I'm a misfit?"

Jordan watched her for a moment. "People on the inside—people who think they fit—won't put up with our shit. We need people who don't have such high standards to get us started."

Rhonda laughed out loud. "So you're settling?" She dropped her eyes to her plate and used her fork to cut a corner off the tender meat.

"Maybe I just have different standards."

Rhonda took another bite. She sighed as the blend of flavours exploded over her tongue.

"Good?" Jordan grinned at her.

She nodded. "Here, try it." Rhonda scooted her plate forward, and Jordan reached over with his fork. "Get all of it, the sauce, the greens."

Jordan obeyed, and then offered her a bite of his steak. All of it was delicious. But sharing it with him–knowing he was experiencing the same thing as her in that moment—made it more. Something about no other people on the planet living in that exact physical experience in those few seconds. It was intimate in a way that made her shiver.

"I don't think I have any standards." Rhonda pulled her plate back.

"No?"

She shook her head. "I didn't think I wanted anyone in my life, so I didn't think about it."

"Hmm." Jordan's blue eyes flicked up. "But you're thinking about it now?"

Rhonda flushed. She took another bite to cover up the heat in her cheeks. She was thinking about it now. But maybe that was why it felt so terrifying. When she started to drive or tried cooking for the first time, there had been a manual. A recipe book. With relationships, there were no rules to follow. No right way to do it.

"Maybe I should get some self-help books or something," she thought aloud.

Jordan leaned back in his chair, grinning. "Tell me more."

"Since I've never done this before—"

"Done what?"

Her blush deepened. "This." She pointed between the two of them.

"Gone on a date?"

Rhonda scoffed. "I've gone on dates, but not where the intent was to actually get to know someone."

Jordan's eyes narrowed. He leaned forward, resting his elbows on the table. "Never?" She shook her head, her heart beginning to pound. Jordan pushed his chair back, then stood and walked toward her. He held out his hand, and Rhonda took it, allowing him to pull her up next to him. He tugged her against his chest, wrapping his arms around her so completely, that she was swallowed up in his warmth, the soft cotton of his shirt, and that same cologne she'd smelled on him when they'd met at the hotel.

He didn't let go. He held her there, not saying a word, his hand curling behind her neck, his fingers resting behind her ear, in her hair. Cradling her. Protecting her.

Rhonda sank into him, her heart swelling until she wondered if light was shooting from her fingertips. Was this what it felt like? *Could you do this?* Tell someone the worst things about yourself, your biggest insecurities, and then have them . . . still want you?

A lump formed in her throat, and she worked to swallow. To breathe. Jordan held her until it passed, then slowly released her. He smoothed her hair from her cheek, then turned and settled back in his chair.

She swayed a little on her feet, trails of heat still buzzing on her skin from where he'd touched her. Rhonda sat, and they both continued eating like nothing had changed. Even though inside of her, everything had.

. . .

———

After sharing a delectable flourless chocolate torte, they stepped out into the night. Rhonda's body hummed with an energy she hadn't felt in a long time, and now that they'd started talking, they didn't seem to be able to stop. They talked about everything, from where they bought their clothes to what they ate on Sunday mornings. They talked about potential pets, gifts they were getting for friends for Christmas, places they wanted to travel, and their least favourite things about their jobs.

Rhonda slid into the driver's seat, sad that for two seconds Jordan was outside while she was in, then exhaled with relief when he got in and she turned on the engine. The heater blasted her legs as she pulled out of the parking lot.

The streets were mostly empty on the way back to their hotels because everything shut down early in Lethbridge. Jordan brushed her arm when he saw a church sign that read, "I'm also making a list and checking it twice. God." They laughed, and then Rhonda nearly choked on her spit when Jordan ran his fingers over her wrist and twined his fingers with hers on the console.

She pulled into Jordan's hotel parking lot, breathing like she needed a ventilator, and turned off the engine.

Rhonda spun to him, her grip on his hand tightening. "What if I'm crazy?" Jordan laughed, but she tugged on his arm. "I'm serious. I'm basically a toddler here. I'm—" She pursed her lips.

"You're what?" He looked like he was staring at a baby kitten in the window of an animal shelter.

Rhonda groaned and dropped her head back against the seat. "You think I'm pathetic."

"No." He lifted her hand and pressed his lips to her skin. "I think you're sexy."

"Jordan—"

His fingers brushed her chin, and he turned her head to look at him. "I have no experience with this either. I told you. Every relationship I've been in, I've done wrong."

She blinked, struggling to think with his thumb burning a hole in her jaw. "That's not comforting."

His smile widened. "It should be."

"Why?"

"Because we can do this however we want. If we don't know how it's supposed to be, we can't do it wrong."

"Was that the problem? Your past girlfriends had expectations?"

Jordan's throat worked. "Yeah. And I didn't know them."

Rhonda wet her lips. She twisted her hands in her lap. "But . . . did we already do it wrong?"

Jordan's eyes dropped to her mouth. He exhaled, his fingers moving just enough that her heart forgot its rhythm. "Maybe doing it right wouldn't have worked for us. Misfits, remember?"

"Mmm." She felt pinned to her seat like a moth on a corkboard. Jordan's gaze the pins holding her wings stretched wide and on display.

"I had a nice time tonight."

Me too. The best time. Rhonda tried to form words, but they wouldn't come. For the first time in her life that she could remember, she wasn't hoping this moment would turn into anything more.

She revelled in the exposure. The nakedness. It was perfect, just as it was.

"Are you heading back tomorrow?" Jordan asked, his hand dropping from her face. She felt the loss like throwing off the sheets on a December morning.

Rhonda nodded. "I need to be back for—"

"The Snowballs game."

She grinned. "You know their schedule?"

"Now that we have to share the same rink."

"Right, when do the renovations end?"

Jordan shrugged. "They said after Christmas sometime." He pulled her hand into his lap, and Rhonda peeled herself off the seat. "I get back Sunday night. Talk then?"

She nodded. "Thank you for dinner."

"You're welcome." He lifted her hand one last time and hesitated before brushing his lips over her knuckles. "Have a good night."

"You, too." Words and emotions tumbled through her head like they were pouring from a torn bag of Skittles. Bright yellows and reds, blues and purples. Love and fear and happiness and desperation flashed like they were torn from magazines and pasted into a collage or vision board she never knew she wanted.

Jordan got out of the car. She watched him walk into the hotel then drove in a daze the block and a half to the Marriott. Since she was on the third floor, she took the stairs, needing to do something physical to clear her head.

She walked to her door, scanned her card, and stepped inside, the silence of the room making her head buzz. Rhonda kicked off her shoes and walked to the bathroom, her mind still replaying every moment of the night. The last three days seemed to take up more space than the past year in her memory, and she wasn't mad about it.

She washed her face, brushed her teeth, and changed into her cotton camisole and matching underwear—for all her talk about black lace, this was her favourite sleep set—then crawled into bed.

She pulled the covers up to her chin. She was just about to turn off the lamp when her phone buzzed. Rhonda's heart leapt as she saw Jordan's name on the screen.

JORDAN

I should've kissed you again

Warmth spread over her skin like massage oil.

There's still time

Jordan

If I come over there, I won't leave

I don't see the problem

Jordan

Sorry to disappoint

Not sure disappointment is the right word

Jordan

What is?

Frustrato

JORDAN

> Hm. How frustrated are you, exactly?

For someone who won't come over, I think that's an asshole question

JORDAN

> On a scale of 1-10

Your assholery? 10

JORDAN

> Lol
>
> Sorry. Couldn't stop myself from texting

I'll forgive you. Maybe

JORDAN

> I'll kiss you in Calgary

Promises, promises

He hearted the message, and Rhonda dropped the phone to her

chest. She was lying in her hotel room alone breathing harder than after she finished a run on the treadmill.

She rolled to her side and picked up her phone, scrolling to her reading app. She should've brought her eReader, though she'd already finished her book on there.

Rhonda opened her app and scrolled for top titles. She tapped on the romance section, her eyes lighting up like a kid that walked into a candy store for the first time. She scrolled the brightly coloured books and perused the blurbs. Hot best friend's brother? Wait, hockey players?

Rhonda sat up and pulled a pillow behind her back. Hell, yes. Why had she never been interested in this before?

She borrowed two available titles with her subscription, then flicked to her messages while she waited for them to download on the hotel WiFi. Her thumb lingered over her texts with "J" but then she tapped on the search bar and typed, *Cassie.*

She scrolled through her text thread with her sister and read through the one-sided messages.

> Hey! Just landed in Calgary.

That was back in January when she'd been in Ottawa for a month

> How are the kids doing??

That was in March. And:

> Got tickets to the Oilers game in April. You and Sam want to come with?

Rhonda's throat tightened. She'd made an effort, but now that she knew what real looked like, none of that seemed to fit the bill.

She thought for a moment, chewing her lower lip. Then she started to type.

CHAPTER

Twenty~Five

Jordan

BACK IN CALGARY the next week, Jordan opened the door to his apartment. His internal organs playing musical chairs. Rhonda wore an oversized sweater and jeans. Her hips looked so damn good in jeans.

"Hey." He stepped out into the hall and let the door swing closed behind him.

Rhonda smirked up at him. "I thought I was coming in there."

"You will." He ran his hands up her arms. Her sweater felt like velvet, but her skin was better. He planted his hands in the hollow of her neck. "I made you a promise."

Rhonda let out a breath, but he didn't give her a chance to speak. He lowered his head, and she tipped her chin to meet him. He didn't waste time warming her up, just kissed her until she had to suck in a ragged breath.

Jordan pulled back, his lips humming. "Glad you could make it." He turned and pulled her into the apartment before he could press her against the wall and spend the rest of the night in the hallway.

Chubs was still in the middle of telling a story about a particularly bad date, complete with hand gestures that, with zero context, looked like he was miming a porno. Ellie, his love interest from the gym whose biceps could rival his, rolled her eyes and dealt out the cards.

Jordan introduced her to everyone. Chubs, Cam, and Patrick were the only members of Pucks Deep there. Well, Patrick was starting in January. He liked to get the new guys plugged in as soon as possible.

But this was a risk. Patrick had communicated with Sean and the Snowballs when he first planned to relocate. He talked with most teams in the area. Not that he had a relationship, but he didn't understand the way Elite League worked yet.

Jordan had made them all promise they wouldn't say anything about Rhonda even though he knew Chubs and Cam were good. Rhonda hadn't said anything explicitly but every time the Snowballs came up, she turtled. If anyone was going to break her cover, it wasn't going to be him or his teammates.

Rhonda slid into the seat next to Jordan, and even after the poker game started, he had to work to focus on anything besides her. Every time he saw her, there was something new to discover. The lines next to her nose when she frowned, studying her cards. The way her fingers tapped on her thigh, or how she let out a little breath before she laughed at a joke.

"So what's Jordan's tell?" Rhonda asked.

Jordan raised an eyebrow. "Good luck. They don't know it."

Chubs laughed. "He gets more confident."

"That's not a tell, that's my homeostasis." Jordan put a few chips in, waiting for the flop.

Cam shook his head. "He changes it. He's pulling psychological BS on us, messing with our heads."

Rhonda's eyes sparkled. "Hmm."

"Hmm, what?" Jordan watched the cards, the feeling of her eyes on him making his blood rush.

Rhonda laughed, then put in her chips to match. "What happens when I run out? Do we barter? Strip?"

Chubs nodded solemnly. "Strip. Absolutely."

Ellie gave him a look. "Did you wear clean boxers?"

Chubs looked down and pretended to pull at the waistband of his pants before Ellie smacked his hand away. Oh, Jordan liked her.

The game continued, and Rhonda fit in seamlessly. She laughed at Chubs' jokes, joined forces with Ellie to heckle Cam, and ended up calling his bluff to win all her chips back and then some.

When the rounds finally ended, Rhonda stood and stretched, her sweater riding up just enough to show a sliver of skin. She glanced down, the sparkle in her eyes telling him she knew exactly what she was doing.

Chubs and Ellie left first, then Cam and his roommate. Rhonda walked into the kitchen with him, watching as he loaded the glasses into the dishwasher.

"Thanks for letting me crash." Rhonda said, her voice breathy. "I should probably get going."

Jordan set the last glass on the top rack and turned to dry his hands. He walked with her to the front door. Rhonda put on her shoes, then turned and paused.

He stepped forward and wrapped her in a hug. "That was fun."

"It was." Her voice was muffled against his shoulder, her breath warming the fabric of his shirt.

She pulled back and dropped her hands from around his waist, then fidgeted with the hem of her sweater. "So. See you soon."

"I'll text you."

Her mouth quirked. "Okay." She walked out of the apartment, and Jordan had the urge to walk with her down to the lot.

To make sure she got into her car okay. But he knew she wouldn't want that. Or at least, didn't know how to handle it.

He had to take things slow. Jordan adjusted himself and went back to the kitchen. Not rushing ahead was for both their good. But it still sucked balls.

———

For the next three weeks, they saw each other as much as possible, which amounted to four face-to-face interactions. Rhonda travelled twice, once to Sylvan Lake and once to Grande Prairie. He joked that she was visiting his hometown, and she almost appreciated it.

She met him once for lunch between shifts, and he met her for a late dinner on the weekend after giving face time with the team after a win against C-Biscuit.

Rhonda told him more about her dad, and he made a point to give up time with her when she needed to see her friends. The last thing he wanted was for her to see any of her old man in him. Since Jordan loved grand gestures, that was already a potential strike against him.

Now it was two and a half weeks before Christmas, and they sat next to each other at intermission for the Nutcracker in the Jubilee Auditorium.

Jordan ran his thumb over the inside of her palm. "What do you know about Curtis and his wife?"

"Snowballs' Curtis?" she asked. Jordan nodded. Rhonda thought for a moment. "He's a family guy. They have four kids. Why?"

Jordan brushed a strand of hair away from her cheek. "I coach his oldest son. He and this other kid aren't sympatico at the moment."

"Ah. Hoping not to tattle?"

He grinned. "No, I love tattling. I just need to know how best to do it."

"Maximize the trouble this kid will get in."

Jordan laughed. "Exactly. See? You get it."

The lights dimmed, and he settled back in his seat. Rhonda leaned over. "I'll call Curtis's wife. I'll let you know if I hear anything that could help."

It was only two days later when he and Rhonda sat in the hospital coffee shop that she followed up. Rhonda had just finished a meeting with Dr. Mallory. She said she'd sweat through her shirt, but he couldn't tell.

Rhonda wrapped her hands around the warm ceramic mug. It was already getting dark at four in the afternoon, the sky outside the coffee shop a deep indigo. He still had three hours on his shift. He'd been storing up time for a couple of absences over the holidays where he was going to need to take time off.

"I think I might be a genius at this now." She took a sip of coffee.

Jordan laughed. "What now?"

Rhonda gave him a look. "Just, being open. Telling people the truth." She set her mug down. "I talked with Sasha."

"Jace's mom."

She nodded. "I told her about how I don't talk with my sister, just put it right out there, and she said that's her biggest fear for her kids. Then she said that Jace doesn't want to have anything to do with his siblings."

Jordan's brow furrowed. "Sad."

Rhonda sighed. "Jace hasn't been the easiest to deal with at home. He's been giving them a lot of attitude, not doing his homework, and generally being a pain in the ass."

"So, teenage boy."

Rhonda frowned. "Maybe. But after everything you told me, I don't think it would be a bad thing to say something. I think they'd be grateful for some insight."

He nodded. "Perfect. Thank you."

Rhonda beamed. "You're welcome."

Jordan took a drink and leaned back in his seat. "So, you helped me."

"I did."

"Which means I get to help you with something. I get a freebie."

She scoffed. "That's not how this works."

Jordan was already scooting his chair back. He stood. "Meet me tomorrow morning. I'll text you the address."

He grinned, then shared a location for his favourite tire shop as he walked down the hall. He'd already called to make sure they had the right snow tires in stock.

He was about to slip his phone back into the pocket of his scrubs when a text came through. Unknown number. He wouldn't have clicked on it, but his name was in the preview.

Hey, Jordan. This is Anne.

And Tina!

Jordan stopped short. Anne and Tina. Those were Rhonda's friends.

Hey?

Anne

Sorry to weird you out. Just wanted to say, we've never seen Rhonda like this

Tina

What Anne's trying to say is: if you hurt her, we will kick your ass

Jordan laughed out loud.

I'll kick my own ass

TINA

Perfect

ANNE

Okay. That's all

Jordan gave that message a thumbs-up, then continued to the nurse's station. Never seen her like this. He'd take that.

RHONDA

RHONDA PULLED into the parking lot of the Ice Centre, the moonlight glinting off the man-made plowed snowbanks that lined the edges. It was mid-December, the kind of cold that bit through your coat and made you wish for the warmth of a fire and a hot drink. She stepped out of her car, her breath puffing out in clouds, and pulled her scarf tighter around her neck.

Tonight, she wasn't there for practice but for the annual white elephant party. It was a tradition, one that felt especially poignant this year. In so many ways, her life had shifted, and Rhonda was beginning to feel more settled in herself than she ever had before. Every routine moment seemed brand new.

Things with Jordan hadn't been perfect since Lethbridge, but that almost made it more so. If something happened and she tightened up, didn't talk to him for a couple of days, he was right there when she was ready. She had gone to the tire shop, but she wouldn't let him pay for even a snack in the vending machine. She did, however, allow him to buy her dinner. Twice.

Since Sunday, they'd been texting and calling every day, but she'd shown up early for this white elephant party for one reason and one reason only.

Rhonda scanned the parking lot. No truck. She thought about waiting in the parking lot, but Kelty had just pulled in and spotted her. She waved, and Rhonda joined her to walk into the lobby where they were meeting everyone after practice.

"Hey, you two!" Emma called out and ran toward them. Apparently everyone was early. "I'm so glad you could make it."

Rhonda gave her a hug. "You promised there'd be rum and eggnog."

Emma laughed, and when Rhonda looked over her shoulder, the prompt attendance suddenly made sense. Delia Melise was standing next to Jack in the entry, who was in an animated discussion with Fly. Rhonda had only met Fly once. Used to be the captain of the Snowballs before Sean.

Jenna ran up and yanked her attention from the celebrities. "I have to talk to you." She pulled her away from the group.

"I thought Delia was still on tour?" Rhonda hissed.

Jenna nodded. "She is. They just flew in for today, and then I think Jack has a game in Oregon or something. She's heading out to New York." She stopped next to the windows and whirled, her eyes gleaming.

"Jenna—"

"We have a baby."

Rhonda's heart dropped into her pelvis. "What?"

"She's sixteen months—"

"Fostering?"

Jenna shook her head, her eyes glassy. "Adoption. We finalize the paperwork Monday."

"What?" Rhonda shrieked, and Jenna motioned for her to keep her voice down.

"I know! Thankfully I already had the nursery set up from the last time—"

"When? When do you get her?"

Jenna shook out her hands. "Christmas Eve."

Rhonda pulled Jenna into a hug so tight, she might've bruised her ribs. "I'm so happy for you." Jenna squeezed tighter, and as Rhonda pulled back, she caught movement at the other end of the lobby. The doors opened. Jenna stepped back, and Rhonda's already racing heart kicked up another notch.

Jordan was the first of his teammates to step through the door, his dark hair curling out from under his backwards baseball cap. He laughed at something one of his teammates said. Not Chubs or Cam. Those were the only two she knew.

Jordan strode across the lobby with his bag slung over his shoulder. The muscles in his arms flexed with each step, and she wanted to scold him for only wearing a T-shirt.

Until he looked up.

He did a double take and his steps slowed for the briefest of seconds. Then he dropped his eyes and kept walking toward the stairs. She turned her head and saw the Snowballs ascending, fresh from the showers. Country and Ryan led the pack with Tyler and Sean close behind.

Rhonda's pulse rushed in her ears. This had happened once before. Back then, the idea of the Snowballs seeing her with Jordan felt like a death sentence. But now? She was going to have to tell them at some point because quitting Jordan wasn't an option.

Her heart fluttered like a moth around a porchlight as she put a hand on Jenna's shoulder. "Hold this? I promise I'll explain." Jenna gave her a puzzled look as Rhonda handed her the gift she'd been holding. Rhonda jogged forward, bolting faster across the lobby until she could reach out for Jordan's hand.

He turned in surprise, and she threw her arms around his neck and his bag slipped from his arm, nearly knocking her sideways. He quickly dropped it as she pulled his lips down to hers.

And then she was floating. The warmth of his skin. The familiar scent of his cologne. The softness of his lips, and the rough stubble on his jaw.

A shockwave ripped through her as his hands pressed into her lower back. His mouth was minty, his tongue cool as he flicked it over her lips.

Then he tensed, and the reality of where they were and who was standing in the lobby rushed back in. She hadn't asked him. She'd only been thinking about herself—about how she was okay giving away their secret. She hadn't even thought to find out if he was.

Rhonda pulled back, her lips tingling. "I'm sorry. I—"

Jordan kissed her again, drawing the breath from her lungs. When she pulled back a second time, he watched her, his eyes dark and hooded. She ran her fingernails over his chin.

"You know what this means?" He asked, his voice low and rough.

Her lips twitched as she nodded. "I know exactly what this means."

Jordan's eyes seemed to liquify. "I didn't know you'd be here."

"I wanted to surprise you. Preferably in the parking lot." She shrugged, her cheeks starting to flush. "Have a good practice?"

Jordan reluctantly let go of her and picked up his bag. "Not sure I'll be able to focus, but I'll try." He winked, then walked on toward the stairs.

Rhonda watched him go, then turned to find every pair of eyes in the lobby trained on her. Her confidence from seconds before waned, so she did what she'd done so well for thirty years of her life and pretended nothing happened. She slapped on a smile and walked back to Jenna, plucking her gift from her friend's hand.

Jenna gaped at her. "Ummm . . . "

"Later." Rhonda linked her arm in Jenna's and started toward the exit.

They walked across the street to One Place and found a central table to sit at. The whole pub had been booked out for them, so there wouldn't be any real competition, but she still wanted a good view of the gift opening.

The others filtered in, and Rhonda busied herself with bringing over pitchers of beer and plates and napkins for the pizza that was about to come out of the brick oven. Jenna watched her like a hawk, but once Country and the other guys were there, they didn't have a moment to hash this out alone. And it was going to take a good hashing.

They piled the gifts on a table in the corner and all drew a number out of Darcy's hat. He got the first pick, which was arguably the worst, so nobody accused him of cheating.

Darcy chose a purple bedazzled bag, then sat back on his stool and pulled out the tissue paper. He reached in and pulled out a large rubber phallus, purple and sparkly, with a suction cup base.

Laughter erupted around the table.

Tyler raised his voice. "Okay, who raided Brett's bathroom."

Brett flipped him off.

Number two, Curtis's wife Sasha picked a medium sized box. Inside she found a pillow with the words "Open for Sex" on one side and "Don't Ask" on the other. She clutched it to her chest, kicking her feet with glee.

The pillow got stolen almost immediately. Darcy changed his grip on the dildo every round in the hopes of making it look more appealing to the masses.

Rhonda just about died when Anne opened up her pair of boxer briefs with the words "I licked it so it's mine" across the front, and then all laughter died when Fly opened up a set of custom shot glasses decorated with the Pucks Deep logo.

Tina's eyes shot to hers. Rhonda waved it off. It didn't need to be a big deal and—

"I think Rhonda needs those," Darcy quipped.

Rhonda's blood turned to ice. "Excuse me?"

He held out his hands. "Not like it's a secret anymore. Everyone saw your tongue down his throat."

Anne cleared her throat. "Okay—"

"No." Rhonda drew a deep breath and grinned. "I can take a joke. Better than Darcy can take purple sparkles."

The group erupted, and she poured herself another beer. But then Sean spoke up from the end of the table. "I just hope you're being careful."

Rhonda's jaw clenched. She exhaled and counted to three to make sure she wasn't going to rip him a new one, then stood and held up a hand. "Alright, let's just get this over with."

Everyone quieted.

This was not how she'd intended to rip off the Band-Aid, but here went nothing. "First of all, I love you all. You know that, right?" She waited for nods. "And I know you all probably think I'm certifiably insane to be seeing Jordan." She paused, looking around the table. "You all think Pucks Deep players are a bunch of assholes and you hate Jordan?"

"We don't hate—" Suraj started, then stopped when he saw Rhonda's eyes flashing.

She pointed at Sean. "You hated Tyler at first. When he started dating Emma." Then she pointed at Jenna. "You hated Country. For like, a minute before you remembered you had a lady boner for him for thirteen years."

Country snorted, and Tyler looked a little smug.

"All I'm saying," Rhonda continued, "is that when you get to know someone, they're usually pretty great." She sat back on her stool and held up her slip of paper with the number nine. "Jordan's great. I was into him before I ever knew he was on Pucks Deep, and I almost didn't do anything about it when I found out he was. He's my boyfriend. Get over it and hand me those damn shot glasses."

CHAPTER
Twenty~Seven

JORDAN

JORDAN CLOCKED out at the urgent care, his shoulders slumping as his shift officially came to an end. He rubbed his eyes, the fluorescent lights glaring down from the ceiling.

"You out of here?" one of the nurses called from the station.

"Yeah, I'm out. Merry Christmas, everyone." He waved and headed for the break room. He opened the bag he'd stashed under the sink earlier and pulled out a variety of snacks. Protein bars, fruit, assorted gourmet teas and coffee. He knew what the other nurses liked, specifically not more candy, and he'd picked up their favourites.

He set the snacks on the table, arranging them neatly, and then pulled out a handful of gifts. Personalized hand sanitizers and packets of gourmet hot chocolate. Nothing fancy. He left them on the counter and avoided the main hallway, opting to slip out the back door to the parking lot.

The early morning frost clung to the streets, the air crisp and biting. He shoved his hands into his pockets as he walked to his truck. The second he closed the door and started the engine, he re-read the messages from Anne and Tina.

ANNE

> Rhonda just cooked the Snowballs

TINA

> She called you her boyfriend. Told them to get over it

ANNE

> I tried to kiss her for you, but she wasn't into it

He'd planned this weekend in the hopes that they'd be at a place to enjoy it, and after Rhonda had kissed him in the lobby? He could barely wait the eight hours until he got to see her.

The best part? Rhonda had no idea. Anne and Tina had been working things behind the scenes, and now all their plans were about to snap into place.

Jordan drove home and trudged to the elevator. He needed to sleep. He knew that. But he could already tell his brain wasn't cooperating. He walked to his apartment, kicked off his shoes, and headed straight to his bedroom.

He stripped off his scrubs and threw them into the washer, then collapsed onto his bed. He stared at the ceiling, willing his thoughts to slow down. He had to be up in a few hours if he was going to get to the hotel on time, and the clock was ticking.

Jordan rolled over and checked his phone one last time. There was a message from Anne confirming everything was set. Tina had responded with a thumbs-up, and Rhonda had apologized profusely that she wasn't going to see him that weekend.

He chuckled and set the phone on his nightstand, then forced his eyes shut.

———

The alarm blared in his ear, and Jordan jolted awake. He blinked, his eyes gritty and his mouth dry. It felt like he'd barely slept, but his heart had already jolted like he'd been defibrillated.

He threw off the covers and leapt out of bed, then stumbled into the washroom and turned on the shower. The hot water pelted his skin and woke him up fully. He washed his hair, soaped up his body, then stood under the stream, letting the warmth seep into his bones.

When he finally shut off the water, he grabbed a towel and dried off, then pulled on the clothes he'd laid out the night before. A pair of jeans, a long-sleeved shirt. He was half tempted to wear a clean pair of scrubs since Rhonda went feral every time she saw him in them.

He grabbed his phone and keys from the nightstand, then put on his socks and shoes and left his apartment.

He was just turning off Deerfoot when a call from an unknown Calgary number came through on his phone. Jordan debated, but answered it just in case it was a problem with the hotel.

"Hello?" Jordan spoke up to make sure he was clear over the speaker.

"Jordan?"

"Yep."

"This is Curtis. Jace's dad."

Jordan tapped the steering wheel. *Jace's dad.* Not Curtis from the Snowballs. "Hey, thanks for getting back to me."

"Yeah, I got your message. I thought since it's the holidays, we'd just talk on the phone. If that's okay?"

"Sure. I wanted to talk about the issue with Jace and Ethan."

Curtis exhaled. "Yeah, we heard about it. I want you to know that we're taking it seriously. We want both boys to feel safe and respected during practice. I'm sorry I reacted the way I did when you first brought it up."

An apology? Jordan blinked. "Thank you. And agreed. I don't expect them to be best friends, but you remember what it's like in the locker room at that age. We can't be in there to police them."

"Wouldn't expect that. He's seventeen. He needs to figure that out."

Jordan hesitated. He didn't want to out Ethan. "I'm not sure what all Jace told you—"

"He filled us in on the attempted kiss, if that's what you're referring to."

Jordan breathed a silent sigh of relief. "That's the one."

"Sad to see a friendship shredded like that. They're going to need each other."

Jordan blew out a breath. "Yeah."

"Well, thanks for looking out for these boys. I'll see what we can do."

Jordan's grip on the steering wheel relaxed. "Great. Appreciate that." He expected Curtis to end the call, but instead he cleared his throat.

"Uh . . . I just wanted to say, I'm open—I mean, some of us are open—to talking about our teams as well."

Jordan stared at the road bending in front of him. "Not sure what you mean, bud."

"Snowballs. Pucks Deep."

Jordan couldn't think of a damn thing to say to that. Luckily he didn't have to because Curtis was talking again.

"We got our asses handed to us the other night. Might be good to clear the air."

Jordan almost laughed. He had to be talking about Rhonda. "That would be good. I'll talk to the guys and see what we can set up."

"Right. Merry Christmas."

"Merry Christmas." Jordan pressed the button on his steering wheel, then hit the brakes. He'd been so focused on the conversation, he almost missed his exit into Canmore.

CHAPTER
Twenty-Eight

RHONDA STOOD AT HER DOOR, gripping her overnight bag, hot pink with black leopard spots and a bright blue zipper. It was her staple for weekend getaways. She quickly rifled through the contents of her bag, making sure she had everything she needed. She'd packed in a rush, so her mind ran through the list. Toothbrush, makeup, a change of clothes, and her favourite shampoo and conditioner. A hot water bottle for her feet—they were always freezing. Her silk hair wrap so her curls didn't go insane while she slept.

Anne's car pulled into the driveway, and she hurried out the door, locking it behind her. She jogged down the steps and climbed into the passenger seat.

Anne grinned at her. "Ready?"

"A hundred percent." She tossed her bag into the back seat, and Anne reversed back onto the street. Maybe she should've said ninety percent. She was excited to spend time with them, but there was a part of her that wished she could be with Jordan.

Anne would've understood, she'd ditched them plenty of times to see Gary. But Anne had been so amped about this weekend. Rhonda couldn't say no.

Rhonda turned in her seat. Anne was dressed in a pair of black leggings and a cozy waffle knit top. "How far to the cabin?"

Anne shrugged. "Should only be forty-five minutes or so."

Rhonda adjusted her seat. "Where did you say it was?"

Anne focused on the road. "It's just outside of Canmore. I think you'll love it." She turned her head, a bright smile on her face. "So, how was your week?"

Rhonda told her about the ongoing discussions with Rocky Ridge, then about her meetings up north. Community pharmacies were about to take major pay cuts after the government promoted opening pharmacist walk-in clinics because of the physician shortage. Rhonda was working to support them, and she was grateful Cantra was making it a priority, as well.

Anne filled her in on all the things they'd been cramming in with Melissa while she was in town. Rhonda felt a little guilty about not being around for that, but Melissa wasn't leaving until after the new year.

She'd never apologized for making her work a priority, but she had been seeing things differently as of late. What was the point of getting promoted if it didn't allow her to live the life she wanted? It had never been about her setting boundaries, it had been that she didn't know which boundaries to set.

"Do you miss all the excitement?" Anne asked, lifting her water from the cupholder and taking a sip from the straw.

"Of . . . ?"

"You know, meeting new people."

Rhonda considered this. "I don't feel like I'm missing anything." It was the truth, but it was accompanied with another thought riding on its back. Instead of stuffing it down, she spoke it. "I am worried that I will someday. That this with Jordan will wear off and I'll feel trapped."

Anne exhaled. "Yeah. I always thought the goal was to feel settled."

"Gross."

Anne laughed out loud. "I said 'thought,' like past tense."

"I always wanted to be in charge, but I never wanted to feel like I'd arrived. Reached the finish line." Rhonda twirled a curl around her finger. "Maybe with work. I guess I did want that with work."

She glanced up at the sign for Canmore, and Anne turned on her blinker.

"I'm going to grab gas." Anne glanced at the dashboard. "I think there's a station just off the highway."

Rhonda nodded. "Sounds good." She looked out the window, the landscape growing more picturesque by the second as they drew closer to the Rockies. Wind swirled snow around the jagged peaks, making the sky around them blur.

They merged onto a smaller road that wound through town. Her eyes snagged on every medical facility they passed. Because Canmore was so close to Banff, there were more per capita than other towns.

Rhonda sat up a little straighter. "Do we need to grab food or anything?" Even though Tina loved to plan, she didn't want to be that friend that showed up and expected everything to be done for her.

Anne grimaced. "Oh, shoot. I didn't realize we needed to turn in there." Anne's hands tightened on the wheel. "I think there's another gas station a bit further in."

Rhonda pulled out her phone and scanned her email while she waited. A few seconds later, she looked up and frowned as Anne turned into the parking lot of a massive stone building. The place looked like a medieval castle with its imposing stone walls and elegant archways.

Anne stopped in the turnaround. Rhonda reached out and pressed her hand against her friend's forehead. Anne laughed and pushed her away.

"Just making sure you don't have a fever."

Anne turned with a huge smile on her face. "No fever."

"This isn't gas."

"Well aware." Anne pointed out the window and Rhonda turned to look. There was a sign with cursive lettering. Canmore Cascade.

The gears turned in her head. *Why did she know that name?*

Anne put the car in park. "I think you should get your bag and—"

"The auction." Rhonda's eyes widened, and her breath caught in her throat. She turned to Anne, her pulse quickening. "December twentieth. The auction. Jordan spent ten grand for a weekend here." She tapped her phone screen and checked the date.

Anne's lips twitched. "Huh."

Rhonda's mind raced, her thoughts a jumbled mess. "Hold on. Hold on." She put her hands out, trying to make sense of it all. "Are Tina and Melissa at a cabin waiting for us?"

Anne practically squealed. "No."

Rhonda's heart pounded in her ears. "So—?"

"Jordan's in there waiting for you! Get the hell out of my car!"

Rhonda spun to look at her bag in the backseat. "I didn't bring lingerie."

"Yeah, we couldn't figure out how to ask you to do that without things getting weird."

Rhonda laughed. "You guys have been texting him? How did I not know this?"

Anne held up her phone. "You did put us in a group chat."

She scoffed. "Behind my back?"

"I think you'll forgive us in about five minutes."

Rhonda's throat tightened. "I don't want you to think Jordan is more important—"

"Get. Out." Anne laughed and shoved her shoulder. "We'll have plenty of girl time next week. You're coming to the spa, right?" Rhonda nodded. "Great, then I'll expect a full report then."

She couldn't think of anything to say other than "Thank you." She opened the door, grabbed her overnight bag from the back seat, and walked up the stone steps to the front entrance. Rhonda turned and waved to Anne, then walked through the spinning front door.

The lobby was breathtaking. Rhonda walked through the double doors and stood rooted to the spot. Wooden beams stretched across a vaulted ceiling. A rustic chandelier cast soft golden light across polished stone floors, and a grand staircase with a hand-carved wooden balustrade spiralled up to the right. In a corner, a stone fireplace rose from floor to ceiling, and plush velvet sofas in deep greens sat around a refurbished farmhouse coffee table atop inset herringbone wood flooring.

She stepped forward, and a man looked up from his computer behind the counter. His face lit up. "You must be Rhonda."

Rhonda didn't speak for a moment. She was still processing the fact that she was there and not still in the car with Anne.

The man grinned. "Your suite is the only one on the top level. Just up that staircase and down the hall to your left."

Rhonda's heart pounded. "Thanks." He didn't hand her a key. That meant Jordan was already up there.

"Enjoy your stay." The man's voice echoed through the lobby as she walked up the stairs, her hands shaking.

Exquisite photographs of the Rockies hung along the walls, each one lit by a singular goosehead lamp. Rhonda's footsteps echoed against the stone, and she tried to breathe through the rushing of her pulse.

When she reached the door, she stopped and stared at the grain lines in the carved wood. Jordan's door. *The right room.* At least she didn't have to pee this time.

She drew in a deep breath, lifted her hand, and knocked.

CHAPTER
Twenty-Nine

JORDAN OPENED the door to their suite. He wasn't shirtless like he'd been the first time. She was only mildly disappointed.

"Hey."

Jordan grinned. "Hey." His eyes drank her in. "I have a washroom if you need it."

Rhonda stepped over the threshold and tipped her chin to look up at him. "Yes, please." She wanted to jump into his arms, but nerves kept her arms clamped at her sides.

Jordan slapped her hip as she passed him, and she took in the room. It was a vision of modern elegance—clean lines, minimalistic decor, and a monochromatic palette of greys and whites, broken only by the occasional accents of brushed steel and gold.

Gorgeous. But ten grand gorgeous? "I'm so sorry."

"About what?"

She turned to him. "You spent a small fortune on this."

Jordan smirked. "I have savings."

"But did you want to spend it on this?" *On me?* Her throat

tightened. That was really what she was asking, but she'd never say it out loud.

The smile on his face shifted into something deep and intense. "Hell, yes."

Jordan stood with his hands in his pockets, and the memory of seeing him for the first time hit her like a bus. They were such different people in Medicine Hat. Each so sure they knew what they wanted.

Well, who she wanted then hadn't changed. But how she wanted him . . . She didn't understand then that she was only seeing the tip of the iceberg.

Which was why this felt a million times more terrifying.

Rhonda bit her lip. She knew him, now. Knew that he flipped his fork upside down when he ate. That he only checked his phone once an hour so he didn't get distracted at work. That he kept a flosser in his pocket just in case.

Her heart felt like a pool pump. She took a step farther into the space, scanning the floor-to-ceiling windows that framed the Rocky Mountains against the darkening sky. But it was the details that made her breath catch. The low-profile coffee table had a bucket with champagne on ice sitting ready to be popped. She glanced around and noticed the fake, glowing candles scattered across the countertops and shelves.

"They wouldn't let me use real ones." Jordan's voice was right behind her, a low rumble vibrating through her bones. His movements were fluid, like a shadow coming to life, wrapping over her so slowly, she was absorbed pixel by pixel.

His arms finally made contact and snaked around her middle. "I heard I'm your boyfriend."

Rhonda grinned, her breath hitching. "Oh? Who told you that?" She turned her head to the side, her hair sticking to his cheek like Velcro.

Jordan lowered his head, nudging her shirt to the side so his lips could find skin. "Your friends."

"You're a sneaky bastard."

He chuckled. "You love it." His hand traced over hers, and he took her bag from her hands, setting it on the floor.

She turned to face him, not able to slow the breaths filling and rushing from her lungs. She searched his face. "Didn't you work a night shift?"

He nodded. "I slept a few hours this morning."

Rhonda pressed a hand to his chest and heat flashing through her. "I swear, if you tell me you only want to cuddle tonight—"

Jordan threw back his head and laughed. He pulled her flush against him, his hand cupping her jaw. "I want to wreck you tonight."

Rhonda's spirit left her body at the mental image of him taking her apart piece by piece, then putting her back together. "Mmm."

"I think we've spent enough time taking it slow." His eyes locked on hers.

She didn't know if it was possible for a human to purr, but she was about to find out. "Agreed."

Jordan's face sobered. His grip tightened. "I want this with you. I'm choosing this with you."

His words were intentional, and Rhonda swirled them around in her head. Choosing. Not reacting. Not just giving in.

That was the difference.

The first time she'd shown up at his door, she was scrabbling for control. For release. She held the paddle, but was trying to push against the current. Now she was learning to lift it and travel faster. To give in to the flow and only choose where she directed the boat.

Jordan's thumb brushed over her jaw, his lips grazing her forehead, and her eyes fluttered closed. "Do I need to stop? Am I influencing your response?"

Rhonda gripped onto his hand. "Don't you dare stop." She blinked her eyes open and looked straight at him. "I chose you in the hall. At the Founder's Event."

That moment had been one of the scariest of her life. To admit she wanted more, but that she didn't know how to get it.

Jordan dropped his forehead to hers. "I know."

"But I'm glad we took our time. I didn't know if I could be that person." With that, every nerve in her body came to life in a rush.

"Now you know?"

Rhonda laughed. "Hell, no."

Jordan brushed her lips to his. "Good. I think that's good."

"How is that good?"

"Because I want to figure that out together."

The flickering light of the candles threw golden ovals on the walls as her breath fanned out over his collarbone. She wanted to devour him. To tear off his shirt and bite into his skin. "I'm so turned on, my thoughts are turning vampiric."

Jordan grinned against her cheek. "I'm excited to see where that leads."

Her hands slipped under his shirt, pressing against his chest. "It's going to lead somewhere real weird if you don't start touching me."

Jordan laughed then pulled at her shirt. Rhonda lifted her arms so he could pull it over her head, and before she could drop them, Jordan's mouth was on her. She gasped, her elbows on his shoulders, her fingers tightening in his hair.

Jordan's lips moved over her bra, her ribs, her collarbone, her neck. Rhonda's knees went weak as he murmured her name, his breath hot against her ear.

He knew it.

And that was why this felt nothing like before. She'd never been this close to someone, never let herself be this vulnerable. She was standing on the edge of a cliff, her toes curling, her mind spinning as she readied herself to leap.

Rhonda pulled back, her breath coming fast as she looked up at him. "What do you think about getting into the hot tub?"

Jordan exhaled, his hands still crimping her waist. "Yes. Sure."

Her eyes flicked down to her bag. *No tits, Rhonda.* She grinned to herself. Tonight there would be *all* the tits.

Rhonda followed Jordan into the bedroom and gasped. The bed. It sat under a full glass roof, illuminated by the deep pinks and purples of sunset. She unclasped her bra and dropped it on the chair, then pulled off her pants and underwear.

It wasn't anything Jordan hadn't seen before, but his eyes still darkened as he scanned her body. Twice.

He ran a hand through his hair, then stalked into the bathroom and grabbed two towels. He set them on the bed and pulled off his clothes. Rhonda watched every second of it, grinning as he freed himself from his boxer briefs.

He picked up the towels, and she walked to the sliding glass doors. She slid them open and stepped out onto the patio, the cool night air instantly making her skin pebble.

Rhonda wrapped her arms around herself, and they walked over to the steaming hot tub. Jordan reached down and hit the button to start the jets, then held out a hand to help her in.

She climbed the two steps then dropped her foot into the water and sucked in a breath. She set her other foot on the second step, then slipped down into the water to her shoulders.

"Shit, that's good." Jordan followed her in and settled on the same side of the tub.

Rhonda leaned back, her eyes fixed on the water, on the bubbles swirling around her hands as she moved them back and forth. The stars started to peek through the twilight sky, and the sun was setting behind the mountains in a wash of deep blues.

Jordan found her under the water and pulled her against his side.

"I got a call earlier today." Rhonda looked up at him.

"Yeah?" Jordan raised an eyebrow.

"It was Dr. Mallory. He told me that they were going to add

Reviact to the formulary on a trial basis." Somehow this felt like foreplay.

A slow smile spread across his face. "I'm not surprised."

She dropped her chin and kissed his cool shoulder. "Thank you."

"For what? You did all the work."

She smoothed her hand over his stomach. "For helping me. For taking care of me." She dropped her hand lower.

Jordan exhaled in a rush, dropping his head back. His hand slid up her arm, eager to stroke. To hold.

The water rolled against their bodies as they touched. Explored. Jordan's hands grew more frantic, and energy flared through her. She loved making him feel this way. Making him desperate.

Rhonda twisted and climbed onto the seat, throwing her leg over his and straddling him.

"Rhonda—"

"Shh." She pressed her finger to his lips. "Let me take care of you for once."

She discovered him. Loved him. The best way she knew how.

And suddenly everything she'd learned, every choice she'd made along the way, didn't feel stuck or wasted. They'd all been leading her to this moment. This person.

This man who knew her name.

Epilogue 1

Rhonda

THE THOMPSONS' house bustled with energy by the time Rhonda parked on the street and walked up the driveway. She stomped the snow from her boots, then slipped them off in the entry and hung her coat.

The aroma of roasted turkey, honey-glazed ham, and spiced mulled wine filled the air. She followed the smell into the living room, where a towering Christmas tree adorned with delicate glass ornaments, twinkling fairy lights, and strands of popcorn stood proudly in the corner. Evergreen garlands draped over the mantel, and stockings hung in a neat row. The room was bathed in the soft glow of a crackling fire, and classic holiday music played softly in the background.

Rhonda's chest threatened to cave in. This. All of this.

She drew a deep breath and scanned the room. She spotted Jenna and Kelty near the dining table laden with real charcuterie and waved.

Kelty motioned for her to join them.

Rhonda grabbed a glass of mulled wine from the sideboard and perched on the arm of the couch near Jenna and Kelty. She took a sip as Jenna gesticulated.

". . . it was normal stuff, right? Breaking down plays, chirping the refs, usual banter. But this guy—this *guy*—he starts commenting, like, every five minutes. Same username. 'Puck-Chaser69.'"

Rhonda raised an eyebrow. "Well, there's your first red flag."

Jenna held up a hand as if to say, *wait for it*. "He's not just commenting. He's analyzing *me*. Like, 'Jenna touches her collarbone at 3:15' And, 'her hand drops below the table, 4:03'"

Rhonda's jaw dropped. "Wow."

Kelty clapped a hand over her mouth. "I'm so sorry."

Jenna lowered her voice. "And then he DM'd me. Asked if I had any pictures of what my feet looked like under the desk."

Rhonda choked on her drink. "Okay, hear me out. New subscription-only option—"

Kelty laughed, and Jenna looked like she was going to be sick. "I blocked him. And then Country responded to his last comment with, 'Appreciate the dedication, bud, but maybe dial it back to, like, a 2.'"

Kelty doubled over. "Country, what the hell."

Rhonda laughed, trying not to slosh her wine. A sudden ache hit her chest. She wanted Jordan there. She wanted him to know these people, for them to know him. She made a resolution right there to force the Snowballs further out of their comfort zone. They didn't have to accept Pucks Deep, but they needed to get used to Jordan being around.

Jenna glanced across the room, her eyes locking onto Country who cradled a baby girl against his chest.

Rhonda sucked in a breath. "Is that her?"

Jenna nodded, her hand fluttering at her throat. "Hope. She's so perfect."

Rhonda was so happy for them, she thought she might burst. She wanted to rush over and ogle her, but Country was surrounded by his teammates like Rafiki from Lion King, his face lit up like a Christmas tree. *Later.*

Rhonda wrapped Jenna in a one handed hug just as her phone buzzed against her hip. She pulled back and checked the screen. *Mom.* Jenna gave her a look.

"Just a sec." She handed Jenna her wine and slipped out of the living room, leaving the hum of voices and clinking glasses behind her. She stepped into the kitchen and then out in her stocking feet onto the porch.

She swiped to answer the call, bracing herself. "Hey, Mom."

"Hi!" Her mom's voice was surprisingly warm. "How's the party?"

Rhonda leaned against the porch railing and regretted it instantly. Freezing. "Great, I just got here."

"Sorry to interrupt—"

"No, it's fine. What's up?"

"Nothing."

Rhonda pursed her lips. "You can say it, Mom."

"Your father called."

Of course, he did. It was Christmas, a time when they were supposed to be enjoying themselves. "That tracks."

"Yeah." Her mom blew out a breath.

"You know what he's doing."

"I know."

It didn't make it easier. Rhonda knew that from experience. "I'm sorry, Mom. Don't say it's okay because it's not. I'm glad you told me."

Her mom was silent a moment. "I'm glad you're coming out."

"Me, too. I'll get there on the thirtieth." She started to shiver. "And mom, I'm seeing someone."

Her mom's voice brightened. "Oh?"

"Don't get all excited—"

"I'm excited. What's his name?"

Rhonda laughed. "Jordan."

"Are you bringing him?"

Rhonda blinked. She'd thought about it, but didn't think her mom would be up for it. "I could, I didn't—"

"Bring him. If you can. I'd love to meet him."

Rhonda walked back to the sliding doors, a smile on her face even though her feet were stinging. "Okay, then. I'll look into it."

She walked back inside and got her opportunity to set eyes on Country and Jenna's new bundle of joy. Country held Hope like a football while André helped him dish up more cheese and crackers.

"I'm just saying, you could introduce me," André said.

Country shook his head. "She's classy, bud."

"I'm classy!" André motioned to his button up shirt.

Rhonda laughed. "Who is this we're talking about?" She walked closer and peeked under the soft blanket covering Hope's face.

She was momentarily stunned by the perfect symmetry, her rosy cheeks.

"I know. I can't stop staring at her." Country gazed down at his new baby girl with stars in his eyes.

There was that pressure behind her eyes again. Jenna straightened and cleared her throat. "Okay, spill."

André ran a hand through his hair. "Grace."

"Who's Grace?"

Country rolled his eyes. "The lawyer that helped us with the adoption."

Rhonda frowned. "Tyler's friend?"

"Tyler's ex-*mom*." André bit his lower lip. "I've always wanted to seduce someone's mom."

Rhonda laughed out loud. "Wait, how old is she?"

Country shook his head. "Younger than me."

Her eyes widened, and André waggled an eyebrow. "Tell him. I speak French. That means I'm automatically more charming and romantic than any of you. This woman is new to the city, she could use a friend."

Rhonda grinned at him and plucked a cracker and slice of cheese from the plate. "Good luck with that, slugger."

She squeezed Country's arm and said another heartfelt congratulations, then walked to the edge of the living room. She paused to tap a quick text to Jordan.

> Home in thirty. Meet me there?

Then wound her way back through the group to her friends.

Epilogue 2

Jordan

JORDAN'S TRUCK idled for a moment before he killed the engine. Rhonda's headlights flashed as she turned into the driveway, and his pulse quickened. He'd been sitting on the street for barely twenty minutes, and it had felt interminable.

He stepped out into the cold as soon as she parked. By the time she opened her door, he was there behind her, boots crunching on the snow-covered driveway.

"You beat me home," she teased.

Jordan followed her in, shaking the snow from his boots. "If you didn't treat every party like a closing ceremony, I wouldn't have."

She laughed, hanging her keys on the hook by the door. "I like it when you're jealous."

Jordan grabbed a handful of her left butt cheek as he walked past to the kitchen. He placed the white bakery box on the counter.

Rhonda sidled up next to him. "Those look amazing."

"You can take one. But the rest are for the breakfast."

She grinned, shoving a hand into his back pocket. "Mm. Generous."

He couldn't take it a second longer. He'd worked three shifts over the past two days, and he needed her clothes off. Immediately.

Jordan turned and pulled her against him, but Rhonda wriggled free. "What's this?" She pointed at the small wrapped box next to the cinnamon rolls.

"Something you can open in the morning."

She scoffed. "You can't dangle that—"

"All I do is dangle." He slipped his cold hands up the back of her shirt, and she gasped.

"Hilarious."

"You set me up for that one."

Rhonda kissed him, then dragged her lips over his jaw and sucked his earlobe into her mouth. He panted involuntarily as she said, "If you let me open it, I promise I'll make it worth your while."

Jordan groaned and fumbled for the gift with his free hand. Rhonda pulled back, her eyes shining. She took the box from him, and he kept his hands looped around her waist as she opened it.

He watched her initial reaction when she saw the gold tennis bracelet, waiting for the moment when—

"Jordan." She stared at the charms. One for Pucks Deep. One for the Snowballs. Rhonda looked up, her eyes glassy.

He smoothed a thumb over her cheek. "I'll never make you choose. Your life can be whatever you want it to be. Just tell me I can be a part of it."

Tears welled up, and he pressed against the corner of her eye, letting them spill over onto his fingers.

"I have a gift for you, too. I can—"

"Give it to me in the morning." Jordan grabbed her hand and pulled her toward the bedroom.

Rhonda laughed. "It's a good one."

He spun and pressed her hand to his jeans. "Morning."

Her cheeks flushed. Her teeth scraping over her lower lip. "Morning it is."

———

Rhonda and Jordan pulled up to Anne and Tina's house, the warm glow of Christmas lights twinkling in the windows. Rhonda's breath fogged the air as she exhaled, her excitement palpable. "Okay, I need you to know why this is funny."

Jordan turned off the ignition and looked at her expectantly. "I'm all ears."

"On the group chat. Anne and Tina wanted to invite the mystery guy to a hot tub night."

Jordan smirked and reached for the door handle. "So this is all women."

"Yes."

"And they don't know I'm coming?"

Rhonda shook her head.

"Fantastic."

They walked up the steps to the house, and Rhonda knocked on the door. A few seconds later, Tina stood in front of them, laughing. "You actually brought him!"

Rhonda grinned. "You asked for it." She scanned the room nervously. Jenna was the only wild card. She didn't know how she was going to react.

Tina stepped aside to let them in, and Rhonda was immediately enveloped in warmth and the smell of spiced cider. Anne was already in her swimsuit. "Well, I'll be damned."

Rhonda shrugged out of her coat and hung it on a hook by the door, then turned to face her friends. "Jordan, this is Tina,

Anne, and—" She paused as Jenna walked in from the kitchen. "Jenna."

Jordan nodded at each of them, his expression neutral. "Nice to meet you. Officially."

Tina pointed to the back door. "Oh this is going to be good."

Rhonda flashed Jordan a mildly apologetic smile as they walked to the patio. They stripped off their clothes—they were already wearing their suits—and Jordan climbed into the tub with four women. It wasn't exactly how he saw this fantasy playing out, but he wasn't going to look a gift horse in the mouth.

The questions started instantly, but as the women got more tipsy, they forgot all about him and he got to sit back and enjoy.

Tina brought out pies around ten o'clock, and when she slipped back in the hot tub, she said, "Your story is way better than the one I made up in my head."

Rhonda's nose scrunched. "About Parking Lot Guy?"

"Oh, I still want to have an affair with my version of Parking Lot Guy." Anne laughed. "Not you, Jordan. No offense."

They laughed and ate, and Jordan mostly just watched Rhonda. Her smile. Her laugh. He loved all of it. Her dark, curly hair framed her face, and he couldn't help but notice the way her cheeks flushed from the warmth of the hot tub, the pink on her cheeks. She was captivating. Magnetic.

Rhonda looked up and caught him staring. She raised an eyebrow. "What?"

He reached out and placed a hand on her knee, and her skin prickled. "Hey." Jordan leaned in, his lips brushing against her ear. "I think I love you." He said it on a breath, then pulled back, rejoining the conversation. He didn't want to pressure her or make her feel like he needed a response. He didn't. He just wanted her to know.

When Rhonda didn't move forward, he turned back. She hung her arms over the edge of the hot tub, her phone in her hand.

"Everything okay?"

Rhonda bit her lip, then turned the phone so he could see the screen. It was a message from Cassie.

Hey. Thanks for that. Merry Christmas

Jordan blinked. "Holy shit."

Rhonda nodded. "She texted me."

"She texted you." He pulled Rhonda into his arms, almost making her drop the phone. That reaction prompted questions from the others, and Rhonda filled them in on the saga with her sister.

It wasn't until ten minutes later that Rhonda turned to him. She nodded toward the deck and mouthed, "Check your phone."

Jordan waited a second as she turned back, laughing at something Tina said. Then he twisted and dried his hand on a towel and pulled his phone from the deck boards next to hers.

There was a text from her. *When had she sent that?* He tapped on it, and his heart stopped.

I love you, too

Next in the Series —>

André's story! Preorder Now!

Find special edition e-books and paperbacks exclusively at www. CindyGunderson.com

See the new Campus Confessions series —>

There's a story I tell people of how my husband and I met. All of it is a lie.

The year: 1992

Living with my boyfriend Jason should have been everything I wanted—until I realized his best friend, Rob Thompson, came with the deal. Rob and I are like oil and water, fire and gasoline, sworn enemies under one roof.

When Jason got selected for World Juniors in Germany, I thought I'd get a reprieve. I could handle the quiet loneliness of his absence. What I couldn't handle was Rob. He's still here, stomping around the house with that cocky grin, pushing every button I have. And somehow, when it's just the two of us, the air feels heavier, charged with something I don't want to name.

It's infuriating how he can see right through me, past every wall I've built, calling me out in ways no one else ever has. But as much as I hate him, I can't seem to look away.

Jason will be gone for two months. Rob will be here every day. And I'm terrified that everything I thought I knew about love—and hate—is about to change.

Sometimes the lines blur. And sometimes, you cross them...